The Knights of Aradia

by

AVERY GALE

PROLOGUE

Aradia, Queen of Witches, pulled the heavy tapestry aside to peer out the castle's open window. The other windows of her bedroom had been sealed with heavy leaded glass, but she'd never enclosed this one, preferring to hear the sounds wafting up from the courtyard below. Shivering when the cool night air caressed her face, Aradia was relieved to see the torches of the knights who stood guard outside.

Letting out the breath Aradia hadn't realized she was holding, the Queen of Witches sent out a silent thank you for the sense of security they gave her. Their loyalty and devotion warmed her soul. Gratitude bubbled up inside her, and she whispered a spell to make certain they understood how much she appreciated all they did. Food magically appeared on the table where they sat, and each of their families would find a basket outside their cottage door in the morning.

The knights were warrior wizards who'd pledged their lives to protect hers—in return, she blessed them, their families, and their descendants. She felt safe in their care, even as the steady vibrations of a coming storm resonated deep in her soul. Sadly, Aradia knew the battle between good and evil would continue as long as there were those who cared more for taking than giving. Individuals whose thirst for power erased their compassion and humanity would always challenge the Universal energy focused on love.

The dark forces were gaining strength and amassing followers. Aradia could only hope she would be ready for the coming fight. *How do I prepare for a battle where my life is the least of what is at stake? There is so much to lose, and I'm frightened. For the first time in my life… I'm afraid for our future.*

Sighing softly, she spoke more to herself than to her life partner and chief counsel standing across the room, watching her intently. He leaned against the fireplace's granite mantle with a casual ease that belied his strength. Aradia's whispered words felt vulnerable even to her ears. "Darkness will always try to overtake the light, but in the end, light surely must prevail, or everything the spirits have foretold will have been for not."

True to his name, Conrad was indeed a wise advisor. His calming presence had been Aradia's source of solace and strength during every battle. His were the arms that held her when she worried, when she no longer had the strength to continue, and it was his advice that had always served her so well. Looking up into his dark eyes, she felt her heart squeeze at the love she saw reflected in them.

"Aradia, have you given any consideration to our prior discussion? The gifts you have been given will not be diminished if they are shared."

Aradia walked softly toward him and smiled. "Your candle analogy was persuasive, Conrad, and I agree magic, like a candle, is not extinguished when it's shared with another. My concerns are about *how* to bestow the gifts, not if it is right to do so." Stepping toward the fire, she held out her palms, letting the warmth of the flames infuse her with energy as she asked the Great Goddess for wisdom and guidance.

The inspiration was so sudden and clear, Aradia felt as if the Goddess had spoken to her directly. She gasped and turned quickly back toward Conrad, pulling him as close as she could, considering her well-rounded belly was making it difficult for anyone to get close. Stepping back, she rubbed one hand reverently over her unborn child and waved the other in the oval circle of life as she cast the spell around her. With sparks flying in an ever-expanding spiral, Aradia's words changed the course of magic forever.

"Grant thy gifts upon the firstborn daughter every seventh generation of my family from now until the end of time. Share with her every tendril of my magic and bestow those talents in ever-increasing strength with each blessed generation. Multiply the blessings each year she works in the light. If she falls to the temptations of the dark side, burn her where she stands, and let her ashes blow away with the breeze. *So, mote it be.*"

Aradia had barely finished speaking when she felt the first contractions of childbirth setting the intoned spell into motion...

CHAPTER ONE

E MERALD STONE WAS running on empty. She was so far past exhausted, she couldn't seem to make her mind and body work in tandem. Hex, she couldn't even remember how it felt. She'd been driving for eighteen hours straight and was mentally checking in and out. All those hours watching the white dashes of the centerline flash by were hypnotizing and had taken a toll. She'd probably been brainwashed and would hear sixties rock in her sleep until hell froze over. Her head was pounding, her eyelids felt like they had small weights tied to them, and the inside of her eyelids felt as though they had been replaced with sandpaper.

At this point, it was hard to distinguish what was doing the most damage—the mesmerizing lines, the beat of her ancient tires over the asphalt, or her love of oldies rock. The latter was probably the result of a magic spell, but she had never been able to coax a confession from her Great-Aunt Ruby.

When her vision started to blur, Ema realized she was a danger not only to herself but to others as well, so she took the next exit off Interstate 70, pulling into a truck stop in Colby, Kansas, for a short break. Driving by a sign sporting palm trees had made her look twice, then laugh out loud. Even though the tropical trees were obviously artificial, they still looked odd, surrounded by piles of snow from what she was certain had been an unwelcome winter storm. Shrugging, she let the thought slide out of her mind. If the small Kansas town wanted to advertise itself as the Oasis of the Plains, then palm trees seemed perfectly reasonable.

Her antique Buick was packed to the gills with everything she hadn't sold or given away in the days following the frantic call from her grandmother. *I love her, I really do, but if she isn't really sick... if she is playing me, I swear I'll spell her right into next week. Oh, frack, who am I kidding? I was lucky to get out of Boston when I did. Why I thought I'd ever make it in the big city is a mystery for Athena.* Glancing at the cloudless sky, Ema muttered, "You'd think the Goddess of Wisdom and Divine Intelligence wouldn't ignore someone who sent a zillion petitions her way." *She probably thinks I'm the biggest nag in the world.*

Ema had left behind a boyfriend whose idea of "living it up" was renting two DVD movies instead of one on Saturday night and a dead-end job at a company that was on the fast-track to receivership if Ema's predictions were right—they always were. It was a curse... her predictions were always right. They were one of the few aspects of magic she hadn't been able to block.

She'd only taken an emergency leave of absence but had no plans to return to Apgate International. There was something dark and unsettling about the owner. Derwood Dupriest had given her the creeps since her first day on the job, even though he rarely spoke to her. Just being near him made her nervous, and the few instances where he'd actually acknowledged her, the brief interaction made her skin feel as though it was covered in marching ants.

Instead of storing her belongings, she'd sold or given away anything that wouldn't fit in the behemoth she called a car, then headed west, all within forty-eight hours of her granny's call. The hardest part of moving was leaving her two best friends.

London Adler-Monroe was setting the world of science on fire. How the brilliant chemist managed twin sons and twin Doms was a mystery to everyone who knew her.

Paris Adler-Stone had married Trinity, the local sheriff. Ema knew her friend kept him on his toes and hated that she'd no longer be nearby to watch the fireworks. Trinity was a distant cousin. His branch of the family tree was filled with men, while Emerald's line was blessed—or cursed, depending on your view—with women.

Leaving her friends, London and Paris, behind was her only regret.

Shaking her head, Emerald whispered the Latin word that best described her willful grandmother. *Pertinax.* Stubborn was a description of epic proportions. Opal Stone was as stubborn as they came, but she also had a heart as pure as her crystal ball. Letting out an exhausted sigh, Ema knew if Granny Good Witch, as Ema affectionately referred to her maternal grandmother, was simply up to her hippy dressed backside in one of her crazy plotting maneuvers... it really didn't matter. It wasn't as if Emerald's life had been on the fast track to being named Ms. Urban Success.

Pulling to the side of the large parking lot, Ema felt an odd tingling sensation, much like the positive charge in the air after a thunderstorm, and could have sworn a wave of sparkles swirled around her car. The feeling passed as quickly as it had moved over her, so she chalked it up to fatigue. *I'll think about it later... a lot later... when my brain works again.* Sighing, she leaned her seat back the measly three inches her cramped space allowed and vowed she was just going to close her eyes for a quick minute.

OPAL STONE WAS the reluctant head of a small coven of witches who lived in and around the small town of Crystal, Colorado. She might be a tiny wisp of a woman, but her heart and personality more than made up for her diminutive size. The women in her ancestral line were what they preferred to think of as diminutive... their smaller size balanced out their large attitudes—and in her opinion, you had to use whatever gifts you'd been given.

Thinking back on the phone call she'd made to her eldest granddaughter, Opal felt a twinge of guilt but shook it off quickly before it put down roots. *No need to let guilt about doing the right thing cloud the issue. We need Ema, and she needs to be here.* There hadn't really been any huge health emergency, well, unless you counted the fact she was "sick and tired" of waiting for her granddaughter to decide she'd had enough of the big city life and move home.

During a conversation last fall with Audric Stafford, the head of the Magic Council, he'd assured her Ema would be ready to make a change soon. He'd asked Opal to wait until early spring to give him time to make certain everything was in place. Opal hadn't asked, and he hadn't volunteered to tell her what he was arranging. She had often joked those in the magical world were more like their nonmagical neighbors than not. Sometimes ignorance was bliss.

After a recent message from Audric, giving her the go-ahead, she'd made the call. Opal gave an Oscar-worthy performance of a woman so desperately ill, she might not live through the end of the summer. She had expected Emerald to hop on the next plane and be on her doorstep within a day or two, so she was baffled and worried when Ema still hadn't arrived several days later.

Standing at the large front of her nearly defunct meta-physical shop, Opal looked out Spellbound's front window, blanching when she saw the local sheriff walking straight toward the store's front door. For one brief moment, she gave serious thought to whispering the invisibility spell she knew would conceal her, but his eyes narrowed in warning as if he'd read her thoughts.

Joshua Bennett was six-and-a-half feet tall, with sun-streaked blonde hair that would have made any self-respecting surfer green with envy. Opal had known Josh his entire life, and he'd always been as tenacious as he was handsome. Damn the luck, he wasn't the type to be put off easily. Believing it was best to delay anything unpleasant, Opal gave a quick flick of her wrist, disappeared, and set the deadbolt lock in motion. As the heavy hardware slid into place, the *Sorry We're Closed* sign flipped over, swinging wildly side to side from the sudden change of position.

"It won't work, Opal." Josh's deep voice sounded from the other side. "I know you're in there. Open up... I want to talk to you about Emerald."

Well, spell me. What's happened now?

JOSH HAD A soft spot for the tiny woman locals swore was a witch, even though her incessant matchmaking was beginning to wear pretty damned thin. Hell, Opal was about to drive him to drink with her annoyingly persistent attempts to set him up with every single woman within a two-hundred-mile radius. Several months ago, he'd finally had enough and simply started avoiding her. Even though he'd seen her do plenty of things he couldn't explain, he still leaned more toward her being loopy rather than mystical. Pounding on the door again, he held up his hands to look inside. When he spotted her reflection in the enormous oval mirror hanging above the fireplace, he shouted at her again.

"I mean it, Opal, this is important. I can see you in the blasted mirror, now open the damned door."

Josh was barely holding onto his control—the urge to give the rickety door a solid kick was almost overwhelming. Hell, it wouldn't take much effort to splinter the ancient, decaying wood. His patience was already worn to a frazzle, as his mother used to say, and what little remained was unraveling fast.

Opal needed to open the damned door before frustration trumped common courtesy. Josh knew Opal and her sister, Ruby, were struggling financially, but as he looked around the outside of the small shop, he was shocked at the building's state of disrepair. He made a mental note to make some discreet inquiries, and hopefully, he could figure out a way to help.

Opal winced at his irritated tone. She'd surprised him when she didn't move from what had to be the worst hiding place in history. He could still see her in the mirror—silly woman. She'd once told him he was a nice enough fellow, even if he was stubborn as a mule and probably kicked like one, too. It seemed they had something in common.

SHE'D HEARD HIS thoughts about kicking in the door, and the last thing she needed was another bill to pay. She didn't want him looking into her finances either, but short of putting a spell on him, she doubted there was much she could do to stem his blasted curiosity. *Damn and double-damn.*

When she looked up and met his eyes in the mirror, she knew she was done. *Drat on a dead rat, I am losing my touch. Hiding never was this challenging before. I may as well let him in, or he's going to raise the dead with that confounded bellowing.* With another snap of her wrist, the door swung wide open, and the sign righted itself just as she hustled out of the backroom as if she'd just run a marathon.

"Sorry Joshua, I was in the backroom cleaning. It's a miracle I heard you." She batted her eyes, but she could tell he'd barely managed to keep from rolling his eyes at her blatant lie.

Is she kidding? How dim does she think I am? I swear if she wasn't a hundred-year-old pixie, I swear I'd.... Opal's expression turned stormy, and Josh would swear on his life, he'd seen lightning flash in her dark eyes. Her voice was icy cold when she finally spoke.

"I will have you know, young man, I am **NOT** a hundred." *Okay, maybe that's technically true, but it was certainly misleading since witches don't age at the same rate as the nonmagical, but he doesn't stand a snowball's chance in Panama of figuring it out.* No reason to tell him how old she was. It was ridiculous how hung up nonmagicals were about age. It was positively annoying.

"Boy, you have some nerve. First, you interrupt my cleaning by pounding on my door like your tail is on fire, then you have the audacity to insult my age. And what do you mean, Pixie? *Spell me.* That is just plain insulting. Pixies are trouble-making little fairies who live in the forest." She shook her head, emphasizing how remarkable she found his naivety. "Good gracious, you know I live upstairs. I'll bet dollars to daffodils you have never even seen a pixie. What on Mother Earth are you thinking?" She was on a roll, and Josh looked like he had no clue what to do aside from letting her wear herself out like a blasted wind-up toy.

Opal watched as Josh bit back a grin. He hadn't missed the fact she'd only protested the residency issue of being called a pixie but hadn't denied the trouble-making part since it seemed pointless. She heard him mentally referring to it as a Freudian slip… why he thought he knew anything about Freud was a mystery to her. Opal remembered meeting Sigmund Freud—she hadn't been impressed. The man was obsessed with sex—he thought everything was sexually motivated. It was borderline creepy.

LEANING HIS HIP against the enormous glass display case near the front of the store, Josh crossed his arms over his chest and waited. He knew from experience she'd slow down in a few minutes. Years ago, he learned it was easier to let her spin herself down. In the back of his mind, he wondered why she seemed bound and determined to avoid talking to him about Ema. It was puzzling, to be sure, but nothing was ever predictable when it came to the Stone sisters.

He'd only met Opal's twin, Ola, a few times over the years, but on the rare occasions he'd seen her, Josh thought she seemed more levelheaded than Opal and more insightful than Ruby. He'd received a vague answer when he asked where Ola Stone lived, and the three women completely ignored him when he asked how she filled her time. *Like I said... nothing about these women is what you'd expect.*

Letting his thoughts wander to Emerald, Josh was more than a little curious why she was sleeping in her damned car in a truck-stop parking lot in Kansas. According to the officer he'd spoken with on the phone, her car looked to be on its last leg and was loaded so full she was practically sleeping sitting up. When the deputy finally managed to rouse her, Emerald had seemed lost in a fog of exhaustion. When she'd surfaced enough to tell them where she was headed, they'd called Josh to give him a heads up.

The officer who called made a strange comment before he'd hung up, something about her car changing colors. Now he felt like he was sitting on pins and needles as he waited for her to roll safely into town.

While he waited for Opal to finish listing all the *reasons* he shouldn't interfere in her business, Josh took an amused inventory of today's get-up. Opal was dressed in a black gauzy skirt with an abstract star pattern in various shades of glowing glitter, topped a neon orange Harley Davidson t-shirt with the words Biker Babe on the back. *Mental head-slap and eyeroll.* When he looked down, he nearly laughed out loud. Opal's small feet were clad in bright pink high-tops that flashed neon lights with every bouncing step. The blinding shoes were topped with purple and lime green socks. It was hard to tell which element was the most offensive to the eye. *What's up with her, anyway? I wonder if she's color blind.*

Opal froze. It was spooky how suddenly she'd gone statue-still. Turning toward him, she raised a thin, snow-white eyebrow.

"Color blind? Really? I'll have you know I'm the most fashionable witch in my coven. Just ask any of our members, they'll tell you it's true. I watch what the local kids are wearing, so I know what's trending."

She stunned him, responding to his unspoken thoughts, but it was her casual admission to being a witch that surprised him the most. In all the years he'd known her, Opal had never openly admitted the rumors surrounding her were true.

Josh knew the locals swore both sisters were magical, but he had trouble believing what he couldn't see. He barely had time to register his surprise before she looked him up and down with barely masked disgust.

Scrutinizing his uniform, she harrumphed. "At least I don't wear the same boring clothes every blasted day. And khaki? Really? I'm not sure you could be any more... well... dull. I recognize your style, though. Ola shops at Fuddy Duddies-R-Us, as well. Hell, the two of you should carpool."

"She watches the kids alright and copies them... all of them. She never was good at knowing how to pick and choose out of chaos. Personally, I think she looks like a refuge from a paintball war... but then, she's never listened to me."

Josh looked up and grinned as Opal's younger sister walked into the room. Ruby's presence brought to mind another question—where was Ema planning to stay? There wouldn't be room in the tiny upstairs apartment for all three women. Something about the entire situation was tripping every single one of Josh's internal alarms.

Ruby Stone wasn't much taller than Opal. The younger Stone was rounder and always appeared to be more the stereotypical elderly widow, though he'd never heard anything about her husband. She'd been a chemist in Denver before retiring, but he never knew exactly who she had worked for. Josh remembered hearing his parents mentioning that Ruby had been widowed at a very young age, but he'd never thought to ask any of the details. Maybe he'd give his mom a call and see what she remembered.

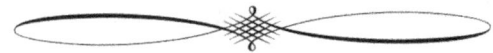

OPAL TURNED TOWARD her sister but promised herself she would not bother responding to Ruby's catty remarks about her wardrobe. *Like I'm going to take fashion advice from someone who dresses like a fifteenth-century nun.* Ruby's raised eyebrow let Opal know she'd heard the remark but wasn't going to rise to the bait. *Too bad. I could use a good fight right about now. Fighting with you would be a great distraction from Sheriff Hot Stuff.*

Turning back to Josh, she felt as if she'd been struck by lightning. When her gaze locked on his, she felt like she'd been hit over the head with her Book of Shadows. *Oh Goddess, are you sure he's the one? Are you absolutely positive? Because he is so... nonmagical. Oh, boy, who would have ever thought this was possible? And here I've been setting him up with every woman I could find. Holy... Well, at least now I know why all those dates failed.*

She wondered why on earth the powers that be hadn't bothered to reveal this to her sooner but shrugged off the question. It was foolish to waste time focusing on questions no one could answer. If she'd learned one thing during all her years as a witch, it was the Universe rarely did things in ways that made sense to her.

Coming back to the moment, Opal rubbed her hands together and giggled before she realized Josh was staring at her. His expression told her he was worried the very last one of her badly cracked marbles had finally rolled off the table and shattered.

"Are you okay, Opal? It looked like you left us there for a few seconds." His voice was laced with concern, and she noted his body language had shifted as well. Gone was the laid back gentle giant stance she always considered too close to condescending for her comfort.

Opal took a deep breath to expel any residual negativity she'd harbored toward the man in front of her and hoped her voice sounded confident—as if she'd been chatting about nothing more significant than the morning's crisp weather.

"Oh, I'm positively peachy. Now, why don't you come over here? Have a seat, and we'll have a lovely chat." She waved a hand toward a ladder-back chair. Josh watched in open-mouthed wonder as it slid forward. A feather duster worked its way over the seat, then disappeared as quickly as it appeared. When he just stared at the chair as if he couldn't believe his eyes, Opal stepped closer and smiled. "I'm so glad you stopped by. What brings you calling on a couple of local helpless, frail senior citizens, hmmm?"

She batted her eyes at him, giving everything she had

in a futile effort to look innocent. From the disbelieving expression on his face, it wasn't working. So much for trying to convince him she hadn't finally gone over the edge. The coughing and wheezing fit Ruby fell into wasn't helping her cause, either. *Damn, my acting skills need work. And, although my performance with Ema was so spot-on, too. Oh, well, maybe it's the pressure of performing in front of a live audience… or a moon phase. Certainly can't be from lack of effort.*

Opal was having trouble holding back her giddiness at the insight the Universe had just given her. She had the solution to one of her biggest challenges, which made her want to dance a jig. A few minutes ago, Opal had been convinced persuading Emerald to stay in Colorado would be difficult at best. Now, the answer was standing right in front of her, and knowing her granddaughter had once carried a torch for the man was a huge bonus. All those hours of worry about how to persuade Emerald to stay were for naught, when a little basic matchmaking was all that was required. Opal could hardly believe it—the delicious answer had been right under her nose all this time.

Josh was perfect for Ema… all that sexiness wrapped up in a nice-guy persona. He came from a great family, and money would never be an issue. He didn't have any major psychological problems that she'd heard about. She'd even heard he liked his sex a little on the kinky side, and as far as Opal was concerned, that was a huge plus. Yes, indeed, he was perfect. *Well, except for the pesky little fact he doesn't believe in anything he can't see… but we'll fix that soon enough.*

JOSH WATCHED OPAL'S eyes glaze over, and her lips moved as if she were speaking with someone only she could see. In a matter of seconds, she was back, her return just as abrupt as her departure. The sudden about-face in her attitude and the direction of their conversation had him stymied. She'd gone from avoiding a conversation with him to overly accommodating, and in his experience, a sudden change in *anyone's* actions sent up warning flags of imaginable colors. Watching the wily woman act like a hapless geriatric would have been comical if it wasn't so suspect. It was unlikely the words helpless and frail would ever find their way into anyone's description of Opal Stone.

Josh put aside his curiosity about Opal's behavior. He needed to get back to his original reason for stopping by the small eclectic store. The Stone family had run the small shop on Main Street for as long as anyone could remember. Hell, the place would probably qualify for the historical registry.

Ruby had always seemed more levelheaded of the two sisters... okay, maybe she occasionally wore skin-tight jeans and t-shirts with leather hiking boots, at least it was all black, and being monochromatic had to count for something. Sighing to himself, Josh tried to remember he'd returned to this rural area tucked away in the Rocky Mountains to escape the craziness of the city, even though most days he was fairly certain he'd merely upgraded to a higher level of lunatics.

"I got a call last night from a Kansas police officer who found Emerald sleeping in her car in a truck-stop parking lot in Colby. He said she was so sound asleep, he was getting ready to break the window when she finally roused." Josh watched Opal's eyes widen and heard Ruby's soft gasp of surprise. He wasn't going to bring up the subject of Ema's car changing color. No reason to give the citizens of Crystal a reason to drop a net over him.

"Ema told him she'd was tired because she'd been driving non-stop. She claimed she was in a hurry to get to Crystal because her beloved grandmother was deathly ill." He paused for a moment, trying to regain the patience he felt slipping when he saw a cloud of guilt cloud Opal's dark eyes. Her expression fell, and he knew her granddaughter had been hoodwinked. "It seems Ema had been driving for almost eighteen hours when she'd finally pulled over for a catnap. The officer wanted me to verify her story." He gave Opal a deliberately slow up and down perusal and noticed her barely perceptible flinch.

"Now, I assured Officer Snook it was entirely likely Emerald received a call from her grandmother. I couldn't imagine Ema lying to a law enforcement officer about something so important. I assured him I would personally check on the sweet shopkeeper. I promised him Ema wouldn't lie about the grandmother I know she adores... and trusts." Josh let his words settle over Opal, hoping she'd realize how true they were.

"Officer Snook made sure Emerald ate something other than the snacks he saw in her car before he let her get back on the road early this morning." Tapping his foot in frustration, he continued, "You want to explain to me why Ema believes you are teetering on the edge of death? Why she's so convinced you are standing toe to toe with your impending demise, she would risk life and limb to get to you? Consider it a dress rehearsal for when your frantic and embarrassed granddaughter arrives on your doorstep in a few hours."

Josh sighed in frustration. With the tiny grandmother dancing a happy jig all around the nearly empty store, it was obvious he wouldn't hear a reasonable explanation why she'd called Emerald home.

Yep, my day is now complete. First, I find out the most beautiful temptation I've ever known is on her way to town, and now I'm watching her crazy-assed, two days older-than-dirt Granny dance around in pink high-tops and a Harley t-shirt. Just shoot me now.

CHAPTER TWO

B Y THE TIME Ema eased her heap of a car into a parking place in front of her family's magical shop, she was nearly delirious with exhaustion and hunger. The breakfast she'd eaten before dawn had long since faded from her memory. *Spell me. At this point, I might enjoy my own cooking.* Her willingness to eat something she'd cooked spoke volumes about how desperate she was since she was affectionately referred to as the Queen of Smoke Alarms by anyone who knew her well.

It was embarrassing to admit how many firefighters she knew on a first-name basis. She'd been invited to join them for dinner on several occasions—interestingly enough, all of those incidents coincided with them watching her walk by carrying groceries. They'd even occasionally brought her dinner in their less-than-subtle attempts to avoid a trip to her apartment. Two really cute, single firefighters even tried to teach her how to make a few "fool-proof" dishes, but after filling the station's kitchen with smoke the second time, they'd deemed her untrainable and hadn't mentioned cooking lessons again.

Ema sat in her car for a few minutes, taking in her surroundings and relishing a movement-free moment. Goddess, she was tired of traveling. More specifically, she was tired of driving. Stretching her cramped hands, she turned her head from side to side, hoping to loosen the tight muscles. When she turned to her left, she gasped. There he was, standing a few doors down, talking to a young couple with a small pink bundle nestled in a stroller.

Joshua Bennett was the best-looking man she'd ever seen, but since he was older, she'd never really gotten to know him very well. *Right Ema, except for that one crazy night at the lake when you...* Closing her eyes, Emerald could still remember how it felt to have Josh's soft lips pressing against hers and the way his touch set her bare skin aflame.

Shaking her head to clear her wayward thoughts, she watched as he leaned down to admire the baby, but she could feel his attention laser-focused on her. *Oh, hex, he probably thinks I'm a special kind of a lunatic for falling asleep in my car in that blasted parking lot.* She still couldn't believe the local police called him to confirm her story.

Nope, nothing embarrassing about THAT....

Ema quickly looked down at her hands and wasn't surprised to see them trembling, though she wasn't sure if it was from fatigue, hunger, or seeing Josh before she'd even had time to exit her car. Hopefully, things would go uphill from here.

JOSH CONTINUED CHATTING with his friends, admiring their beautiful new daughter, but his attention was lost the minute he saw Ema sitting in her battered blue monstrosity of a car. She was every bit as beautiful as he remembered. Her mahogany hair fell over her shoulders in a soft cloud of waves, her face still reminded him of an angel, and her eyes were overly large for her small heart-shaped face. He wondered what her life had been like in Boston. Josh didn't like the haunted look in her eyes. Was it worry for her perfectly healthy grandmother or something else? Pushing his concerns aside for the moment, Josh focused on the memory of how fascinated he'd been at the ever-changing shades of her green eyes.

Trying to stay focused on his conversation without letting Ema out of his sight wasn't easy. His thoughts kept returning to the overwhelming sense he was missing something, but couldn't figure out why. He hadn't missed the fleeting expression moving over her beautiful face. The look made Ema look lost, and the flash of loneliness he'd seen haunting her shadowed eyes made his heart squeeze. After saying goodbye to the new family, he ambled slowly down the wooden planked sidewalk and approached the driver's side door of her relic of a car.

Josh pulled the handle just as she put her shoulder against the door, giving it a hard shove. The door seemed to stick just before swinging open. The damned thing was obviously in need of a major adjustment, and he wondered how long she'd been using the linebacker move to open the damned thing. Distracted by his observation about the car, he missed the more pressing problem. Looking on in stunned horror, Josh realized too late Ema was tumbling out of the car, landing in a tangle of arms and legs at his feet. Stepping back so he could kneel beside her, he tried to help her to her feet as everything became a comedy of errors.

"Damn… Ema, are you alright? What the heck was that about? Don't men open doors for ladies back east?" His voice sounded gruffer than he'd intended, but he was shocked and flustered, and neither of those things happened to him often.

Josh had retired from his Navy SEAL career a little over a year ago after a mission went so far south, it had hung precariously from the tip of the South Pole as penguins gathered around, laughing at him. The lingering effects of that night helped convince him it was time to walk away. When you lose faith in your leaders, no one is safe. Without that unwavering trust, nothing works—people die, and everybody loses.

Once she finally stopped flailing, Ema dropped her eyes to the ground and heaved out a sigh of defeat. "Well, if this was how things are going to go, I'm tempted to get right back in my car and hightail it on down the road. Or I would, except for the pesky Granny Good Witch problem." He looked on in admiration as she seemed to pull herself together before looking pointedly at the sky and storming, "I mean it, Goddess Almighty, if that old woman is playing me for a song, I'm going to spell her, so everything she wears is age-appropriate!"

Josh laughed out loud at her rambling threat. He remembered how Ema had always blushed when the kids at school teased her mercilessly about her grandmother's crazy fashion choices. If you asked him, the only thing scarier than Opal's clothing ensembles was her driving, which gave everyone in town nightmares.

EMA TRIED TO get her feet under her without flashing Josh—no need to show off her ratty granny-panties. Her squirming was making his attempts to help her up exponentially more difficult, but just thinking about giving him a glimpse of her thrift store lingerie was enough to make her shudder with mortification. His hands skimmed over her body, and his touch was starting to feel more like a full-body pat-down than assistance. When his palm gently brushed the outside curve of her breast, her breath caught. Every cell in her body went on alert in the blink of an eye, heating to the point of near spontaneous combustion. *Goddess, please tell me he didn't notice my reaction.* The whole scene was making her look as though she was channeling a slutty version of Lucille Ball. *Yep, just another day in the sitcom life and times of Emerald Stone, super klutz.*

Even the thought of how his hands would feel caressing her bare skin with a smooth, sensual touch kicked her pulse into high gear, and for several seconds she forgot to breathe. Giving herself a mental head-slap, Ema reminded herself Josh was merely trying to help her to her feet. *He's probably just checking me for injuries. After all, he is the Sheriff, and it is his job to look out for the citizens of Crystal. There is no way he is as haunted by that long-ago night as I am. Hex it all.* She doubted he even remembered the night they'd spent at the lake, and she damned well wasn't going to tempt fate by mentioning it. Hearing confirmation that he'd forgotten the single most interesting night of her life would be even more humiliating than falling out of her car at his feet... *almost.*

The night they'd spent together felt so much more significant than two friends who'd merely become lost in a moment of shared boredom. Josh genuinely seemed to enjoy talking to her and had been incredibly patient when she'd asked him dozens of questions about his job. Of course, most inquiries were met with tactful avoidance or only answered in the sketchiest terms.

Ema understood much of what he did was classified and appreciated how he'd still answered candidly when he could. Josh's ability to compartmentalize the horrors he'd been exposed to both impressed and worried her. After that night, she'd sent up many prayers to the Universe for his safety, physical and spiritual.

Much to her Granny's eternal frustration, spells had never seemed particularly important. Her granny was dismayed by her lack of interest. Despite her general apathy, Ema had made a point to learn several protection spells and repeated them often since that starlit night.

"I'm alright." *Totally humiliated and mortified by my clumsiness but not physically injured.* Ema could feel Josh watching her closely as she tried unsuccessfully to get her feet under her. Josh seemed to have finally decided she wasn't making any significant progress and reached under the arms, lifting her as you would a child who'd fallen and couldn't get back on their feet. He was smiling at her, and when she looked around and saw they'd attracted a small crowd, she groaned.

"Geez, I tell you... if this is in next week's local newspaper, I'll move. I swear it, and if Granny Good Witch isn't on her death bed, I'm going to go positively postal."

EMA'S WORDS HAD been spoken so quietly, Josh knew she hadn't intended for them to be overheard. But, years of training had taught him to listen to everything—not just the words a person spoke aloud. Josh listened to their self-talk as well—and you could be sure he damned well listened when the woman who captivated him whispered to herself. He was sure she was more embarrassed than angry, but just on the off-chance she was going to lose patience with her grandmother, perhaps a small intervention was in order.

The last time he spoke with Emerald was the night they'd spent together at the lake. He often wondered if she remembered that night as clearly as he did. They'd been sitting on the hood of his car, eventually reclining against the windshield as they talked about anything and everything. Josh didn't think there'd been a topic they hadn't at least touched on.

Ema had been remarkably insightful for her age, and he'd been grateful for the glimpse of her gentle spirit. Her sincere questions about how he dealt with the violence of his job indicated a level of maturity that astonished him. Over the years, he often thought about how effortless their conversation had been. She'd exhibited wisdom well beyond her years, and when they'd parted in the early hours of the following morning, she'd left him with a new outlook and a renewed sense of purpose.

To this day, he couldn't tell you much about the specific points of their conversation, but he could sure remember how she'd seemed to reach inside his mind and soothed his deepest fears. After the time he spent with her, his worries about losing his humanity had ebbed away. Following that night, there had been times he felt as though he was protected by an unseen force. *Hell, maybe she was a witch after all.*

Josh found himself lost in the memory of their night together. Only a few seconds passed, but that was all the time he needed. Recalling the sweet scent of her hair wafting around him, Josh could practically feel the silky-smooth locks slipping through his fingers. He'd been amazed at the warmth of her bare skin despite the cool evening air, and the feel of her satiny heat was imprinted on his mind. Even now, if he closed his eyes, he'd be able to see the way her ivory skin seemed to sparkle as the light of the full moon highlighted the unblemished surface.

The night at the lake had been one of the most romantic moments of his life. Pulling the skimpy, cropped shirt over Ema's head was like unwrapping the most beautiful gift he'd ever been given. Josh wasn't sure he'd ever felt the world was better aligned... until a few minutes later when he slid his aching cock into her tight passage. She hadn't told him she was still a virgin, but he'd known as soon as his tip pushed through the fragile membrane of her innocence. That night was still one of his most treasured memories. To this day, he was humbled, knowing he'd somehow been able to earn her trust.

Coming back to the moment, Josh reached down,

easily lifting her to her feet, but didn't immediately release her. He frowned when he realized his hands spanned her tiny waist. The warmth of her slim body so close to his seeped into the depths of his soul, making it difficult to release her when it became clear she was steady enough to remain upright. When she seemed to have her bearings, he grinned down at her.

"Well, now that I see you're all right, how about walking with me to the diner? I saw Opal earlier today, and I can assure you she will be fine until you have eaten." He held up his hand when she started to protest. "I know what time you left, Colby. I also know how long the drive is, so it's a simple calculation to figure out you haven't stopped long enough to eat. It's a small miracle you made it here without running out of gas in that boat you're driving." He chuckled as he waited for her to retrieve her purse from the front seat. "Any chance you could get one more thing in that car? Mercy, how long are you planning to visit, anyway?" *Wait. Didn't Officer Snook say the car was blue? It was blue a minute ago... wasn't it? The damned thing is pink now.*

Josh watched as the sweetest flush moved up her slender neck to color her cheeks.

"Umm. Well, about that.... It's not exactly a visit, but Granny doesn't know that yet. I'd appreciate it if you wouldn't share that tidbit with her until I find out exactly what's going on. If she's playing me, I may well move on sooner rather than later. It's not that I don't trust her manipulative little self... it's just that... well, I don't trust her."

Josh laughed. Hell, he knew her skepticism was justified. He pushed aside his concern Ema might decide to move on if she'd been played because he didn't have any doubt that was exactly what she was going to discover. Opal Stone could write a book on manipulation. Ema's wily, meddling grandmother would be thrilled her favorite granddaughter was planning to stay.

Crystal had always been one of those small towns where everyone knew more about your business than you knew yourself, so Josh had known for months how much Opal hoped Ema would return home. He also knew she would likely start matchmaking before dawn, but for some reason, the thought didn't bother him as much as it probably should.

"Do you think I'll have trouble finding a small room to rent until I can get the upstairs apartment ready? I have a sleeping bag in my backseat." Looking around as if she was assessing the weather, Ema shuddered. "I'm afraid it might not be enough for Colorado nights this time of year. Heck, any time of year, for that matter."

Josh hated the lost look he saw coloring her expression. It was gone almost as quickly as it appeared, making him wonder if his imagination was playing tricks on him. Damn, she was so beautiful, she stole his breath. The thought of anyone hurting her made him see red.

Emerald's face had always made her an open book. His friends had disagreed. The guys he'd hung around in school didn't see past the girl who kept to herself because she never seemed to fit in, thanks to her unusual family. Mentally rolling his eyes at the thought of her sleeping in her damned car, Josh took a deep breath. Good God, not only would it be too cold, but it also wouldn't be safe.

JOSH STOPPED WALKING and turned to face Ema, his brows arching above his sky-blue eyes. "You don't have a place to sleep tonight?" He'd bet his last nickel Emerald didn't know about her Granny and aunt's financial struggles. What he'd learned after leaving the small metaphysical shop this morning painted a bleak picture. The women had been struggling financially for a couple of years, but the past twelve months had been devastating. They'd leased out the family home and were currently occupying the small apartment over the store.

"Well, it's not like I'm homeless... not really. I can always crash downstairs at Granny and Aunt Ruby's until I get everything in the store's upstairs cleaned out. That apartment hasn't been used for a long time. I shudder to think what condition it might be in. Granny mentioned it wasn't available at this time... odd verbiage, don't you think?"

Josh watched as Ema tilted her head to the side as she considered the way her grandmother had sidestepped what had likely been a delicate dance around a minefield of honesty. Ema was lost in her thoughts for several seconds before her eyes focused. With a small wave of her hand, she dismissed the concerns.

Josh blinked in surprise. He could have sworn, he saw

sparkling bits of glitter follow the gentle, arcing motion of her hand. *What the hell? Damn, I really need a day off!*

CHAPTER THREE

E MA TURNED AND walked the last few steps to the diner as if it was perfectly ordinary for silver sparkles to follow the movement of her hand.

"Anyway, I don't think the little upstairs apartment can be *that* messy. I'll probably just tough it out up there. That little one-bedroom place will be plenty big enough for me."

Josh was glad she didn't notice his grimace as they entered the small eatery. He certainly wasn't looking forward to seeing her frustration when she discovered her grandmother's deception.

Ema stopped so suddenly when she stepped over the threshold of the small diner, Josh almost walked right over her. Grasping her shoulders to keep them both from faceplanting, he heard her pull in a deep breath and sigh. The delicious aromas of the diner washed over them, and Josh smiled as he turned her until they were face to face. Watching her eyes flutter closed and her lips turn up in a sweet smile of anticipation was the hottest thing he'd ever seen. He completely understood the feeling. Every time he'd returned home on leave, he'd made a beeline for the diner.

"Are you okay, Em?" When her long, dark lashes fluttered over the dark shadows below the eyes, a surge of protectiveness steamrolled through him. The harsh lighting in the diner emphasized subtle signs of exhaustion he'd missed in the dim light of late evening shadows on the street. Seeing her obvious lack of self-care and dangerous level of vulnerability due to exhaustion brought his long-suppressed Dom instincts surging to the surface.

Josh had never been totally immersed in the lifestyle, but he appreciated the added spark certain elements of kink could add to sex with a like-minded partner. He hadn't been able to visit the nearby BDSM club for so long, he'd wondered if his sexual predilections had actually changed. The ShadowDance Club was close—almost *too close*—which was part of the problem. He'd planned to get better established in his position as County Sheriff before risking fallout from local scuttlebutt.

Now, seeing how delicate Ema appeared, despite her efforts to fight back the fatigue threatening to melt her into a puddle, Josh wanted to wrap her in his arms and protect her from the disappointment he knew was coming. He wasn't sure what Opal was up to, but if Ema's heart was being put at risk, he planned to keep a close watch.

Josh took Ema's elbow, ushering her to a seat near the large plate-glass windows looking out over Crystal's main street. It always surprised him how little the town where they'd both grown up had changed over the years. Hell, when he looked at the pictures in the local museum, he'd been shocked to see how much Crystal looked like it had in the late 1800s. The flurry of mining in Colorado meant there'd been many small towns nestled in picturesque locations. Small communities sprang up more from necessity than their picturesque views and easy access for tourists. Only a handful of those early settlements survived, and it amused him how many became refuges for hippies and other members of the counter-culture movement of the 1960s and 1970s. The rest were now little more than ghost towns frequented by tourists and tumbleweeds.

Crystal was surrounded by some of the most stunning mountain landscapes in North America. The small community was stunning and remote, but it was also often completely cut off from the outside world. There was only one main road leading into town, and it was frequently closed due to snow or falling rocks. There were lesser roads if you had a high-clearance vehicle and an even higher tolerance for adrenaline.

Main Street was only two blocks long and was wide by most modern standards. Many of the homes looked as though they'd been pulled directly from a children's storybook, and the wooden sidewalks had always reminded Josh of the westerns he'd watched on television as a child.

Ema studied the menu, but her eyes were so unfocused, Josh sensed she wasn't able to see anything but words swimming on the page. Watching as she struggled for several seconds, he finally plucked the menu from her hands and ordered for them both. He fought back his smile when her eyes widened, defiance flashing for a split second before she gave a resigned sigh and rolled her eyes, grinning.

"Thanks. I'm not usually this disconnected… I swear."

He ordered the daily special, knowing their food would be delivered in less than a minute. True to form, the waitress slid steaming plates of roast beef and mashed potatoes buried under thick gravy in front of them exactly fifty seconds later. Watching Ema lose herself in her dinner was one of the hottest things he'd ever seen. *How does she make eating look so sensual? It's as if she's lost in ecstasy. I never imagined eating roast beef could be so damned sexy.*

"Oh, my Goddess, I didn't realize I was so blessed famished. Thank you for insisting I eat something, Josh. You're an angel." She grabbed his hand, giving it a quick squeeze.

Electricity raced up his arm, and he felt his eyes go wide. Her quick inhalation let him know Emerald felt the same jolt. The sizzle between them was like a bolt of lightning racing up his arm. Josh saw her eyes go wide as a white-hot feeling of intense connection, so strong he wondered if he'd ever find the words to describe, steam-rolled over him.

"Wow! What the hell was that about Ema?" Josh was so stunned, he knew he sounded harsh and hated the way she'd flinched. Softening his tone, he added, "That's some powerful static electricity you have sparking through you, sweetheart." If she was surprised by the endearment, she didn't let it show. The sweet pink staining her cheeks told him she'd either been shocked by the power of their touch or more affected by his use of a sentiment usually reserved for intimate partners than she wanted to let on.

"I have no idea. I thought you shocked me. Oh, hex, Granny is going to have a field day with this..." Her last words trailed off softly, but he hadn't missed them. She was probably right. Opal Stone could make a mountain out of a molehill faster than anyone he knew.

Before they finished their meal, Josh and Ema were interrupted several times as people from town stopped to welcome her "home" and to express their hope she'd be able to help her family during her visit. She seemed confused by their comments, keeping her responses vague enough to conceal the growing number of questions he sensed she struggled to work through. Ema remained reluctant to answer inquiries about her plans for the future despite being asked by almost every person they spoke with.

Josh was convinced her car was packed with everything she owned, and everything about the situation sent up warning flags. Shaking his head, Josh wondered what happened in Boston that made her walk away. Why hadn't she taken time to hire movers? Not that he didn't want her here. Hell, he was thrilled she was back, but he couldn't shake the feeling things weren't as simple as they appeared.

There were plenty of single men in the area who would be equally pleased, and that was more unsettling than it should have been. Josh also knew if any of the local busybodies walked by her car, they would ask the same questions floating through his mind. The local rumor mill would crank out theories at an Olympic pace within hours. News of Ema's return would spread through town like a raging forest fire.

Once the flow of well-wishers finally slowed, they enjoyed a casual conversation, chatting about people they knew and how things hadn't really changed all that much while they'd both been gone. Out of the corner of his eye, Josh noticed Tyler looking their way. The younger man stood frozen in his tracks at the other side of the narrow diner. Josh saw his friend's gaze lock on Ema. Hell, it looked as if he'd lost all focus as he dropped the large tub of dishes he'd been carrying. Josh looked between them, puzzled.

"Ema, do you know Tyler?"

"Oh, my stars and garters, is that you, Tyler?" Scrambling from her seat on the other side of the booth, Ema rushed across the room to embrace the young man. "It is you. Oh heavens, let me look at you. I have to say, you look very handsome in your uniform." Josh sat back and watched Tyler's expression fill with pride, and he looked as though he was glowing from the inside. Tyler's broad smile was almost as big as when he'd won a gold medal at a Special Olympics event a few months ago. Tyler's obvious delight made Josh smile. Ema was chattering a mile a minute, filling in the silent gap while it took Tyler a few minutes to find his words.

After his high school graduation, Josh only returned home a few times after enlisting. After joining the SEALS, trips home became even more infrequent, but he always asked about the young man who'd so often been pushed to the sidelines during local activities. Tyler's father had worked for the Bennett family for years, and Josh's mom had always taken a special interest in Tyler, including him in several of their educational excursions over the years. Caitlyn Bennett had been relentless in her pursuit of improved opportunities for kids with special needs in the local schools. Josh remembered his mom mentioning an older girl who became Tyler's champion when he entered high school.

Josh's mother was a force to be reckoned with when she was passionate about something, and she'd always been frustrated by their small town's refusal to see Tyler's potential. When he moved home, Josh had been pleasantly surprised to see things had finally changed. Several locals told him one young woman's friendship and unconditional acceptance led to Tyler being virtually adopted by everyone in town.

Josh had never known the name of the young woman, and now he chuckled as he watched the scene playing out a few feet away. Didn't it figure the woman in question would be Emerald Stone? The girl who'd been teased relentlessly was the one person who'd understood what it felt like to be an outcast. The irony had never been lost on Josh. He was damned impressed with the way Ema turned her negative experience into something positive and changed Tyler's life in the process.

Hell, Emerald Stone might be able to do magic after all, but to Josh, her real magic was the way she effortlessly brought out the best in everyone around her. People practically glowed when they talked to her. He'd seen it several times since they entered the diner. The effect she had on people was remarkable.

Thinking back on the hour he just spent with her, at least twenty people had approached their table, and she'd greeted each one as if they were long-lost best friends. Emerald Stone was a virtual people magnet. Every person she'd talked to had been the center of her focus for the few moments they spent with her, and they'd known it.

The woman missed her calling. She would be a hell of a politician! If this is how it's going to be with her, our future dates will have to be out of town. That thought brought him up short. *Dates?*

As much as he enjoyed her company, he would be wise

to think carefully and take the time to consider the wisdom of getting involved with the granddaughter of a woman who claimed to be a witch. Hell, after he saw those sparkles following Ema's hand, he wondered if there might not be at least a shred of truth to the rumors. He could only imagine the scrutiny he'd be subject to if he married a witch. Hell, it would be a story The Denver Post wouldn't let slip through their fingers, especially with his family's political and financial connections.

Josh continued watching as Tyler finally appeared to recover. The younger man picked Ema up, swinging her around in a circle with her small frame crushed to his chest.

"Miss Ema, I am so happy to see you again. I'm so glad you are moving home. I'll be able to come and visit you and sit on your porch and watch the stars again. Nobody does star gazing as good as you. We can be star friends again." Once he'd set her on her feet, Ema pulled back from Tyler and laughed before he hugged her tightly again. "You are my best friend always and forever... see, I never forgot!"

The joy on Ema's face was easy to read when she stepped back and smiled up at her admirer's luminous face. "You sure didn't, but I knew you wouldn't. And you know what else? Nobody back east has any clue about stargazing. Can you imagine that?"

Just then, a bellowing voice sounded from the back, "Damnation, if Tyler dropped another tub of dishes, I'm gonna have his hide." Tyler's eyes widened in alarm, but Ema placed her hand on his arm, and Josh looked on in amazement as Tyler instantly settled. With a small wave of her other hand, the shattered dishes fixed and restacked themselves as if invisible hands had placed them back in the large rubber container. Josh gaped at the Rubbermaid® tub, unable to comprehend what he'd just seen.

"Thank you, Miss Ema. You are the bestest friend ever. Can I come by your Granny's store later on and see you? I have to get back to work now, or I'll be in big trouble."

Josh frowned as he thought about rumors he'd heard recently. Not everyone thought Tyler was treated properly by his new boss, a situation Josh needed to keep a close eye on. Tyler looking anxiously toward the back of the diner, which made the hair on the back of his neck stand on end.

"You sure can. I'll be looking forward to it. Let me know when you're coming, and I'll make snacks. And don't you worry a thing about your boss. He's new to Crystal and doesn't know how things work in our small town, but I have a feeling he'll treat you a lot better from now on, okay?"

Josh wondered how she'd been able to make that assurance because the diner's new owner was a first-class ass. Hell, on the man's best days, he was like a bear with a thorn in his paw.

If she could make Sam Tucker behave, Josh would have no choice but admit she was gifted. As if on cue, the burley bastard slammed through the swinging doors separating the kitchen and dining room. Before he could speak, Ema flicked her wrist in his direction, freezing the loud-mouthed bastard in place, then walked to the diner's ill-tempered owner and took his meaty hand between her own, looking him directly in the eye.

"Well, you must be Tyler's boss. I've heard a lot about you...." Josh almost laughed out loud as she deliberately paused several beats, giving Sam an opportunity to wonder about what she might have heard. "Isn't Tyler just the most amazing fellow you've ever met? Talk about somebody who can put a sparkle in your day. I've never met anyone else whose smile can light up a room the way his smiles do, have you? Of course, you haven't. You've obviously recognized his special gifts, which is why you've kept him on, right? Oh my, where are my manners? It's so nice to meet you... Sam. I'm Ema Stone, Opal's grand-daughter. I'm sure we'll be seeing a lot more of each other. Now, I see my dessert has been served, and I'm neglecting my dinner companion, so I'll let you get back to work, but we'll talk again soon."

Sam smiled—the jerk actually smiled at Ema—before muttering, "It's nice to meet you too, Ms. Stone, and any friend of Tyler's is always welcome at the diner." He nodded to her, turned on his heel, and retreated the same way he'd come.

Josh would have never believed it if he hadn't seen it himself. Everyone in the diner seemed to hold their breath, then Josh felt relief sweep through the room when the man disappeared through the large, swinging kitchen door. In all the time Josh had known Sam Tucker, he'd never seen him so docile. It was positively spooky. Sitting across from Ema once again, Josh looked up at her and smiled, even as he shook his head.

"What? I didn't do anything." Her voice might have sounded contrite, but the underlying thread of humor was easy to hear. "Well, maybe a little public relations work, but that's all." She flashed him a cheesy grin that assured him it had been anything but simple PR work.

"You don't say? You seem to be quite popular, Ms. Stone. You have a remarkable talent for pulling people to you. What did you do for a living back east?" Josh would bet if she'd had any client contact, her boss was regretting his loss.

"I have been doing marketing since I got out of college, most recently for Apgate International, an art trading firm."

Josh wasn't an expert on Greek Mythology, but he was sure Apgate was the Goddess of Deception. It seemed an odd name for an organization that should want to put as much distance as possible between themselves and any perception of dishonesty.

"I loved my job… at least in the beginning." Ema's voice softened as she rotated her glass on the table, forming an interesting spiral pattern with the condensation sliding down its smooth surface. She paused, but Josh knew she wasn't finished and wondered why she was choosing her words so carefully. He hoped she'd be more comfortable with him soon. Sighing, she finally added, "I was good at it, too. I brought in a lot of business, but it never seemed to be enough."

Her eyes lost some of their shine, and he regretted bringing up something that so obviously made her unhappy. He waited, sensing there was more to the story, and planned to make some discrete inquiries if she wasn't more forthcoming. When she realized she'd drifted off into her own thoughts, she gave him a shy smile.

"I didn't feel bad leaving because they'd made it painfully clear, I would never advance beyond my entry-level position. Truthfully, I'm not sure the business will stay afloat much longer, anyway. It's weird because they seem to move artwork all around the globe, but the company always seemed to teeter on the verge of financial collapse. If I hadn't known better, I'd have thought it was a start-up or a shell company. Odd that..."

Ema drifted off into her thoughts again, but Josh's interest was piqued by several things she'd said, and he made a mental note to send out some feelers. He certainly didn't need trouble following her home, and the hair on the back of his neck was standing on end. His sixth sense had saved his ass more than once when he'd been a soldier, and the one time he'd ignored it, he and several others had paid a hefty price.

Refocusing his attention on the beautiful woman in front of him, he asked, "What about a boyfriend? Did you break some guy's heart when you packed up and moved?" Josh tried to keep the inquiry casual but wasn't sure how successful he'd been. An angry ex-lover could be a problem, so he could claim professional concern. That was his story, and he was going to stick to it. *Keep telling yourself that, Bennett.*

"Well... I was dating a guy from work. Dating is a completely inaccurate description of how we spent our time. It was more like he came over and watched movies at my house and kept me from doing anything interesting. Now that I look back, the whole thing was actually quite strange."

Something about Ema's observation seemed more than odd, but Josh wasn't sure why he'd gotten the impression. What kind of loser would treat a beautiful woman so poorly? Hell, she'd only been in town a couple of minutes when he'd invited her to dinner. She'd obviously been hungry because she polished off her dinner and a decadent dessert in record time. He almost laughed out loud when she blinked in surprise at the empty, chocolate-smeared dish in front of her.

Josh hadn't planned to ask such a personal question, but it just seemed to bubble up from deep inside him and burst out of his mouth. "Were you sleeping with him?" The minute the words left his mouth, he wished he could pull them back.

Ema looked up at him, blinking her big green eyes for several seconds, trying to bring both him and his words into focus, then raised her eyebrows in questions. "No." She said nothing else, and Josh was sure the simplicity of her answer was loaded with a hidden meaning but damned if he knew how to interpret it. Hell, he thought women were supposed to love complicated verbal exchanges. His sisters had never given a one-word response when they could use two hundred.

Mentally shaking his head, Josh couldn't help wondering why the years the two of them had spent apart hadn't weakened his attraction to the bewitching woman sitting across from him. He was grateful to the elderly couple who stepped up to speak with her, giving him a chance to sit back and regard her closely. Fuck, he needed to find his damned social filters and kick them into gear again.

Sitting quietly, watching as Ema charmed the older couple with her enthusiasm and self-effacing humor, he tried to pinpoint how she was able to connect with each person she spoke with. She regaled people with tales of the trials and tribulations she'd faced living away from home, and Josh caught himself laughing out loud several times.

Ema seemed to take care of everyone around her, but who took care of her? Once again, his inner Dom pushed to the surface. *Who takes care of you, Ema?* Even though Josh appreciated her nurturing nature, she had trouble magnet written all over her. As they stood at the cash register, Ema reached into her purse. Shaking his head, Josh placed his hand on her arm, halting her attempt to find her billfold in the enormous bag she called a purse.

"Let me buy your dinner… please. Consider it a welcome home treat from an old friend." She smiled and thanked him politely, but he didn't miss the fleeting look of relief in her eyes. Josh schooled his expression, hoping she wouldn't notice his concern. Why would she be worried about the cost of a simple meal? Evidence was mounting—there was more going on with Ema's decision to return to Climax than simple concern for her grandmother.

Earlier she'd described her apartment as a hole-in-the-wall, so he assumed she hadn't been paying much rent. Even an entry-level marketing job should have allowed her to put away some money each month. The only thing that made sense was she was giving money to her no-account mother and sister. Sending money to those two worthless women was tantamount to setting it on fire.

How Opal had raised such a worthless daughter was a mystery for the ages. Ema's younger sister was a real piece of work as well. The last time he'd asked Opal about them, the older woman said they were both living in Miami, and he'd sent up a silent prayer they stayed there.

Ema reached over the small glass case to introduce herself and shake hands with the young woman running the register, holding the woman's hand for long seconds.

"He'll be okay... your dad, I mean. I know you are worried about his medical tests tomorrow, but he's fine... you'll see. Oh, and congratulations... you're going to be a beautiful June bride." Josh wasn't sure Ema saw the shocked look on the young woman's face, but he hadn't missed it, nor had he missed the pretty cashier's audible sigh of relief.

Ema had already moved toward the door when the young woman looked up at him with eyes shining with unshed tears and asked, "How did she know? We just got engaged last weekend. We haven't told anyone yet. We were waiting to find out about my dad. I don't understand."

Josh just laughed. "Ask around, Rita. I'm sure someone will be happy to fill you in on Emerald Stone." Josh moved quickly to catch up with Ema before she reached Spellbound.

"Ema, hold up a minute. I want to say something before you go in and talk to your grandmother." He took a deep breath and waited for her to look up at him. "I might have a suggestion for a small apartment if you are still interested tomorrow... or later tonight. Let me see your cell phone." When she handed it to him, puzzled by his request, Josh quickly programmed in his work and personal numbers before setting it back in her outstretched hand.

"Call me if you need anything, and please try to remember, well... your grandmother is kind of a cool old lady. I'd hate to see you go postal on her like you mentioned earlier." He smiled when she gave him a strange look. Nothing really new there—women had been giving him that confused look for years, and more than one of his dates had accused him of being deliberately vague. It was more that he was accustomed to the military's "need to know" basis communication, and old habits obviously die hard.

"Thanks for the dinner and company, Josh. I'm sure I'll be fine. How bad can it be? I'll catch you later. Good night." When she turned and breezed through Spellbound's front door, Josh let out a breath he hadn't realized he was holding.

How bad, indeed.

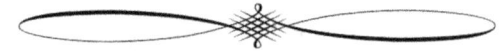

CHAPTER FOUR

EMA STEPPED INTO the metaphysical shop that had been in her family for generations and bit her lip to keep a shocked scream from escaping. The entire store was covered in a thick layer of dust, making it look as if it had been abandoned for a decade or more. Holy Hannah, she could actually see footprints in the filth covering the floor.

Shelves that were usually filled with brightly colored, uniquely shaped decorative apothecary bottles stood nearly empty, and labels were missing from the few dust-covered bottles that remained. The bins that had always been filled with dried herbs and roots were empty, and many of them were missing their hinged wooden lids. She stood stock-still, taking in what looked like an abandoned business. How had things gotten so out of hand, and why on earth had her grandmother kept this from her?

"Oh, my Goddess above… what's going on?" Raising her voice, she called out, "Granny? Aunt Ruby? Is there anyone here?" Moving quietly toward the backroom, she heard a noise that sounded as if someone was moving around in the small upstairs apartment on the second floor. Alarmed, she looked for something she could use as a weapon, but the only thing she could find was a child's broom. The irony wasn't lost on her, but she grabbed it, anyway. Holding it like a baseball bat, she started up the stairs as stealthily as she could.

Ema didn't realize she was holding her breath until she started seeing black dots floating in front of her eyes. Taking a deep breath, she leaned against the wall, trying to calm her racing heart. When she'd almost reached the top, she peeked around the corner, coming face to face with her diminutive grandmother. Gasping in surprise, Ema dropped the broom, collapsed onto the top step, and dropped her head to her knees, trying to stave off the dizziness engulfing her.

Looking up when she could finally pull in enough oxygen to speak, Ema squeaked, "Spell me, you nearly scared me to death. Why are you up here?" When she stood and stepped forward to give her five-foot-nothing Granny a hug, Ema glanced around the room and let out an excited squeal. "Oh, you guys are the best. You've already fixed the place up for me. You didn't have to do this. I could have crashed at your house on the sofa tonight, then started on this tomorrow, but it's perfect. You've set everything up... and... hey, wait a minute. Isn't this your furniture?"

Ema was so relieved she wasn't facing an intruder, then excited about the apartment already being set up and ready for her, she forgot she was hugging and kissing a woman who was supposed to be deathly ill. Stepping back and focusing her gaze on Granny Good Witch, she let her eyes move over her remarkably healthy appearance. Ema's brows pulled together as she frowned. When she noted the guilty expression on her tiny trouble-making grandmother's face, Ema wanted to scream.

"You sure seem to be fit as a fiddle for someone who was knocking on death's door just a few short days ago. Are you planning to tell me you've made a remarkable recovery, or are you going to admit you lied to me?" Ema was working up to a real good mad when her Aunt Ruby stepped between them.

"Oh, Emerald dear, we are so happy to see you, aren't we, Opal? I'm afraid you're right. It seems my sister may have exaggerated a bit about her ill health, but it's still wonderful to have you here." Ema didn't move or speak, so her sweet, peacekeeping great-aunt blustered on. "About the apartment... well, we've been living here for a while. Money was tight... this darned economy has just been a bad spell for everyone. Then there is that pesky issue with the neighboring coven—they are beyond shady. Black magic pressure has been the devil's spit for sure."

Ema held up her hand—she'd heard enough for now.

"Why didn't you tell me there wasn't room for me? I could have made other plans. Now I'm homeless, and well... hex it all. I feel damned foolish for thinking moving home might work out." She didn't even want to think about how cold she would be sleeping in her blasted car tonight. Now she understood why Josh had insisted on programming his numbers into her phone. Nothing like the public humiliation of having the hottest man she'd ever met clued in on what a freaking disaster she was walking into.

OPAL STEPPED AROUND her sister to enfold her favorite granddaughter's cool fingers in her own. When her small, wrinkled hand wrapped around Ema's slender, pale hand, Opal was stunned by the feeling of desolation rolling off the beautiful young witch. It was obvious there was more troubling Ema than her grandmother's deception and the troublesome issue with the apartment. Evidently, her granddaughter was keeping some secrets of her own.

Emerald had always underestimated her magical abilities, never truly recognizing the strength of her Goddess-given powers. Opal had told Emerald the legacy of Aradia, but explanations of how relevant the story was to her personally seemed to fall on deaf ears. As the firstborn daughter of a seventh generation, Emerald had always been destined for greatness, but first, she needed to believe in herself. The training would be intense, but Emerald's natural abilities would make it easier to bring her quickly up to speed. The only problem Opal could see was the fact Emerald had always been prone to a lack of interest that made her careless and a general belief that magic wasn't necessary. The lack of faith wouldn't be difficult to remedy, but clumsiness in the world of magic could be downright deadly.

Opal knew it had been wrong to trick Ema into coming home, but now it appeared the Fates might have orchestrated a blessed rescue for everyone involved. Neither Opal nor Ruby had ever talked about Emerald's status to her mother, though it seemed unlikely Jade didn't know. Hell's bells, even Opal knew her daughter was a flake.

If Jade had fully understood Emerald's destiny, she'd never have agreed to leave her in Opal's care. Jade would have used Ema's "value" to the magic community as leverage for every privilege she could swindle. While she would have received more in the exchange, she would have sealed her own fate. It didn't matter how little regard Opal had for her flighty daughter, she didn't want to see any harm come to her. Now the trick was going to be not losing Ema before she even had a chance to unpack.

"Now, Ema, we really are thrilled that you are here, and don't you worry, we'll figure out something with the sleeping arrangements. You'll see." Smiling brightly, she waved in the general direction of the teapot, and it started whistling. Ruby moved into the tiny kitchen and set about making their tea while Opal and Ema sat at the small kitchen table.

The two sisters spent the next hour filling Ema in on all the problems they'd been experiencing over the past couple of years and how much worse they'd become over the past several months. They also explained how they thought she might help. Neither of the elderly witches mentioned that they were convinced some of the financial pressure had come from the Council of Magic to encourage Emerald back to Crystal.

Opal's twin sister, Ola, was a member of the Council and had assured them magic's governing body wanted the store set to rights, but the timing seemed awfully suspect. Opal could hear the questions rolling around like a tempest in Ema's sharp mind. The cresting storm was barreling their way, and Goddess help those who dared challenge a seventh-generation witch.

The catch is… as much as the Council wants you here, the dark forces don't want you anywhere near Mother Earth's power. Opal sent the subtle message to her granddaughter, hoping it would take root. Ema needed to be here, but even more important was making certain she understood what she was up against.

Exhausted beyond any expectation of being functional, Ema walked down the steep steps leading to the store's backroom in a haze-like stupor. It took everything she could muster to put one foot in front of the other. She felt herself sliding headlong into a maze of scattered thoughts as she reached the front of the store.

Reaching forward with her right hand to grasp the ornately carved knob decorating the elaborately carved wooden door, she screamed as glass exploded all around her. She was paralyzed in fear for a split second, but when the sharp crack of what sounded like lightning or a rifle registered in her fatigue clouded mind, she was yanked back to the moment. Dropping to the floor, Ema pulled her phone from her pocket, dialing before she realized her fingers were moving.

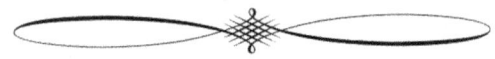

BY THE TIME Josh reached Spellbound, his entire body was pulsing with adrenaline. The only thing he hated more than feeling out of control was knowing he was behind the curve of whatever happened across town. He tried unsuccessfully to push back his growing panic, barely putting his truck in park before leaping out of the still-rocking one ton and dashing through the open door of the small store, searching for the woman who'd called him moments earlier.

He'd been thrilled to see Ema's number on his Caller ID, but that had changed the instant he heard her frantic cry for help. Even though he'd only been on the other side of their small community, it felt like a lifetime before he made his way to Crystal's main street. Bursting through the front door, Josh skidded to a stop and felt his knees almost fold in relief when he found her unharmed.

Ema was sitting on the floor amid shattered glass, shaking like a leaf. He was grateful she appeared uninjured and equally puzzled that she didn't appear to have a single scratch or cut anywhere. Stepping gingerly toward her, his heart squeezed when she finally realized someone was close. Damn, how the hell had she lived in Boston without developing a basic level of situational awareness?

The look of raw fear in her beautiful green eyes made his breath catch. He was swamped with relief when she scrambled to her feet and launched herself into his arms. Ema wrapped around him like a spider monkey, and he enclosed her in his embrace. Pulling in a calming breath, he sent up a silent prayer of thanks to whatever guardian angel had been looking out for her.

When Josh inquired about Opal and Ruby, Ema simply pointed to the upstairs apartment. He didn't want to think about why the two hadn't heard the shattering glass.

Hearing them thundering down the stairs, Josh wondered if he'd jinxed himself by thinking about the dynamic duo. Waiting for several beats, he wanted to roll his eyes. Evidently, thundering down the stairs only equated with noise—speed was obviously a different consideration.

Opal and Ruby burst into the room, their raised voices inquiring about the siren they'd heard. *Holy shit, they didn't hear a rifle shot or glass exploding, but they heard my siren?* Knowing Ema had been alone downstairs meant she'd been the intended target. Realizing someone intended to harm her sent ice racing through Josh's veins. Hell, the only people who knew she was in town were the few they visited with at the diner. She'd only been home a matter of hours, and someone was already trying to kill her? It didn't make any sense.

As Opal and Ruby surveyed the mess, Josh noted the silent exchange between the two. As quickly as their meaningful looks appeared, they vanished. With a few waves of their hands, the large glass window was repaired, the entire mess evaporating into thin air.

What the ever-loving hell? So much for denying magic... or gathering evidence.

Moving to stand in front of them, Opal directed her question to Josh rather than her granddaughter. "Is she alright? Does she need anything? Holy hexes on a half-shell, can you believe that mess? What happened to the glass? How did it break?"

Josh looked at her with narrowed eyes as he answered. "Gunshot. Probably a high-power sniper rifle, if I had to guess. Didn't you two hear *anything* upstairs?" There was something about Opal's overly eager demeanor that gave

Josh the impression she knew more than she would willingly share, but at the moment, all he was concerned about was Ema.

Opal's eyes widened, and he heard Ruby's sharp gasp before she answered, "No Josh, we... well, we were sort of playing the music loud and dancing along with those cuties on Dancing with the Stars. Those young studs are just the hottest...." Josh's mind blissfully blocked out the rest of her chatter about shirtless men on a damned television show. Looking chagrined, Opal shrugged. "Oh, well... I guess that is a little too much information, huh?"

Not knowing how to respond, he moved to the side of the room and sat on a wooden bench away from the windows. Shaking his head, he wondered just how loud that music had been. Hell, rifle shots were *loud* unless they were silenced, and now that he considered it, that sort of crack should have been heard all over town. The thin air at this altitude would have amplified the sound, yet he hadn't gotten a single call other than Ema's.

Josh was still holding Ema close when he heard her giggle. Pulling back, he studied her as she started laughing. He recognized her response as the hysterical laughter people used to distract themselves from something frightening and knew the adrenaline crash wouldn't be far behind. Smoothing the backs of his fingers down her pale cheeks, he watching her pupils dilate. Seeing her reaction made him wonder how she would respond to the other ways he wanted to touch her.

Helping her to her feet, Josh kept his hands clamped around Ema's tiny waist until he was sure she was steady on her feet. Standing, he looked down into her dark green eyes.

"Ema, are you alright?" When she blinked without answering, he quickly ran his hands over her, making certain she was indeed unharmed. "Can you tell me exactly what happened? Don't leave out a single detail. Tell me everything."

For the next half hour, Josh listened as Ema answered every question he threw at her, her responses consistent, clear, and concise. It was mesmerizing to watch the way the various shades of green changed, depending on the emotion of the moment. Ema's story never varied, and as impressive as her recall was, she hadn't given him a clue who would want to hurt her. He sighed with frustration. Ema hadn't seen anyone or realized she was in danger until the window exploded around her.

When she finally leaned back in her chair and closed her eyes, he conceded they were finished. She was wilting fast. He felt guilty for having pushed her when she looked up at him.

"Josh, I really have told you everything I know," she whispered. I know it isn't much, but I just don't have the energy to continue. I need to find a place for my sleeping bag, so I can get some rest."

Josh nodded and turned to Opal. "I don't think it's safe for Ema to stay here tonight, and you obviously don't have room for her. The guesthouse at the ranch is vacant. It's small but a damn sight better than sleeping on the floor, and she'll be much safer there. I'll help her get what she needs from her car and drive her there myself. I'm worried she's too tired to make the drive safely."

Shifting his gaze back to Ema, he softened his tone.

"Don't even get me started on your car, sweetheart. You'll be hard-pressed to make it much further than the nearest garage. Whatever possessed you to think that car would make it two thousand miles boggles the imagination." Without waiting for a response, Josh led Ema to the door.

Stepping out into the cool night air, Josh laughed to himself. Calling the ranch "safer" was a gross understatement. Hell, he wasn't any more paranoid than other former Special Forces operatives on the planet—as a rule, they were all obsessive about security. It was a simple fact of his former life—he'd made enemies, some of them with long memories and plenty of money to hold a grudge.

When he moved home, he'd upgraded the perimeter security, making certain the property surrounding the ranch's main compound was protected by a state-of-the-art monitoring system. The system used technology so advanced, many of the components weren't available on the civilian market. With the underground pressure sensors and above-ground motion detectors, no one would get within a half-mile of the main house or the smaller guesthouse without him knowing. There was a safe room in the main house and a hidden underground tunnel between the guesthouse and the main residence.

Josh's parents moved to Denver when he returned home, so he lived alone in the sprawling main house. Hell, he and Ema could both live in the massive home and only see one another in passing. He doubted Ema would feel comfortable with that arrangement, so he would stick to his original plan of settling her in the guest residence.

The small guesthouse was approximately twenty-five yards behind the main house, and in his opinion, it was perfect for Ema. The kitchen was extremely small, but it had never been an issue since guests were always invited to share the family meals in the main dining room. Ema had commented during dinner she wasn't particularly interested in cooking, so he didn't expect any complaints. He was certain the heated floors in the newly refurbished bathroom would more than make up for the small kitchen.

Walking out of the store, Josh led Ema to the ancient yacht on wheels she called a car. Keeping his arm around her slender shoulders, he tried to shelter her from the shifting breeze, suspecting her shiver was as much from adrenaline as the sudden biting chill of the wind. Damn, he could feel the weather changing and wanted to get her settled before the storm hit. *Wait... wasn't her car blue earlier? And I'm sure the officer in Kansas said it was pink.*

Keeping her anchored against his size, Josh realized he'd never really considered their height difference until this moment. Emerald's larger-than-life personality was so captivating, he hadn't thought about how petite she was. When they reached the driver's door, he turned to her and held out his hand for the key.

"What do you need to get out of your car to be comfortable tonight?" When she just stared at the car without blinking, he tried again. "Sweetheart, can you tell me what you consider the most valuable thing in your car? We'll take that, and I'll get a couple of friends to drive it out to the ranch later." *Or maybe I'll have them deliver her possessions and lock the damned thing up. If I'm lucky, they'll let it roll off a cliff.* The thought no sooner moved through his mind than he felt a heated blast of air. Blinking in surprise, Josh could have sworn the car's color shifted to black for a split second before settling back to a different shade of blue. *What the fuck?*

"My Book of Shadows... that's the most valuable thing... I won't leave it. It's in the satchel on the passenger seat." Her voice pulled him back to the moment, breaking the trance he'd fallen into, staring at the mechanical mystery in front of him. "My car doesn't lock, so maybe if it's not too much trouble, could they lock it somewhere safe until they can deliver it? I don't have much, but everything I own is in this car."

For a few seconds, he'd wondered how a book about shadows could possibly be her most valued possession, but it was quickly becoming too damned cold to debate the point standing in the street. He'd ask her later when they were somewhere warmer. Frankly, concerns about a book ranked low on the list of questions he had about the woman who was becoming more mysterious by the moment. Hell, for all he knew, she was still too shaken to think clearly. As he started around the car, her words finally registered.

Her car doesn't lock? How did she travel more than halfway across the country and not lose everything? Hell, how did she keep from getting herself killed? Shaking his head, at least now he understood why she'd taken a nap in her car rather than opting for a motel room. Leaning into the behemoth, he looked around, planning to grab as much as he could. He had already promised to make certain his friends at the garage didn't leave her car vulnerable too long, so he wasn't worried about getting everything.

Josh set the small suitcase on the car's battered roof before gathering up several other small bags and reclosing the car's heavy door. He quickly stuck the keys in his pocket, and when he turned back to where he'd left Ema on the other side of the vehicle, she was gone. Frantically looking around, he finally ran to the other side of the car and found her collapsed in a heap in the street.

"*Shit*. Ema, are you alright?" Damn, he should have known better than to leave her alone. He'd seen adrenaline crashes many times working with the teams and knew the signs. Hoping she'd been past the crash point turned out to be a mistake. Leaning down, he scooped her into his arms and carried her to his SUV. After strapping her in and reclining the seat, he tossed her bags into the back seat and headed to the garage at the end of the street.

Leaving the keys to her tank on wheels with his friends, Josh thanked them when they agreed to move her car into their shop right away, even though they'd been confused by his vague response about the Buick's color. Telling his friends the damn thing seemed to change colors would send them into fits of laughter, and he wasn't prepared to have the locals dropping a net over him just yet. When he pointed down the street at her monstrosity on wheels, their jaws dropped open.

Rolling his eyes, Josh asked Buck and Tag to inspect the car and let him know what it would take to make it roadworthy. His friends grinned and shook their heads, assuring him they'd deliver her belongings within the hour and let him know in a few days what it would cost to update Ema's monster mobile. Didn't it figure they'd already given the car a nickname?

Once they were finally on the road to the ranch, he called his housekeeper to let her know they'd have a guest for the foreseeable future. As he ended the call, Ema's beautiful green eyes fluttered open.

"Oh, my Goddess, Josh, I'm so sorry. I can't believe I've put you to so much trouble. Curses, I just got here, and I'm already a nuisance. I'm a disaster magnet." Guilt clouded her pretty green eyes as she let out a breath that sounded too much like defeat. "I swear I'm not always this much trouble to have around, not most of the time, anyway. Well, okay… it seems to happen with frightening regularity, but it isn't like I try to be a pain or anything." She pulled in a deep breath, then let it out slowly.

"Probably wouldn't do any good to deny it. You'd find out eventually since you're the sheriff. *Spell me.* Who am I kidding? The firefighters near my apartment have probably posted my picture on some sort of website, warning other departments in advance, like a 'Most Not Wanted in Your City' list or something. Half of Hades seems to have me on speed dial. Maybe I should check the Post Office. That's where the Most Wanted posters are, right? I'll bet those guys would use that resource. They were pretty creative in their taunts when they found out I was moving. Drat, a couple of them even offered to help me pack. They tried to pretend they were teasing but weren't very convincing." When she finally seemed to surface from her rant, Ema blinked in surprise when she noticed he'd pulled to the side of the road and was smiling at her. Shaking her head in disbelief, she let out a frustrated sigh. "Oh hex, I said all that out loud, didn't I?" When he merely nodded, she shook her head, turning back to the window to look out at the trees lining the two-lane highway.

"If it makes you feel any better, I'm fairly certain there

isn't a website like the one you described." He chuckled and added, "Even if there was, I wouldn't care. You've livened things up, that's for sure, but I'm glad you are home, Ema. I missed the friendship we'd started building." Pausing for a few seconds to let her mind catch up, he noted some of the tension appeared to drain from her slender shoulders.

"I'm glad to see some color back in your cheeks. I was worried about you there for a while. We'll be at the ranch in a few minutes, and I've already called Reyna to give her a heads up. She's already started the heat in the guesthouse, so it'll be ready for you by the time we get there. My pals at the garage are bringing your things up in a little while, and they'll check out your car in a couple of days. By the time I give you the grand tour and help the guys unload, Renya will have baked a dessert worthy of a five-star resort, so be ready."

Pulling back onto the road, Josh smiled to himself. He wasn't kidding. Reyna had been with the Bennett family for longer than Josh had been alive. The feisty woman liked to remind him she had seniority, teasing him about pushing his way in after she'd taken the job.

"We'll sit down and brainstorm. Maybe we can come up with some ideas about who might have been responsible for what happened at Spellbound." *We'll chat if I can keep her awake long enough.*

"Before you put up a fuss, I'm well aware you just ate a little while ago, but Reyna was so excited about having someone to cook for, I didn't have the heart to tell her we'd already eaten dessert. So, mum's the word, okay?"

Josh didn't remember the last time he'd actually looked

forward to eating at home. Hell, for that matter, he couldn't remember the last time he asked a woman out to dinner. He didn't invite them into his private domain because it gave them ideas. Ema was different from the women he usually spent time with, and everything about bringing her home with him just felt *right*.

He was still sorting through his unexpected and unsettling need to protect her. It wasn't just because it was his job to serve the people of Crystal—there was something more meaningful. Josh could sense there was something deeper, a more significant piece of information lingering in the background just out of his reach. Shaking his head, he set his concern aside. Returning his full attention to Ema, Josh focused on making certain she was settled and that he had all the information he could before she crashed.

The one thing he knew? There was *something* about Emerald Stone that made her important to everyone she met. *She's damned important to me.* It was a sobering truth, but there it was. Finally, admitting it to himself was as terrifying as it was a relief.

CHAPTER FIVE

N IGEL LANCASTER STOOD deep in the shadows, cursing the events unfolding on the other side of Crystal, Colorado's ridiculously wide main street. Damn it, how had his plan imploded before it had barely begun? He'd been watching over Emerald Stone since she was a toddler—he should have everything down to a damned science by now.

As the firstborn daughter in the seventh generation of direct descendants of Aradia, Queen of Witches, Emerald Stone's arrival had been greatly anticipated by the Magic Council. The group charged with overseeing the world of magic had closely monitored her developing special gifts and assigned him as her overseer before she started nursery school. The first time she scrambled onto his lap, the petite beauty with the sparkling green eyes had stolen his heart.

He visited her several times each year while she was growing up. His assignment included monitoring her progress, making suggestions related to her training, and overseeing the various magicals hired to be by her side during her day-to-day activities. Emerald wouldn't remember any of her early interactions with him. Nigel remained diligent about erasing her memory of their encounters. She'd captivated him as a child. He'd never met anyone with her unique ability to draw people to her. The skill was so rare in magic circles, there was very little written about how it would affect her future. The downside? She'd become overwhelmed and left Crystal.

When she moved to the east coast, the council worried she would permanently turn her back on magic—a concern he understood but disagreed with. Hell, anyone with her hideous mother and sister would probably want as much distance between themselves and family as they could manage. He'd always known she would return. The power of the Crystal Cavern would pull her back home, eventually.

Emerald Stone was many things, but most importantly, she was destined to become his partner. He'd known from the moment he'd set eyes on her, the two of them would be a force to be reckoned with. Their combined power would be unlike any seen in several generations. Having her remember he'd visited so often would have steered their relationship in an entirely different direction, changing her view of him forever. The last thing he wanted was for her to see him as was a kindly old uncle intent on using her magic for his own selfish purposes. The truth wasn't his friend when it came to Emerald Stone.

The fact he was indeed much older than Emerald was irrelevant in magical circles. The life spans of witches, wizards, and sorcerers were exponentially longer than nonmagicals, so age was little more than an arbitrary number. Nigel's family was one of the oldest in England— the House of Lancaster was a dynasty of English kings. His grandfather headed the family as one of the opposing factions in the fifteenth-century War of the Roses. As a reminder of his heritage, their family symbol, a deep red rose, was handstitched on every article of clothing Nigel wore.

With each passing year, Emerald's progress seemed to slow until he'd understood the council's concern. After moving to Boston, Emerald had virtually stopped using magic. Nigel knew Emerald felt pressured from every direction. Her grandmother was trying to talk her into returning home, her mother's monetary demands over the past year nearly bled her dry, her sister's jealousy was exhausting and borderline pathological, the man she thought was interested in her was little more than a casual companion, and her career stalled almost before it started.

The last time he saw her before she'd moved home, Nigel had known she was close to breaking. It had been difficult for him to walk away, knowing it was in his power to fix, but he'd stuck to his original plan. The only thing he left behind after their later visits was a comfortable familiarity she would feel but not fully understand each time they were reintroduced. More often than not, over the past couple of years, he'd only checked on her through third parties or briefly in disguise. Right now, that was a decision he regretted since he hadn't been the person she called when she'd been frightened.

Nigel always underestimated the powerful magic pulsing along the ley line beneath the small town. What he'd planned to sound like a rock hitting the small metaphysical shop's front window ended up sounding like a damned rifle. Luckily, he'd been able to contain the sound. *Yeah, all I needed was to start a damned avalanche. Is it avalanche season? Who the hell knows? I swear Colorado has the most unpredicta-*

ble weather I've ever encountered.

He'd only meant to startle Emerald, then race to her rescue. What he hadn't planned for was Dudley Do-Right's involvement. Hex, he'd heard the man's truck roaring across town before it slid to a stop in front of Spellbound's front door, lights flashing and siren blaring. Great Goddess evidently, magicals weren't the only ones with a flair for the dramatic.

When Emerald first arrived, he'd watched the local sheriff move to her car within minutes. The damned cop had been hanging out on the sidewalk, chatting with anyone who happened by. The damned Sheriff of Nottingham was checking his watch for an hour before she'd docked that damned boat she called a car, making Nigel wondered who alerted him to her pending arrival. The man's body language remained professional for all of sixty damn seconds before he'd unceremoniously dumped her onto the dusty street by pulling open the driver's door as she made a Herculean effort to force the damned thing open.

Nigel understood the logic behind the Council's desire to allow individuals to make their own way and letting the fates play their hand, but that damned car was a menace. Judging from the sheriff's scowl, their mutual contempt for her mode of transportation might well be Nigel and Matt Dillon's only common ground. *Not entirely true. You share an interest in the gifted witch, blushing furiously as Sheriff Bennett hoists her back to her feet.*

Before Nigel could move to her side, Sheriff Rosco P. Coltrane bundled Emerald off to the small eatery down the street. Damnation, she hadn't even made her way into her family's rundown store before Andy Fucking Taylor marked himself as a problem. By the time they'd reemerged, Nigel had been vibrating with frustration, and the strain of holding back his anger was taking a toll.

He shamelessly eavesdropped during Emerald's conversation with Opal and Ruby. When he'd heard the defeat in Ema's sweet voice, the final edge of his anger collapsed in an avalanche. His vision had turned blood-red as he wondered if he and the Magic Council hadn't gone overboard in their exertion of pressure on Opal and Ruby to get Emerald back to Crystal.

Nigel shook off his useless second-guessing. It was too late to change things now. Hex, he'd been so lost in those thoughts he nearly missed his cue, and rushing meant the magic he'd sent toward the fragile glass at the store's front was more powerful than intended. *When will I ever learn everything in Crystal is amplified?*

The magic he'd used to shatter the front window was lightning fast and way more intense than it should have been. Ema had mistaken the ear-splitting crack for a gunshot. It had essentially been the same effect as a clap of thunder—something Ema would have recognized if Opal had been doing her job.

Slipping back into the shadows, Nigel could only watch as the scene played out. It was mind-boggling how quickly things could spin out of control when Emerald was involved. The only predictable element was Opal's immediate recognition of his magical signature. The petite witch was a damned whirling dervish. She'd known the instant she stepped into the room who broke the glass, and if Nigel was betting, he'd put his money on her knowing what his plan had been as well.

The damned woman not only instantly erased all traces of his magic, she also fixed the window and cloaked the small, dilapidated shop in a silence spell. He'd been equally surprised and impressed by the strength of her magic. No doubt it was a direct result of her frustration with him, so he'd taken his time reversing it. When he'd worked through the final layer allowing him to hear their conversation again, Emerald's knight in shining armor was pulling things out of her car before quickly whisking her away.

Swearing under his breath, Nigel paced along the rock wall across the street, hoping to work through his frustration as Bennett's truck drove down the wide street, taking Emerald Stone farther and farther from Spellbound. Finding her was never a problem. He'd tagged her Book of Shadows years ago with a tracking spell. No witch would leave their book behind unless their life was in mortal danger, so Emerald would be easy for him to locate, but that didn't ease his frustration.

Once he'd spent some of his irritation, Nigel didn't waste any time making his way into the dismal metaphysical shop. The damned placed sat atop one of the most powerful crystal deposits in the world. Anyone sensitive to the energy created by the rich mineral deposit would feel the power sizzling in the air around them. The size of the crystal resources below the town was a carefully guarded secret. If nonmagicals had gotten wind of what lay just beneath the surface, they'd have ravaged the site years ago. The monetary value of the minerals in today's market was staggering, but the mystical value was truly the most significant.

Striding toward the front door of Spellbound, Nigel thought back on the months he'd watched that nitwit Frank Black attempt to spy on Emerald. The low-level magical reported to the dark forces with an unusually high level of regularity. Even more importantly, his negative energy drain on those around him had done untold damage. Why on earth the senior members of the council let Black run unchecked for so long was one of the many unanswered questions only the Great Goddess above understood.

Hexing hell, Black was as lazy as a rotten log and not nearly as smart. The cretin's connections to those practicing the dark arts were well documented. Nigel had argued against his involvement. Even if the man was an incompetent boob, Emerald shouldn't have been exposed to the ever-increasing amount of powerful negative energy surrounding Black.

Shaking his head in frustration, Nigel knew it was all water under the bridge at this point. Even though Frank Black was no longer an immediate concern, Nigel was beginning to think the good Sheriff of Crystal might well be a bigger challenge. He'd heard all the bullshit about Bennett and Emerald being fated… blah, blah, blah. Nigel didn't want to marry the girl—he wanted her as a magical partner. If there were other benefits, he wouldn't turn them down, but it was their professional partnership that would benefit them both.

One problem at a time. Right now, he needed to face a very pissed-off witch and her sister, who had the ability to poison him without breaking a sweat. Nigel knew he was walking into a shitstorm. Opal Stone was territorial on her best day, and there wasn't any doubt his interference would have her as spitting mad as a scorched cat. As an alchemist, Opal's younger sister, Ruby, might well mix a potion designed to impart a slow, torturous death for no other reason than to stem her sister's fury.

Stepping through the store's front entrance was tantamount to traveling back in time. Nigel sighed at the dismal state the shop had fallen into. Looking around, he regretted how far the Council had allowed things to spiral out of control. The financial pressure they'd allowed the dark magicians to put on the Stone family had certainly been overdone. The interior of the store was a disaster. There should be a limit to how much interference was allowed when dealing with dark magicals. Great Goddess, this was a fucking train wreck. If Emerald didn't agree to help turn the business around, there was a very real possibility the property would fall into the wrong hands.

Nigel was certain those interested in annexing the tiny coven Opal led were well aware the store held something special. He was equally certain they didn't know how vast the resources were or the extent of the power at stake. Forces playing on the wrong end of the magical spectrum wouldn't have let anything stand in their way if they understood the full potential of the limitless power pulsing beneath the Stone family's store. It was a small miracle Opal's family had shielded the energy for as long as they had. The dark magicals had been ramping up their efforts to absorb the Stone's coven, and the Council expected the efforts to become exponentially more aggressive now that Ema was home.

Sighing, Nigel straightened his spine and walked directly into the storm. It was too much to hope Opal and Ruby would think he'd left town. It was impossible to mask a magical signature as powerful as his when dealing with a gifted witch. Frankly, it required too much energy to maintain the illusion. His presence alone would send ripples far and wide through the magical community, so he needed to bring all three of the Stone women on board quickly.

Looking up into Opal Stone's narrowed eyes and seeing the rippling, angry waves of energy radiating through her aura confirmed his suspicions—she was seven kinds of pissed. Unfortunately, there wasn't much he could say to help the situation. Less than a second later, Ruby Stone joined her sister. *Just fucking dandy.* Ruby crossed her arms over her chest, her dark eyes filled with almost as much venom as her sister's.

Opal Stone was the more powerful of the two witches, but Ruby was a formidable opponent in her own right. The younger Stone was also blindly loyal to her family. Ruby's background as a chemist scared the hell out of anyone with a lick of sense, and he hadn't even considered what Opal's twin, Magic Council member, Ola Stone, would do when she discovered his faux pas.

Deciding a direct and honest approach, along with a sincere apology, were his only options, Nigel greeted the women and explained exactly why he'd shown up. When he offered the embarrassing details of his mistake and miscalculation of the strength of the spell, they appeared to relax marginally. Some of the tension drained from their narrowed shoulders when he apologized, but he knew it was far from over. What he didn't mention was the extent of the Council's involvement in the store's steady decline and the fact he'd be sticking around for the foreseeable future. There was no sense in giving two angry old women any unnecessary ammunition. Hell, they were already going to put up enough roadblocks to his pursuit of enlisting Emerald as a magical partner.

EMA TOOK IN her surroundings, blinking to bring everything into focus. She couldn't believe she was sitting at a small table in the Bennett mansion's kitchen. She'd never seen a kitchen this large outside a commercial setting. *Holy potions and parrot feathers, how many people do they feed here every day? Maybe they run a soup kitchen or do catering on the side?*

Looking across the table at the man who'd starred in every hot dream she'd had since she was a freshman in high school was enough to make her blush. Joshua Bennett was the man Ema had compared all others to, her gold standard for a perfect boyfriend. Unfortunately for her social life, Josh had set the bar so impossibly high, no other man could ever hope to measure up.

Hex me. Josh Bennett has been turning every girl's head since he was a teen, and now it appears he's destined to one of those blessed people who age to perfection like fine wine. I'll probably end up more like Granny Good Witch—a color-blind geriatric whirlwind who looks like she flunked out of clown school.

Ema sighed as she remembered all the times she'd

stood to the side, watching women's heads swivel on their shoulders as though they were trying out for a part in *The Exorcist* whenever Josh entered a room. For Goddess' sake, all the man had to do was walk down the damned street, and women walked into poles or tripped over their own feet. Who was she kidding? It wasn't just women. Men were equally entranced, locking their attention on Josh, their eyes becoming unfocussed as their minds went blank. He always seemed blissfully unaware of the effect he had on people. She'd frequently wondered if that wasn't part of his charm. He'd never been arrogant despite having every reason to be.

Josh's family was not only rich, they were also honest, fair, and genuinely well-respected people. Holy hexes, Ema considered decent people so rare, they might well be the next entry on the endangered species list.

Everything always seemed easy for Josh—he was popular, exceptionally bright, and athletic. There'd been plenty of gold-diggers trying to claim the heart of the most eligible bachelor in western Colorado. Only one had ever gotten close, but thanks to a whispered truth spell, Meghan Morris blurted out her tainted intentions during a large family dinner planned to announce their rushed engagement. Ema might have been young, but she'd known the other girl wasn't pregnant and hadn't wanted to see Josh stuck with a lying wench.

The only other significant challenge she knew Josh had faced was a mission the local rumor mill reported had gone horribly wrong. Of course, any of the information the local gossips swore had been leaked by officials was nothing more than pure speculation, but whatever happened was serious enough for Josh to walk away from a career she knew he'd loved.

Too bad there aren't more heroes willing to walk into hell in defense of others. And it's a damned shame all wildly wealthy people don't help their friends and neighbors the way the Bennetts do. The world would be a lot better place with more light magic.

When Ema was a senior in high school, she'd been thrilled to learn Josh would be home for a few weeks right after graduation. His service in the Special Forces had both impressed and terrified her. As much as Ema worried about him, she'd been completely captivated with their conversation the night they'd kicked back on the hood of his car, talking about his job and watching the stars move across the summer sky.

Josh's enthusiasm and dedication made him seem almost larger-than-life in her young mind. His service to his country earned him a lifetime of respect, but the single trait that had always called to her was his kindness. She'd never seen him be rude or unkind to anyone. When she had mentioned that observation during their conversation at the lake, he'd ducked his head, and the light of the full moon had shown the tinge of pink in his cheeks.

Ema hadn't been surprised tonight at the diner when Josh mentioned he was volunteering with the local Special Olympics. He explained how his long-time friendship with Tyler spurred him to work as a volunteer. When Josh invited her to attend an upcoming meeting, she'd enthusiastically accepted. *Bet he regrets that invitation now.* She could almost hear him in her mind… *Sure Ema… come along to meet people doing amazing work… oh, and be sure to bring your sniper along, too. We'll set up a lottery to figure out how many citizens you can put in danger by just being in the general vicinity.*

No doubt his generous offer to let her be a part of the organization was off the table now. She'd have to be content hearing how the organization had grown from the local scuttlebutt. They hadn't spent much time discussing the special group helping even more special people, but watching his eyes light up when he'd spoken about the participants warmed her heart. The more she'd heard, the more her respect for him had grown.

From what little she'd been able to find on the internet, Josh brought that same single-minded focus to his public service in Crystal. Their small hometown had very little crime, but when Ema's family was involved, a little went a long way. Women in the Stone family were trouble magnets. She made a mental note to put another protection spell in place. *Face it... with me in town, he's going to need it.*

AFTER THEY FINISHED the sweet treat Reyna served, Josh leaned back in his chair and sighed. Stretching his long, muscular legs out in front of him and crossing his ankles under the table, he flashed a smile that made her heart skip a beat.

"We need to revisit what happened at Spellbound. Let's start with the rifle shot, then move on to how things seemed to right themselves. After that, I'd like to know why you thought it was a good idea to drive a clunker car across the country." *Oh brother.* She didn't even want to think about explaining how Granny Good Witch and Aunt Ruby fixed everything with magic. And calling Berta a clunker wasn't going to earn him any points with her enchanted automobile. He sighed when she didn't respond immediately.

"Are you absolutely sure you don't have any idea who might want to hurt you?" The question surprised her because she'd been expecting his focus to shift to magic, but who was she to look a gift horse in the mouth. Given a chance to delay that difficult discussion was a welcome reprieve she intended to grab with both hands.

Over the next hour, Josh pushed Ema to explore every conceivable scenario, but in the end, they were no closer to figuring out who might have fired the shot at her inside the small store. Ema couldn't imagine anyone disliking her enough to hurt her. She didn't have any enemies. Hell, she barely had any friends. The only person she'd seen socially in a year was Frank Black. She doubted Frank would have access to a weapon, let alone know how to fire one. Hex, he wouldn't notice she was gone until he wanted a place to watch television. Ema knew Josh was frustrated with their lack of progress. He wasn't the type to let something like this go without resolving it. Unfortunately, the energy she'd gained from her dessert-fueled sugar rush and adrenaline surge was fading fast, leaving her on the cusp of collapse.

When Josh placed his much larger hand atop hers, Ema felt the warmth pull her back from the edge of exhaustion. Assuring her his deputies were working on tracking down the culprit, Josh reluctantly admitted with no tangible evidence. *Thank you very much, Granny.* There wasn't much chance they'd be able to build a case, even if they got a solid lead.

The light touch of his hand atop hers was enough to let his frustration slowly filter into her mind. Ema hated putting him in a position where he felt helpless. It had to be the worst possible scenario for a man accustomed to being prepared for every outcome. She had said nothing to Josh, but Ema was certain her grandmother knew more than she was sharing—she always did.

Taking a deep breath, she blinked rapidly, fighting a losing battle to stay alert. There wasn't anything to be gained by rehashing the same information again and again. Nothing else could be done tonight, and grilling her grandmother would have to wait until tomorrow morning.

Unless Aunt Ola pops in, Granny and Aunt Ruby are my best hope to figure out what's happening.

Paris and London warned her the Magic Council didn't always willingly share what most magicals considered pertinent information, but in Ema's opinion, that was par for the course with governing bodies. It would be useless for her to speculate, and nothing she could say would ease Josh's mind tonight.

Ema was clueless about the nuances and political maneuvering of the magical community. It was humbling to admit she didn't know much about the organization, but now didn't seem like the best time to point it out to the man who was valiantly trying to deny magic's existence. She'd avoided involvement in all things magical when she could. Frankly, she was tired of all the references to her destiny and duty when no one seemed willing to *adequately* explain what either of those things meant. If there was one thing Ema found annoying as hell, it was *vague*.

Ema's Book of Shadows was the only magical thing she kept close. Her compulsive attachment to the enormous leather-bound book was as much a mystery to her as everything else about the blasted *prophecy* her grandmother had been preaching about since she was old enough to remember. The only thing consistent about her magical background was how irate her mother became anytime her gifts were mentioned. Ema learned at an early age to avoid the topic whenever possible. Hell, she avoided her mother and sister at every opportunity, as well.

Just as Ema stood to leave, she heard an alert sound from Josh's phone. After checking it, he'd told her his friends were coming up the drive. The three men made short work of moving her things into the Bennett's beautiful guesthouse. She almost cried when she got her first look at the lovely cottage. The living room alone was larger than her entire apartment in Boston, and when she spotted the large, jetted bathtub, Ema practically swooned. Staring longingly at the tub, Ema wondered whether or not to indulge in the temptation. Josh's laughter from the front of the small house broke through the fog of her internal debate.

Once his friends said their goodbyes, the reality of being alone with Josh settled in. Within seconds, Ema felt the sizzle of static electricity arcing between them. She tried to take a step back, hoping tiny lightning bolts wouldn't be so noticeable, but it had only made the colors leaping in the air more vivid. When she finally found the courage to look up to see his expression, she was relieved to see he was watching her with a confused grin. He finally shook his head, his soft chuckle more about amusement than disbelief.

"Get some rest, Ema. You look like you are dead on your feet. Keep your cell phone next to the bed. Don't hesitate to call me if you need anything." She nodded her understanding. "You can relax here. Remember, this place is wired for sight and sound. I'll know if anyone is anywhere nearby. Do you remember how to access the tunnel?"

Ema smiled to herself since he'd already shown her three times. If she didn't know by now, her friend Paris Adler would slap a Romper Room reject label on her forehead and call it a day. She nodded and quickly repeated the simple steps back to him. Josh looked satisfied, moving slowly toward the door. His hesitance made her realize he was as nervous as she was.

Holy mystic mysteries. Josh Bennett, Mr. All-American Hero... every woman's wet dream, is nervous about being alone with me? Oh, hex. He's probably trying to work out a tactful way to remind me he's simply doing me a favor, and I shouldn't read anything into his generosity.

"Josh, I just wanted to say... well, I... I know you're just being nice. I really appreciate you letting me crash here. I wasn't looking forward to sleeping on the store's cold floor. I promise I won't overstay my—"

Josh pulled her into his arms and sealed his lips over hers, halting her words. His kiss sent her ass over teakettle into the pure pleasure of having his strength wrapped around her. His hot lips pressed firmly over hers made her knees weak. When she felt the tip of his tongue slide along her lower lip, Ema sighed, allowing him to push through.

The kiss was hot and sweet, the mix leaving her emotions rocketing between a burning desire for more and fear she'd disappoint him. When she moaned and opened more to him, the kiss changed to searing between one heartbeat and the next. Ema felt as if the floor disappeared beneath her, and the circle of his arms was the only thing keeping her from crashing into the seven levels of darkness below.

Ema's skin tingled, the surface felt as though it was being electrified from the inside, and her sex had come alive. All the sensitive folds and hot spots of her pussy were pulsing with an unfamiliar need. She tried to isolate each of the individual feelings, hoping the mental effort required would bring her traitorous body back under her control, but the lines were too blurred to make the necessary distinctions.

Over the years, several members of Ema's family had accused her of choosing to function from a place of logic and reason without allowing the magical side of her personality to become involved. She'd never argued the point because they were right. After her mother and sister moved, leaving her behind, Ema focused every ounce of her energy on school and helping others. In her young mind, if she became *perfect,* maybe her mom would love her. Unfortunately, nothing she'd done had ever been enough. Her mother hadn't returned or invited Ema to visit.

For only the second time in her life, Ema let emotion and need cloud her thinking to the point she was happy to fling common sense aside if Josh would just keep kissing her. *What is it about Josh Bennett's kiss that launches logic out the window?*

CHAPTER SIX

F OR THE FIRST time in as long as Josh could remember, he'd rushed headlong into something without taking time to consider the consequences. Truthfully, he wasn't sure he could have stopped himself, so it was a mute issue. Grabbing Emerald Stone and kissing her might not have been the smoothest he'd ever been with a woman, but at that moment, his heart hadn't given a rat's ass what his brain thought.

What started as a sweet kiss between old friends quickly morphed into a raging inferno. Everything about the moment reminded him of the soul-stealing kisses he shared with Ema years ago. Every cell in his body was screaming at him to strip her, spread the petite beauty on the nearest horizontal surface, and worship every delectable bare inch. If he didn't get out of the small entryway, fighting the urge to claim her would be a lost battle.

The scent of her arousal swirled around him, ratcheting up his desire and making him wonder if she would taste as wild as he imagined. Emerald fit in his arms perfectly despite the significant difference in their heights. Josh hoped their years apart hadn't amplified his memories of their stolen night at the lake. Too many times to count, he gazed up at the night sky from some hellhole Uncle Sam had sent him into and wondered if his sleep-deprived mind was playing tricks on his memory. He couldn't believe how perfectly they'd seemed to mesh, how her petite frame molded to his much larger one, or how honored he'd been when he realized what a precious gift she'd given him.

Now, once again, Josh was thrilled at the feeling of her small body pressed against his—hell, it was as if a greater power had made her for him alone. Pulling back to catch his breath, Josh didn't hesitate to press his lips back against hers. This time their kisses held a deeper level of intimacy. For the first time, Josh understood how sweet a woman could taste. Several long minutes later, he reluctantly pulled back. Damn, he loved seeing her eyes unfocused and clouded with passion. Ema's lips were swollen and deep red from his attention. He smiled to himself when he noticed her tightly peaked nipples outlined by the thin blouse she wore.

Using his fingers to push the wayward strands of hair behind her delicate ear, he leaned forward and whispered, "God in heaven, you are so beautiful, you take my breath away. It is taking every ounce of self-control I have to walk away from you tonight, but I want you to get some rest. When we make love, I want you to lose your mind with pleasure, not float away from sheer exhaustion."

Josh deliberately said *when* rather than *if* and was thrilled when she didn't protest his presumption. Her expression reflected a hint of disappointment, so he was counting it as a win. Feeling the need to reassure her, Josh brushed his fingers from her temple down to follow the curve of her jaw.

"I want you, Ema, more than you know." Sighing, he

shook his head, hoping to pull himself back from the edge. "You need to take a relaxing bath, then get some sleep. I'll check on you in the morning, sweetheart."

The entire time he'd been talking to her, Josh caressed the side of her face with the tips of his fingers. Her eyelids fluttered before closing, and he'd bet she wasn't even aware she was pressing the side of her face into his palm like a sweet kitten seeking affection. He pressed a quick kiss to her forehead and relished the feel of her smooth skin against his lips.

Her soft sigh of resignation made him smile. "Alright. I am awfully tired... thank you again... for everything. I'll talk to you in the morning. Hopefully, your deputies will have some information or at least something we can use as a starting point."

He nodded before giving her another quick kiss, then walking away. Making his way over the cobblestones, Josh covered the short distance between the guest and the main house in seconds, but it felt like an eternity. He fought an internal battle of epic proportions to keep from turning around. His body was clamoring for him to finish what he'd started, and his mind was quickly running out of excuses.

He'd had other women, both before and after the night he'd spent with Emerald. Hell, he never claimed to be a fucking saint, but it had always been Ema's face he saw during those moments of passion. No other woman had ever captured his interest the way Ema did, and he'd never felt another woman understood him as she had during their late-night conversation. The connection had been on a whole different level of intensity and ease.

Watching Ema's eyes cloud with desire before he left the guesthouse had been the most beautiful thing he'd ever seen. Walking away from her had been torture. He meant what he'd said—he wanted everything to be perfect when he finally had her beneath him again, and a bit of anticipation would serve them both well.

Stalking across the main house's enormous patio, Josh shook his head and chuckled. Hell, Ema had already gotten under his skin. From the moment she'd tumbled out of her car onto the street, Josh had taken every opportunity to touch her, no matter how fleeting the moment. Each stroke of his fingers, every subtle scrape with the back of his hand, or the secure grip of his hand wrapped around her upper arm was electrified. Power, unlike anything he'd ever experienced, passed between them, and he had the strangest feeling it would have taken very little effort for him to hear what she was thinking.

It had been easy to see Ema was completely spent. He marveled how lust and desire were winning the battle as her body fought for rest. The sexual dominant side of his personality he'd pushed to the dark recesses of his mind came roaring to the forefront, reminding him it was his responsibility to provide what she needed above what she wanted.

Josh wouldn't pretend to understand the strong connection he felt, but he couldn't deny it, either. Sighing as he entered the house, he pulled his phone from his pocket. He planned to check in with his office, then try to wade through some of the paperwork piling up along the edges of the massive desk in his home office. God, he hated the never-ending need to file crap he knew he would only need if he pitched it.

Looking out the kitchen window, he watched the bedroom light in the guest house wink out, relieved to know she was settled for the night. Taking care of a woman like Emerald Stone would never be easy, but the sexual chemistry between them was going to burn down the night. What he needed to decide was whether or not it would be worth the effort and aggravation of dealing with her crazy family.

Keep telling yourself it's a question, fool.

EMA LEANED AGAINST the inside of the closed door after Josh left, trying to reclaim her equilibrium. His reaction to her promise not to overstay her welcome had been a pleasant surprise, and her entire body was still vibrating in the aftermath. She dated Frank Black for months, and he'd only kissed her once. Frank's kiss paled in comparison to the heated lip lock she'd just shared with Josh. Taking several deep, cleansing breaths, she rolled her eyes when she realized her hand was splayed over her chest as if that alone could calm the frantic beating of her heart. For the first time, she understood what people meant when they spoke of kisses so intense, they set off fireworks in your brain.

Moving unsteadily down the hall to the beautiful bathroom adjacent to the small cottage's only bedroom, she looked longingly at the enormous bathtub that would more accurately be described as a small pool. It was complete with underwater lights and soothing jets that could be adjusted to massage just about any part of the body. She grinned when she thought how appropriate it was a former Navy SEAL would have installed a tub designed for "water sports." Finally giving in to her crushing case of "tub envy," she started the water but promised herself she wouldn't linger for fear she'd fall asleep and drown—considering the way her luck usually ran, it was a distinct possibility.

Flipping off the guest cottage lights, she lit a couple of candles and set them on the bathroom counter. Ema lowered herself into the steaming tub of bubbles, the hot water, and pulsing jets easing the muscle fatigue from her long hours of driving and the few cat naps she taken in her car. All too soon, she felt herself drifting off and knew it was time to move.

It took more effort than it should have, but Ema finally pulled herself out of the bath and dried herself quickly. Pulling on the first thing she found in a suitcase and collapsed on the enormous bed. She didn't even pull the duvet completely over herself before falling into a restless sleep.

Unsettling dreams chased through her mind like an old-time movie reel, the fast-moving stills keeping her from sleeping peacefully. Ema's unconscious mind processed the scenes as a series of warnings, but she wasn't sure why. She woke up several times during the night, worried about their significance. The one time she'd been awake enough to take in her surroundings, Ema had been surprised but not frightened to see a tall Native American warrior standing in the corner. His arms were crossed over his chest, his expression stoic. She had been too sleep-dazed to question her conclusion but had somehow known he was watching over her.

As strange as it sounded, her fogged mind hadn't been alarmed by the strange man in her bedroom, and when she'd finally raised her hand in a small wave, he merely nodded in acknowledgment. Slipping back into sleep, she decided his presence was a question for another day.

SHARING BREAKFAST WITH Josh the next morning, Ema subtly tried to ask about the history of the land surrounding his family's estate, but he didn't seem interested in discussing it, so she'd dropped the subject before he started asking questions about her sudden interest. Hopefully, her granny or aunt would know the answers because she didn't want to explain her curiosity to her handsome host. *As if he doesn't already think you are a few billion stars short of a constellation.*

The ride to town had been quiet as she'd taken in the beauty surrounding her and wondered what the future would hold. The entire time Ema lived on the east coast, she'd been plagued by nightmares and headaches. In the beginning, she'd tried traditional and holistic solutions, but nothing helped. After a phone conversation with her great-aunt, she'd hoped Ruby would send one of her famous concoctions, but all she received was an email with a map of the world's crystal deposits and ley lines. *Thanks so much.* Not at all helpful or what she'd expected from a chemist.

Today, for the first time in two years, she felt a renewed sense of energy and purpose unfurling. She wasn't sure if it was because she was finally home, Josh's kisses, or because she finally got a few hours of sleep, but she was basking in a blessed feeling of contentment as she watched the mountainous splendor move past the truck's windows.

She'd assured Josh she could drive herself into town, and he politely reminded her she didn't have a car. Actually, his comment had been more along the line of not allowing her to drive her gas-guzzler until he was convinced it wasn't a death trap. He also grumbled under his breath about the condition of her tires, something about oil draining from beneath the beast, and a clattering sound beneath the hood that sounded like a ghost dragging chains at last year's haunted house. She tactfully chose to ignore his negative observations since they were impossible to refute.

Josh parked at the curb in front of Spellbound, then turned to face her before she got out. "I'll stop by later to take you to lunch. Maybe we'll have something more concrete to go on about last night." She grinned and nodded, even though she didn't hold out much hope of finding out anything useful unless her family was more forthcoming. Bounding up the wooden sidewalk to Spellbound's entrance, Ema paused. Taking a deep breath, she squared her shoulders and stepped through the door. Coming to a hard stop, she looked around, wondering where to start. She'd never seen her family's business in such a state. The whole place was a wreck. Taking another deep breath, Ema wondered where to begin.

Tossing her jacket aside, Ema decided cleaning was the first order of business. It would be easier to assess what little inventory remained if she wasn't sneezing every few seconds. *Look at the bright side, it'll be easier to clean empty shelves, and Goddess knows, the entire store is all but empty.* Shaking her head, hoping to clear her thinking, Ema moved to the backroom for supplies. As she gathered a few things from the nearly depleted supply cabinet, she started rolling ideas around in her mind. She needed to update the displays and set up a web page for the business. The last time she asked, she'd been told the store had almost no on-online presence. But... the first order of business was digging out from under what appeared to be several layers of dust and grime.

For once, Ema didn't feel the least bit guilty using magic. The mess was too much for one person to tackle. The deplorable condition of the small shop hadn't been her doing, and damn it all to dumpy daisies, she wasn't about to waste a week or two setting things right. When her granny and aunt finally made their way downstairs at the 'crack of ten-thirty,' she sent them out to run errands, hoping it would keep them busy and out of her way. *Pickled pixies, no wonder the place is a wreck. Who on earth starts their day at ten-thirty?*

Ema covered the windows with plain brown paper decorated with bright colored letters announcing the store was undergoing a major revamping. One section of the brown paper advertisement alluded to the store's history in Crystal, reminding those passing by to watch for updates. Jotting a note to ask about local internet providers, Ema started mentally designing the store's website. She planned to pull together information for pages highlighting the local tourist attractions along with tie-ins for her family's part in Crystal's success.

She knew the window coverings would generate enough buzz to create interest, but her biggest concern had been hiding her magical assistants from the view of anyone passing by. The vast majority of Crystal's nonmagical residents took little interest in the ever-present rumors about the two eccentric women living in their small mountain enclave. Of course, there had always been a few who made no secret of the fact they found the rumors of witches and magic offensive. Most people in town accepted the members of the small coven. There was a lot to be said for the remnants of the sixties counter-culture mentality that were such a large part of Crystal's history.

Like other towns, there were always those few people who were so judgmental, they rejected anyone who didn't think the same way they did. Rather than seeing all the similarities, they focused on the differences and refused to admit how easily they could live in harmony.

While Ema jotted notes on a clipboard, the brooms swept the hardwood floors, and the feather dusters moved over every inch of the floor-to-ceiling shelving. Once the fog of dust finally settled, Ema went out the back door and dusted herself off. She shook her long hair back and forth to rid it of dust, then brushed the long waves back into some semblance of order. Just as she stepped back inside, Granny Good Witch and Aunt Ruby burst through the front door, full of enthusiasm when they saw the progress she'd made. Her pint-sized grandmother was practically bouncing in place as she'd clapped her hands and giggled.

"Oh Goddess, I knew you'd be able to breathe some life back into this old place. Are you going to sell any of those hip sexy things I see on the internet? Clothes and accessories. Oh, and slinky undies." Ema shuddered as she laughed at the horrified look on Aunt Ruby's face. "I would like to get some new work clothes. Look at these rags I'm wearing. My wardrobe has become so bland, it's practically geriatric. When the younger people come in, I want to fit in, you know? I've had my eye on a pair of black ankle boots and fishnet stockings I saw in a magazine at the library."

Ema cringed, realizing her grandmother had not only made that speech with a straight face, now she was dancing around the room in high-top tennis shoes flashing neon purple and pink lights. Opal Stone was wearing an orange-and-yellow broomstick skirt topped by a lime green Harley Davidson t-shirt sporting the words "Ride Me Baby" in hot pink glitter... and her clothes aren't colorful enough? *This outfit is geriatric?*

The world's fashion industry hadn't invented an article of clothing her granny couldn't conjure into her wardrobe without breaking a sweat. What she lacked was an audience. She wanted people, particularly young people coming into the store—it was the energy surrounding people her granny craved.

Ruby's voice pulled Ema back to the moment.

"Oh, I can see where that's a real big issue for you, sweet sister!" Her aunt looked over at Ema and rolled her eyes, making Ema giggle. "Hex, all we need to do is put a spotlight on you, and they'll be able to see you from space.

Mercy, not bright enough? Seriously? You keep telling me you'll tone it down when you get older. You're almost four hundred. Just exactly how much older do you need to be?"

"I'M ONLY A three hundred and seventy-two for pity's sake…." Opal was feeling put upon and let it reflect in her expression. She hadn't told Josh her real age yesterday, but he wouldn't have believed her, anyway, so she felt no remorse about the lie. Opal turned back to Ema, letting the animation returned to her expression. "Anyway… what are you planning to stock? We were experimenting with some lotions and creams a few months ago… a few of the ladies in our coven made suggestions. Several of the products we made were quite popular." She was looking at Ema expectantly and was pleased when her granddaughter's interest was piqued.

"That really is a great idea." Ema tapped her finger against her chin, taking a moment to consider her grandmother's suggestion. "How quickly can you plan a coven meeting? I'd like to get as many of the members together as possible. It would be really helpful to hear what all you've tried and how it worked."

Opal felt a wave of energy as Ema's excitement grew, fueling her own. If they could get Ema focused on making the store a success, she might decide moving home had been the right decision after all.

NIGEL STOOD TO the side in the store's main room and watched as Ema used magic to clean the filthy space. Seeing her finally utilizing her skills, even if it was merely for convenience, was encouraging. He was well aware of her aversion to using magic, preferring to fit in with her nonmagical co-workers. What she hadn't known was how many of those co-workers shared some of her magical abilities. He'd always made certain there were magicals nearby, ready to protect her if danger presented itself. Their instructions had been simple—watch and only watch unless she is in danger.

He smiled to himself as he listened to her sing along with music only she could hear. Watching her dance around the room while making notes on her tablet, gave him a renewed sense of hope. With a little luck, the two of them would be working together soon.

Even though he wasn't technically *visible,* Nigel was surprised she hadn't sensed his presence. He didn't know if she was simply distracted or if her lack of awareness was one of the magical elements Opal had failed to help her develop. Either way, she was far more at risk if she couldn't identify the trace magic of other witches and wizards, whether or not they were visible.

Emerald Stone had grown into a beautiful young woman. Her hair comprised layers of different shades of brown reminiscent of the way Mother Nature painted the earth with variations of the same color, so even things that were the same, like trees, were easily distinguished one from another.

As a young child, Emerald's brilliant green eyes had sparkled brilliantly, but the longer she'd lived in Massachusetts, the more their shine diminished until they were shadowed and much too dull for Nigel's liking. Making certain she met London and Paris Adler was a brilliant move on Audric Stafford's part. The sisters revived some of Emerald's earlier spark. Audric was relatively new to his position as head of the Council of Magic. Stafford had only held the prestigious appointment for a few decades, making him a newbie by their ancient group's standards. Despite his short term, he'd made impressive changes. His more progressive views were likely influenced by his youngest daughter, Brigitte. Nigel smiled to himself. Brigitte Stafford had always been a handful, and he could see her ending up as an updated version of Opal Stone.

Even from across the room, Nigel could see Emerald's eyes were regaining their twinkle. The crystal line they were standing over was amplifying her power and reenergizing her. All magical beings drew power from crystals, but some were certainly more sensitive to the intense level of energy than others. Emerald was particularly attuned to the mineral's benefits, and living so far from the radiating power beneath their feet had taken a significant toll on the young witch.

The power of crystals was widely recognized, used by everyone from ancient celestial visitors to NASA to amplify space communication. The Council of Magic had received updates on Emerald's gifts beginning a few days after her birth. By the time she'd entered school, Council members already had safeguards in place, ensuring Ema would remain with Opal when her no-account mother had decided living and working in the small town where she'd been raised was boring. Jade had been convinced she had too much to offer a rich man to stay in a tiny hamlet hidden in the Rocky Mountains.

Nobody had believed Jade Stone actually wanted to take her oldest daughter, but she'd made enough noise the Council elders provided her with plenty of financial motivation to move on quietly. It was anyone's guess how Opal had raised a daughter as undisciplined as Jade. Jade had never exhibited even a fraction of the gifts other members of her family had been blessed with, and her youngest daughter, Garnet, possessed even less magical skill. What both women lacked in magical gifts, they made up for with hideous attitudes and monumental senses of entitlement.

The last time Nigel checked on Jade and Garnet, they'd been living with an aspiring young musician who was quickly tiring of their company. The only reason he hadn't already walked away was their ability to sense his frustration and shower him with gifts. The financial support Jade received from the Council allowed her latest romantic interest to live in the lap of luxury, but it came with a hefty price tag. Although Nigel always joked about Jade and Garnet being energy vampires, it was much closer to the truth than anyone wanted to acknowledge.

Leaning against the fireplace's marble-topped mantle, Nigel watched Ema lose herself in the moment. She was usually overly cautious about her appearance and whether or not she was accepted by those around her. He often worried she would be swallowed up and lost forever in a sea of others' expectations.

Nigel wanted to see her blossom and grow into the witch she was meant to be and wanted her as his partner. Together they'd be a force to be reckoned with, and she would be just what he needed to quickly work his way upward through the ranks of wizardry. His goal was to become the youngest wizard ever seated on the Supreme Council—gaining Ema's trust and cooperation was a central part of his plan.

CHAPTER SEVEN

S EVERAL DAYS LATER, Ema stood at the back of Spellbound's clean but very empty main room. Looking
around, she was pleasantly surprised to see the interesting
mix of people greeting one another with more enthusiasm
than she'd expected. Ema had been thrilled to learn it
wouldn't take long to pull together the meeting she'd
requested. She was even more impressed now after seeing
the impressive number of people crowded in the small
shop.

"Granny, are all these people in your coven? There
must be fifty men and women here." Her Aunt Ruby's
earlier comments about their dwindling numbers included
several observations about infighting among their
members. She'd explained there were differing opinions on
the neighboring coven's continued efforts to *absorb* their
membership. *If this is a significant decrease in the membership,
how many people were members at the coven's peak? Where did
they meet? This room wouldn't hold many more.*

"Yes, they are. I'm sorry everyone couldn't make, it but
it was pretty short notice for a non-emergency meeting.
Hopefully, you'll get a chance to meet the others soon."

Wow. The power that could be generated by a coven
this size would be amazing if everyone was tuned in and

channeled their energy as one. It was hard to imagine how powerful they'd been at full membership. Ema mentally rolled her eyes at her sophomoric observation. For the first time, she wished she'd listened more to the lessons her grandmother had so patiently tried to teach her.

It quickly became obvious how well-respected Opal Stone was among her peers when every witch in attendance made a special effort to greet her. In turn, her grandmother spent one-on-one time with each person. Ema appreciated the opportunity to see firsthand what a skilled leader her pint-sized grandmother was.

Ema loved her scooter-riding granny and often rolled her eyes and giggled at the wacky way Opal made everyone laugh with her outrageous behavior and comments. Watching her now, Ema wondered if it was an act. Maybe a large part of her granny's craziness was simply her way of putting others at ease. How could anyone feel like an outcast or oddball when their priestess was a complete wild card?

Opal Stone was constant motion, and more than once, Ema saw her huddled with a member of the coven, fully engrossed in an animated conversation. When Ema tuned in to those discussions, they were always about the group's ongoing efforts to fight back against the dark forces. From the bits and pieces, Ema put together, most of the coven's members were under attack. The specifics of those assaults varied, but there was a consensus the neighboring dark coven was to blame for the ongoing pressure.

After the coven members finished brainstorming ways to turn the shop around, they formed a circle saying their blessings for the safety of their members and their families.

They invoked a welcoming blessing for Ema and asked the Goddess to bless her with help and guidance as she worked to rebuild Spellbound. In Ema's view, the metaphysical store should not only supply the coven members with the things they needed for potions and spells, it also needed to be a resource.

Most of the members had already said their goodbyes, and Ema had already started clearing the tables when she suddenly came face to face with a young woman. Milk-white skin, high cheekbones, and beautiful long red hair made her stunning, but it was the energy flowing around her that drew Ema's attention. The woman appeared to be near Ema's age, even though her turquoise eyes danced with the enthusiasm of someone much younger. Before Ema could speak, the other woman's face lit with the most contagious smile she'd ever encountered, and positive energy was literally pulsing around the pretty witch.

"Hi. I'm so happy to meet you. I just wanted to tell you how thrilled I am you are finally here." *Finally, here?* After Ema nodded and thanked her, the effervescent woman continued, "There aren't a lot of young witches around here. It will be great to have someone to talk to about... well, everything. I'm looking forward to a conversation where I don't have to explain what every bit of slang means. Oh, Goddess, where are my manners? My name is Kit... well, actually, it's Kathleen... Kathleen Ryan. I'm the local librarian... real exciting stuff that." The young woman rolled her eyes, and Ema couldn't hold back her grin. By the time Kit finally stopped to take a breath, Ema felt an immediate connection to the bubbly bundle of energy standing in front of her.

"I'm happy to meet you, Kit. It will be wonderful to have a friend here, and since I'm planning to stay... at least for a while, I'm sure we'll have plenty of opportunities to spend time together." Ema was about to ask the other woman to join her for a cup of coffee when she looked up and saw Josh leaning against the wall just inside the front door.

Oh, my Goddess and Guardian Angels, he has to be the sexiest man on earth.

The pose should have made him look like a casual observer. Instead, it made him look like every woman's sexual fantasy come to life. *The damned man is sex on two legs.* Sensual energy was coming off him in waves as his gaze locked on hers. Everything about him set her senses on fire. His body language, telegraphing passion, and desire took on a blistering energy all its own.

Josh Bennett's laser focus made him look more like a sleek jungle predator than the local sheriff. During the past couple of days, Ema had noticed the fluid grace of his movements. Damn, she hoped some of his natural athleticism rub off on her. The novels she'd read talked about *economy of movement*, but she hadn't understood the concept until she watched Josh move around his kitchen— he didn't bumble around the way she did. Watching him was fast becoming one of her favorite pastimes.

Josh drove Ema to town each day, insisting her car was a hazard to the local citizens he'd been sworn to protect. She knew he was teasing her... mostly... probably. He'd given her car keys to his friends that first night, and she hadn't seen her car since. She'd giggled when they'd told her the "beast" had refused to start, and they'd been forced to tow her "yacht" to their garage. When Ema tried to tell them the car "didn't like anyone but her," they'd glared at her. When she'd gotten in the automobile, she affectionately named Berta, it started immediately. The shop's mechanics stood nearby, shaking their heads in disbelief. Ema was fairly certain Josh was planning Berta's demise, but he was still refusing to directly answer the question.

JOSH STOOD IN the doorway while Ema chatted with Kit. He was happy to see they'd met and appeared to be developing a fast friendship. Josh had planned to introduce them since he'd thought they might hit it off. Kit was a pleasant woman, even though she seemed to be a bit of a recluse. Josh had talked with her a few times about local community concerns and had assumed she kept to herself because there were so few unmarried women in town. Now it might seem he just hadn't been hanging out in the right places. Josh wasn't sure what her connection was to Opal Stone but pushed the question out of his mind when Ema looked his way.

He was thrilled to see the smile spread over Ema's heart-shaped face when she looked up and saw him watching her. *Damn, she is so beautiful.* He'd started planning a special dinner for Ema several days ago—everything was in place for their candlelit meal this evening, and he was anxious to get her home. They hadn't had a repeat of the soul-stealing kiss they'd shared that first night but keeping to their roles as friends was wearing damned thin. Josh was eager to move things along.

Planning to step things up tonight after an Italian feast he knew awaited them meant waiting for Ema's meeting to wrap up was pushing his patience past its limit. Shoving his shoulder away from the wall where he'd been leaning, Josh headed her way. When he reached the spot where the two women stood chatting, he wrapped his arm around Ema's slender shoulders and nodded toward the town's only librarian.

"Hi, Kit, how's it going?"

Kit dropped her gaze to the floor before returning her attention to Josh.

"Okay, I was just telling Ema how nice it will be to have someone my age nearby... someone who shares my interest in... well, you know... magical stuff. Well, I guess I should probably head home." *Magical stuff?* Well, that explained her connection to Opal. Her comment about going home was amusing since she made no effort to move. Several awkward seconds ticked by before she spoke again. "You haven't... by any chance... seen Matt lately, have you?" Josh could tell that the minute the words crossed her lips, she wanted to call them back.

He raised his eyebrow and smiled, "Well, as a matter of fact, I spoke with him a few minutes ago. He was headed to the diner." He hadn't realized Kit was interested in his friend—wasn't this going to be fun to watch. Matt Goering was as shy as the blushing woman standing in front of him. It was entirely possible Matt wouldn't even notice her interest without some encouragement. Hell, anytime he was in the presence of a woman who wasn't a customer or a member of his family, Matt didn't look anywhere but the floor.

When Josh saw the shy librarian's eyes widen, he was fairly certain she'd be heading to the diner. Maybe he'd send a quick text to the elderly waitress who worked evenings. Billie was always looking for new lives to meddle in, and God knew the woman was second only to Opal Stone when it came to matchmaking. Billie would enjoy the challenge, and Matt could use a sweet woman in his life.

"I'll let you ladies finish up. It was nice to see you, Kit." He turned to Ema and cupped her small shoulders with his hand. When she looked up at him, he grinned when her eyes dilated. "I'll go out and start the truck, so it will warm for you. Bundle up, sweetheart. It's freezing and starting to snow." Spring kept teasing them, but in the Rockies, Old Man Winter liked to linger. He was wearing out his welcome, and Josh looked forward to warmer weather. Skinny dipping with Ema was high on his list of spring activities. Heading outside, Josh pulled his phone from his pocket to send a quick heads up to Billie.

Billie Prescott was pushing seventy but had more energy and enthusiasm than most twenty-year-olds. Her extra energy was a blessing, considering she'd run the small eatery by herself for over a year after her husband died suddenly. The vivacious woman recently sold the business but still worked almost every day helping out.

Josh suspected her decision to keep working had more to do with her fear of missing out on local gossip than a need for money. She replied immediately and assured Josh she was all-in on gently guiding her two timid customers toward one another. Josh laughed to himself. The idea of Billie being subtle was definitely in stark contrast to her usual method of operation.

Josh watched Ema make her way down the steps in front of Spellbound, lost in thought and totally unaware of how slick the snow-covered steps had become. Jumping out of his truck, Josh planned to help her navigate the slippery wooden walkway, but she'd disappeared from his view. Rushing around the truck, he knelt beside her. When her eyes met his, he could see her stunned expression.

"Jesus, Ema, are you alright?" She'd landed flat on her back in front of his truck. Shaking her head as she pushed herself into a sitting position, he laughed to himself as a grin spread over her face. Her eyes twinkled, making her look like an excited kid.

"Wow… that was a big surprise. Don't worry, I'm fine. I got used to being a klutz a long time ago." Giggling, she let him help her to her feet, then smiled up at his worried expression, "I suppose this isn't the best time to ask you how long until I get my car back, huh?" She leaned her head back and laughed out loud at the horrified look on his face. "Oh my, I haven't laughed that hard in a long time. Goddess, but you are fun!"

"Jesus, Joseph, and sweet mother Mary, sweetheart, you are going to be the death of me yet. Let's get you in the truck and warmed up." Settling her in the passenger seat, he was glad he'd started the truck, so her leather seat was already warm. Leaning over her to secure her seat belt, Josh lingered a few seconds longer than he knew she'd expected, smoothing the pads of his fingers over her cheek before brushing a butterfly kiss on her plump lips. Her quick intake of air told him he'd surprised her. *Perfect.* This was the first of several special moments he'd planned for this evening. "I have a surprise for you at home, and I can't wait to get you there, so let's get moving."

STEPPING INTO THE huge entry of the main house, Ema felt a wave of warmth roll over her a split second before tantalizing aromas surrounded her. Ema's stomach rumbled in response, and Josh chuckled. "Oh, my stars and garters, please tell me you're planning to share whatever smells so delicious." Ema wasn't sure why, but each time she entered the house, the structure felt like it was pulsing with positive vibrations. The place had a core of strength she hadn't been able to identify.

"This house has the most remarkable energy. I don't know exactly how to describe it, but it's like walking into a positive ion chamber." Josh tilted his head to the side as if he was trying to decide if she was joking or if her last thread of sanity had finally frayed enough to snap. "You know how clean and fresh the air feels after a thunderstorm? After storms, the air is positively charged by the static electricity generated by the rain moving through the air and lightning. Well, that's how this house feels each time I walk in. It literally recharges me."

She wasn't sure how much he knew about the land his family home sat on. Ema didn't feel like it was her place to repeat what her granny and aunt shared about the land his home sat on. The Bennett estate's elaborately landscaped flower garden sat atop a tract of land considered sacred by the local Native Americans. It was easy to see why the spirits of those who'd passed were well pleased with the pristine way the site was maintained.

Josh smiled and stepped closer to stand in front of her. He cupped the side of her face in his warm, calloused palm, and Ema felt the now familiar zing of electricity pass between them.

"I've had a lot of compliments on this house over the years from a wide variety of people, including the editors of Western Living magazine when they featured it as 'The Ideal Mountain Retreat' a few years ago, but I can honestly say, none of those observations compares with the pleasure your words have given me. To know my home fosters that kind of feeling for you humbles me. Having you here makes me eternally grateful to whatever angel had the misfortune to be tasked with looking over me. It's a miracle my guardian angel didn't throw the towel in years ago."

JOSH'S WORDS WERE sincere. One thing Ema once said she admired most was his honesty. The night at the lake, she'd told him about hearing people say he was honest to a fault. When he laughed, she'd turned to him, shaking her head. "Promise me you'll never change, Josh. Honesty is a blessing." Now, even after so much time had passed, he'd never forgotten her words.

He'd been genuinely humbled by her observation about the house, and for some strange reason, her words sent a strange shiver of awareness through him. Looking down into her bright green eyes, he remembered his mom frequently saying the same thing about their home. Caitlyn Bennett had seen to every detail of the estate. When she learned the location they'd originally chosen for the house itself was sacred, she hadn't hesitated to change the plans. Moving the home's foundation forward twenty-five yards delayed the project six months, but she hadn't cared. To honor the Native American legacy of the land, she'd designed a beautiful garden accented by twisting stone walkways, all leading to the center where the stones were laid in an intricate replica of the local tribe's symbol for an all-seeing deity.

Hearing Ema's words felt significant in a way he couldn't explain, almost as though he'd been given some kind of sign—as if the Universe wanted him to hear the assurance. *Here she is.*

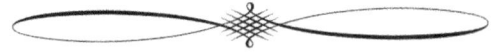

CHAPTER EIGHT

O PAL WATCHED FROM across the room as Ema grabbed her coat after speaking with Josh and made her way out the front door. It was impossible to hold back the smile she felt tugging the corners of her lips. Looking around the large room for her sister, Opal wasn't surprised to find her peeking out the door. Ruby was fond of Ema, and Opal had expected her to keep a close watch on her favorite great-niece. As a child, Ruby Stone had been insatiably curious, always watching, observing the smallest details of situations others missed. Those skills continued to serve her well as an adult.

"Ruby, things are working out perfectly. If I'm right and Josh is her *one*, there won't be any question about her staying. You can feel how intense her magic is… it's practically boiling beneath the surface, trying to break free—so much talent and so little awareness of what she's been given. Her mother always craved the power she thought magic would bring her. Emerald has no desire for power, even though it is her birthright. It's exciting to watch history playing out right before our eyes."

Ruby pulled back the paper covering the heavy door's side window and burst into laughter when Ema slipped on the ice, landing flat on her back. Even from their place inside, they could see Ema giggling like a carefree young woman.

"There is such a childlike wonder about her, an innate goodness that's impossible to adequately explain. My concern is she'll continue to be a target for those whose power comes from darkness. They'll try to recruit her, and when that doesn't work, their focus will shift to destroying her. We have to help her prepare for what's to come."

"I agree," Opal responded without taking her eyes off her beloved granddaughter. "We have so much to teach her, but it's important to give her a bit of breathing room. I want her to settle in a bit before we begin. The depth of her roots in Crystal will determine our success." Opal knew her sister would understand—once they started, the energy shift wouldn't go unnoticed by either side of the magical power struggle, so it would be important her training regime had the best foundation possible.

"Staying at the Bennett's on Mystic Mountain is the best possible place for her." Ruby's opinion mirrored Opal's.

"I nearly fell over when she mentioned the Native American spirit standing guard in her room. The Knights of Aradia are timeless and all-powerful. The assurance they are watching over her is comforting." Opal knew Aradia continued adding Knights to her guard, and the fact she'd let Emerald see one who lived on the mountain spoke volumes about the young witch's importance to the world of magic. As the Queen of Witches, Aradia's influence spanned the globe with no time limits. "The energy from the mountain is elementally positive and will restore the holes I've seen in her damaged aura. I don't know the details of what happened to her back east, but I don't believe for a minute it's over. There is a storm brewing all around us."

"Oh dear, I'm not sure we can take on an additional challenge right now. Our coven isn't as strong as it once was." Opal understood Ruby's concern. Blocking the energy assaults they knew were coming would be a challenge. "Emerald looked so unhappy when she first got home, and she hasn't had time to fully heal. I hate to think about her facing trouble so soon." Opal noted the worry in Ruby's voice and agreed things would likely be damned unpredictable for a while.

In times like these, Opal's gift of empathy was as much a curse as an asset. Opal had known for months things weren't going well for Emerald in Boston. What she hadn't been able to determine was whether the problem was really a threat to the young witch's life or just discontent. Ema hadn't wanted to admit she wanted to move home. She'd seen it as taking a step backward when the exact opposite was true. Her connection with Josh would prove the move had been in her best interest.

Ruby's excited voice brought Opal out of her thoughts.

"What do you say to a little margarita party tonight? I'm sure we can get that little Hamilton Beach caldron bubbling in no time. There are several people still hanging out in the backroom, and well... I feel like dancing. That 'Put a Lime in the Coconut' song keeps playing on a loop in my head."

Opal laughed as her younger sister literally danced out of the room. Ruby had always loved music, and what she lacked in musical talent, she more than made up for in enthusiasm.

Peering through the sliver of exposed glass, Opal watched as Josh drove away with Ema buckled safely in his truck before she put the paper back in place and moved toward the store's backroom. A glint of light caught her eye, and the air around her seemed to crackle and sizzle. The last time she'd faced an energy surge this strong in the store, Opal found herself face to face with a demon who had mysteriously slipped past the magical seal the coven had placed over a nearby portal.

She'd shifted to a defensive stance, wand in hand as the hair on the back of her neck stood on end. It took her a few seconds to realize what she'd seen was actually a reflection from outside as the source of the flash, but once she recognized the magical signature, Opal let out a breath and wondered if it would have been easier to deal with a demon.

Nigel London strode across the street toward her, and Opal fought the nearly overwhelming urge to lock the door. Not that it would do a spell's bit of good, but the idea held tremendous appeal. The door swung open before he reached it—a pompous ass like Nigel couldn't be troubled to actually turn a doorknob like a mere mortal.

"Opal, how lovely to see you again. My my, look what you've done with this place. Mercy you have... well, what shall I say? Oh, yes... *cleaned*."

Opal smiled at him, knowing the asshat would see it for the snarl she intended it to be. Crossing her arms over breasts that had surrendered to gravity many years ago, Opal stared at the meddling power-monger. It wasn't that Nigel was evil—he was simply a machiavellian ass of the first order. Opal would admit she could be a bit manipulative, though she preferred the term outcome engineering, but she'd never been ego-driven the way Nigel was.

Nigel's aristocratic background had long ago gone to his head, and his phony English accent grated on Opal's last nerve. She'd seen him portray a variety of roles over the years, and he was damned good at convincing others that the face they saw was genuine. Opal knew better.

"What do you want, Nigel?" She'd given up trying to play nice with the wizard years ago. Now that he'd been promoted to Deacon of Covens for the western hemisphere, she probably should rethink her approach, and she would... but it wasn't going to happen today. *Yeah, and tomorrow doesn't look promising, either.*

Opal locked the door and pulled down the blinds out of habit, grimacing when she remembered the paper-covered windows. *Damn, I hate looking like a twit.* She'd intended to play his game—the man loved his damned parlor tricks—instead, she'd made herself look like a damned brainless hussy. When she saw his lips twitch, Opal wanted to roll her eyes. Listening to someone's thoughts was as intrusive as it got, but the man had not an ounce of shame.

She should probably thank her lucky stars the windows were covered since Nigel's love of hocus pocus was always exaggerated when he had an audience. Given the opportunity to show off to someone passing by would be too much temptation for him to pass up. Knowing it would make Opal's life difficult would be seen as an obvious bonus.

Turning to him, she noticed he seemed to have lost interest in her as he walked up and down the narrow aisles of the store, looking more entranced than anything else. He kept reaching out with the palm of his pasty-white hand as if he was checking for something she couldn't see. She watched him for several seconds and quickly noticed he was only checking things Opal knew Emerald had touched.

Well, spell me. The last thing I need is Nigel sniffing around Ema. Hell, I'll never get her to embrace her powers and stay in Crystal if he's here nosing around.

Deciding it was better to let him join the party than watch him drool over the trace magic he was picking up, Opal turned and walked toward the backroom. She knew Nigel had a real weakness for liquor and dancing, so this evening's diversion should be right up his alley. Hopefully, she could keep her friends from mentioning anything about their plans for Spellbound. The less he knew, the less he could use against them. Shaking her head and letting out a soul-deep sigh, Opal wondered if Ruby could whip up a good potion for delusional thinking.

Watching her friends' reactions when Nigel sauntered into the room was a study in contrasts. Most melted when he cranked up the wattage of his slick grin. Nigel could be charming, but it was a façade to hide how conniving and arrogant he was to the depths of his soul. Opal had dealt with him from the time the Magic Council assigned him as Emerald's overseer, and she'd never been convinced his focus was on what was best for Ema.

Opal had known Nigel Lancaster his entire life, so she wasn't fooled by his charm. Every nuance of his behavior was calculated. She didn't believe in coincidences. His arrival so close on the heels of Ema's return was anything but serendipity. Why was he making such an effort to fit in? Why schmooze the locals if he wasn't planning to wheedle something out of them, they wouldn't ordinarily volunteer?

Sighing, she watched Nigel work the room. She should probably be ashamed of the secret pleasure she felt when a couple of the more powerful witches in their small coven maintained their distance. The two women had enough experience to scent a predator in their midst, so they were appropriately cautious.

To Nigel's credit, he didn't pump anyone for information, and to the casual observer, he seemed to be genuinely enjoying himself. His efforts to blend in didn't extend to sharing their margaritas, though. The citrus and tequila concoction would have been much too lowbrow for his blue blood. He'd politely declined, saying he preferred to sip the wine he was suddenly holding. *The only thing worse than a meddling wizard is a meddling wizard who is also a snob.*

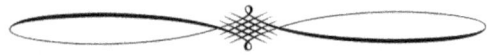

THE MOMENT EMERALD spoke openly about the positive feelings she felt whenever she entered his home, Josh knew something significant had shifted between them. Any semblance of *casual* faded away, and the surrounding air crackled with desire. When she'd first come home, he wondered if the charged air between them was nothing more than his imagination. The more time he spent with her, the more convinced he became there was something undeniably special about Ema... a unique quality he decided defied explanation.

He was reluctant to fully concede she was a witch, but it was impossible to deny there were things about her that undoubtedly fell outside his ability to explain. Ironically, the more time he spent with her, the less he cared about ferreting out reasonable explanations.

Fuck me, the biggest problem is the peculiar feeling I get when I'm near her. It's as if some small bit of knowledge is simmering just below the surface... a memory that's just out of my reach, intriguing and damned annoying at the same time.

He'd hedged long enough—tonight. Tonight, Josh had very specific plans for the woman looking at him from under long curling lashes. The desire he felt was reflected in her eyes, and Josh knew in that instant, he needed her as much as his next breath.

Sighing to himself, he wondered why Mikel Snowden suddenly popped into his head. There was a part of Josh that was certain he'd never see Mikel Snowden again, but the man's face suddenly floated through his mind, and he couldn't help wondering why. Josh met Mikel just a few days after making love to Emerald at the lake.

When Josh returned to San Diego, his new neighbor had wasted no time introducing himself. They'd hit it off immediately, and even though Josh always made friends easily, the connection he'd felt with Mikel had seemed oddly significant from the onset. One night, after a particularly stressful day, they were sitting on Josh's patio enjoying the cool evening breeze and more cold beer than was wise when Mikel commented about the unique marriage of his friends. Josh had been intrigued and asked him to explain.

Listening as his friend described how polyamorous relationships worked challenged everything Josh thought he knew about marriage. His head protested the unusual approach, but his heart understood there might be instances where it would serve everyone's best interest. Josh had listened intently as Mikel explained how there were times when one husband was the traditional head of their household, the other described as a professional colleague. While Josh understood the concept, he wasn't sure it was something he'd be interested in pursuing.

Mikel had traveled almost as much as Josh, so they hadn't seen each other as often as they might have liked, but the time they spent together always seemed to solidify their connection. Josh had never been certain what Mikel did for a living. Anytime he asked, his friend had merely referred to himself as an "overseer."

Despite their erratic schedules, the two years they lived next to one another, they'd had numerous discussions about ménage relationships and their mutual interest in light BDSM play. They'd agreed to stay in touch, but all those plans evaporated during Josh's last mission as a SEAL.

After coming back stateside, the last thing Josh wanted to do was return to his condo on Coronado Island. Instead, he'd retreated into the wilderness behind his family's estate, spending weeks camping beside the largest of a trio of crystal-clear lakes nestled in the deep recesses of his parents' land. Searching his soul while staring into the lake's depths, Josh wondered if he'd ever regain his sense of self. During those long weeks, his parents hired a moving company to pack and ship everything in his condo. He'd returned home the day his belongings were delivered to the front door of the Bennett estate.

Josh hadn't thought about Mikel in months and had no idea why his face had moved through his mind now. Maybe it was their strange conversations about marriage. There hadn't been a woman in Josh's life he'd even considered settling down with—not until Emerald Stone moved home.

Josh had always believed in living without regrets and actually had very few regrets for a man who'd seen the horrors of war up close and personal. In fact, Josh could only think of a few instances where he'd done something he later regretted. He didn't even regret his last mission because nothing he could have done would have changed the outcome.

The one thing he *had* always regretted was letting Emerald leave the lake that night without making certain she knew how special she was to him.

EMA LOOKED ON as Josh's thoughts meandered. She'd only been able to catch a few bits since she'd never been a particularly gifted empath. Even as she let the thought of a magical limitation move into her thoughts, something deep inside Ema instinctively pushed it aside. During the rare occasions when she'd paid attention to her grandmother's lessons, Ema learned the power of internal dialogue. Her grandmother told her time and again, "If you say negative things to yourself, the words will manifest and become a self-determining prophecy. It's important to be kind to others, but it's even more important to be kind to yourself."

Deciding to put her grandmother's lesson into practice, Ema rephrased the comment in her mind. *I'm not a strong empath... yet. It's a skill I know will develop the more I practice.* Immediately, she felt the floor shift beneath her feet.

So, mote it be.

The words moved gently through her mind, and Ema noted the voice sounded oddly familiar, yet the soft Old English accent was unlike anything she'd heard outside a movie or the theater. When she looked up at Josh, his brows were raised, questions reflected in his clear blue eyes.

"Did you feel the floor move?"

Ema couldn't hold back her grin. She knew how difficult it must have been for him to admit he'd felt something he couldn't explain. Magic was a subject they would have to discuss eventually, but she was hoping to steer things in a different direction tonight.

"I did, but I've learned to appreciate the interesting things we all encounter. I prefer to think of the unusual events in my life as splashes of color rather than viewing them as challenges I need to waste time trying to sort out. If the world is waiting for me to find logical explanations for the odd behavior of my fellow man or Mother Earth, they'll be waiting a long time." His eyes darkened, the color shifting from its usual sky blue to deep azure, which always made her think of the southern Caribbean Sea.

"My mother will want to adopt you." Oh hex, the last person she wanted him thinking about when they were on what felt like a date was his mother. *Yikes!* She heard him chuckle and cringed, hoping she hadn't spoken out loud. "Stop worrying. I have no intention of letting my mother intrude on our evening, though it wouldn't be the issue you imagine. I just meant, she will recognize you as a kindred spirit." So much for hoping she hadn't spoken aloud.

Okay, Ema admitted it was a relief to hear what he'd been thinking. Letting her shoulders relax a bit, she hoped the distraction was enough to gloss over the odd shaking beneath their feet. Moving back to Crystal seemed to have revived the magic she used to feel surrounding her. She would ask her granny and aunt for an explanation first thing in the morning. When she first moved to Boston, things seemed fairly normal, but the longer she was there, the more she noticed what felt like a down-shift in the surrounding energy.

"Come on. You look a bit shell-shocked, and I'm starving." Hearing amusement in his tone made Ema grin. She'd been too busy to eat, working on orders for the store and doing a mock-up of the website, so she was going to blame hunger for her inability to stay in the moment. Following him into the kitchen, Emerald gasped when she saw the beautiful table set with fine china. The low floral arrangement in the center would allow her to see him across the table—she'd always been frustrated by arrangements she was forced to move or peak around. The candles cast soft light around the room, and the scent of their dinner teased her senses.

"It's beautiful, Josh. I've never... no one has ever."

"If no man has ever made certain you enjoyed a romantic dinner, you've dated fools, Ema. I won't say I cooked, but I wanted to make sure this evening was perfect for you. You've been working hard since you came home. I've been watching, and it seems you take care of everyone around you." He held out her chair. Once she was seated, he poured wine into sparkling crystal glasses.

Rays of flickering candlelight reflected from the crystal stemware, sending dancing lights over the walls and ceiling. Those colorful points of light reminded her of the fairies she used to watch in the meadows as a child. She hadn't thought about those nights in a long time. Admitting how amazing her childhood had been despite the heartache of dealing with her mother's rejection wasn't easy.

"Who takes care of you, Emerald Stone?" Josh's question pulled her back to the moment. It took her a few seconds to refocus and remember where their conversation had been headed. When she didn't immediately answer, he nodded once as if her silence had spoken volumes. "Let's enjoy our dinner and talk. There will be plenty of time for the more intimate discussion I want to have—and we will have that chat, I promise."

The time seemed to pass too quickly as they shared the food he pulled from the warming drawer. She couldn't remember the last time she'd enjoyed a meal more or been more surprised by the fare. Her smile must have given away how pleased she was when he set a steaming pan of lasagna on the table. The night they'd talked at the lake, she'd mentioned how much she loved the dish. Knowing he'd remembered, touched something deep inside her. She couldn't remember the last time someone other than her grandmother had made an effort to do something special for her.

Emerald's heart squeezed, and she swallowed down the swell of emotion that kept her from answering his simple question. *Who takes care of you, Emerald Stone?* The simple query kept playing on a loop in her mind.

CHAPTER NINE

J OSH COULDN'T REMEMBER the last time he enjoyed a date this much. The intimate dinner he'd planned with Emerald had been relaxed and fun, their conversation flowing easily. She hadn't played coy, pretending that eating a hearty meal was some sort of mortal sin. Ema hadn't held back, eating not one but two servings of lasagna. He'd laughed to himself, wondering where she put it. Hell, Ema was the very definition of petite. Five-foot nothing, she was eighteen inches shy of his six-and-a-half-feet height.

Ema was easy to spend time with. Neither of them felt the need to fill the natural lulls in the conversation with inane chatter. Her innate ability to enjoy moments of silence was a trait he appreciated. Pushing to his feet, Josh held out his hand. It was time to test the waters.

"Come." Her eyes widened for a fraction of a second before she laid her hand atop his open palm. He wondered if her body responded to the command before her brain formulated a protest. Those objections would come—she was too independent for it to go otherwise. He wasn't interested in a full-time D/s relationship, preferring to keep his kink confined to sex play. Having his suspicions about Ema being a sexual submissive was hotter than hell. Josh was eagerly anticipating how beautiful she would look tied to his bed with her bare pussy spread wide, taking his tongue, fingers, and cock.

"I want to show you around the house. Please feel free to spend time in the main house. The guest house is nice, but it's awfully small." Her tinkling laughter made him stop at the bottom of the stairs. Wrapping his hands around her waist, he set her on the second step. It didn't put them eye to eye, but he only wanted to even the score a bit. "Tell me why you think that's funny, sweetness."

He didn't need her answer since he'd already done his homework. The place she'd rented in Boston had been so tiny, he'd shaken his head at the outrageous rent he'd learned the rental agency charged her. It hadn't been that long since he rented a home in the city, so he wasn't naïve to the costs. Either Boston was in a state of real estate mania, or some jerk seized the opportunity to take advantage of a single woman. If Josh was taking bets, he'd be all-in on the latter. When he'd tried to determine who owned the small home Ema had called home, he'd hit a wall, and the bureaucratic roadblock made him even more curious.

"The house I lived in was pretty small. Okay, it was minuscule. The guest house is much larger, and the energy is entirely different." He nodded his understanding but didn't move, sensing there was more, and he wanted to hear it all. When her head dropped forward, so she was looking at his chest, Josh sighed. Using his finger beneath her chin, he lifted her face back to his.

"No, Ema, I won't let you hide. Talk to me." Damn, he loved the pink stain of embarrassment coloring her cheeks.

Hell, she had to be the only woman he ever dated who could still blush.

"The house seemed normal when I first moved in, but everything seemed to shift. It was odd. About the time I noticed strange things happening at work, the house... well, for lack of a better description, the personality of the place became less welcoming." Ema pulled her bottom lip between her pearly white teeth, nibbling on it as worry vibrated around her. Was she remembering how uncomfortable she'd been in her own home? Or was she concerned he'd judge her for the confession? He wasn't sure, but he planned to make certain it wasn't the latter.

"I want you to listen to me, Ema. This is important, and I'll repeat it as often as I need to, though I hope that won't be necessary. You can tell me anything. I won't judge you. I'm not convinced magic is real, but I'm not certain it isn't, either." He saw the corners of her lips pull up into a tight smile. "The more time I spend with you, the easier it is to believe there's magical credence to things I can't explain, but I don't want you to focus on that." He paused, making sure she had time to process what he was saying.

"I think you know how much I want you, but it's important you know there is more to it than a monumental physical attraction. As we explore things together, you'll gain a deeper understanding of what I'm talking about." He could practically hear the wheels of her mind spinning as she tried to wrap her head around what he was saying as well as what he'd left unspoken. Flashing her a flirty grin, Josh hoped would lighten the mood, he pressed his lips to hers in a quick kiss.

"I'm looking forward to finding out what you know about dominance and submission, but first, let me show you around. The house has a few features I doubt you've heard about." Truer words were never spoken.

An hour later, Josh stood beside the indoor pool, watching Ema stepping purposely around the edge as if she was trying to take in everything all at once, and he knew it was a lot to absorb. He tried to see the space from her perspective, but the truth was, he'd grown up with the perks of his parents' wealth, so it was difficult to remember how lucky he was. The expansive space had recently been redesigned by a pool builder from Florida. The man and his crew hadn't batted an eye when they saw the substantial obstacles presented by the area's mountain roads.

"It's amazing, Josh. I've never seen anything so remarkable. A tropical paradise in the middle of the Rocky Mountains." He watched as she skimmed her fingers over the edge of a rock ledge beside the grotto, the movement so fluid, it was sensual. If there was anything he found more attractive than Ema's inherent sexiness, it was perhaps her clear connection to Mother Nature or the way she moved without pretense. Hell, he wasn't sure what made her different from every other woman, but it was undeniable.

"Take off your shoes and socks." When she looked up at him in surprise, Josh didn't try to hide his grin. "Do you trust me, Emerald?" Without answering, she did as he asked, setting her tattered shoes aside after stuffing threadbare socks inside. *For fuck's sake, what has she been doing with the money she earned?*

He'd done enough research to know what she'd been

earning the past few years. Although it wasn't an enormous salary, it should have given her enough spare cash to keep her wardrobe updated. If he found out her mother and sister were the reasons Ema was dressed like a damned street urchin, he would be pissed. Nothing was ever enough for those two.

Taking her hand, Josh grinned when he saw her brightly painted toes. Each nail was a different iridescent color, making him chuckle to himself. *Irrepressible.* The woman was absolutely remarkable. Stopping beside the bubbling spa, he nodded to the steps.

"Step in, close your eyes, and tell me what you feel." When they'd originally dug the pool, they'd hit a natural spring. When the builders couldn't identify the source of the heat, they'd closed it off. During the redesign, Josh did his homework. Understanding geology and digging deep into local archives, Josh was shocked to learn about the crystal deposit beneath his hometown. It hadn't taken much imagination to figure out why it was a closely guarded secret.

He kept the information to himself but opened up the spring, using the natural heat and tapping into the restorative powers of the crystal. When the world seemed to close in around him, or flashbacks stole his nights, Josh always found himself sitting in the healing warmth of the spa, letting Mother Nature soothe his soul. Ema took his outstretched hand, letting him steady her as she closed her eyes and stepped into the water. He was pleased with her show of trust and smiled when she gasped in surprise.

"Oh, Goddess. The crystal vein must be right beneath us. I didn't think it came this close to the surface." Her eyes flew open, and he knew immediately she hadn't planned to speak the words aloud.

"I know that look. Stop right now. Your panic is unwarranted, Ema. The secret of the crystal is safe with me. I have no desire to see roves of rowdy miners destroy our lovely community." Her shoulders relaxed, but only marginally.

"I'm sorry, I don't mean to imply I don't trust you. It's humbling to know you discovered the power of the crystal caverns before I did."

What? Hell, he certainly hadn't seen that one coming.

"You're joking."

"Not even a little. That isn't to say Granny and Aunt Ruby didn't tell me... or at least tried." Josh struggled to hold back his grin as he got a glimpse of the disinterested teen she must have been at home. "They tried to teach me so many important things, but I wasn't interested. Heck, I'm still struggling with the same questions."

Josh watched as she trailed her toes through the warm water. Damn, he wished they were further along in this process. Seeing her spread out naked in his hot tub was something he looked forward to, but right now, he needed to build a more solid foundation.

"What sort of questions, Ema?" When her gaze returned to his, he could see she was struggling to put her feelings into words. During their long talk at the lake, she mentioned a heritage she worried about living up to, but she'd been vague, and he'd been too young and arrogant to entertain the idea magic might be real. He still wasn't convinced, but it was fair to say he'd seen enough he couldn't explain to be a lot more open-minded.

"I'm envious of you." Josh wasn't sure where she was going with this, but he'd bet his last nickel it had nothing to do with money. "You've always known exactly where you belong." She looked at the water, studied the plants lining the grotto's rock wall, and stared longing at the glassy surface of the connected swimming pool. "No matter where your military career took you, this was home. Your parents, your sisters, heck, the whole town knew you belonged here. No one ever questioned whether or not you were worthy of your station in life. Confidence and purpose practically ooze from you. I swear those two traits are written in your DNA."

When Emerald's gaze finally returned to his, the stark look of loss and deep-seated loneliness made his heart clench. He knew Opal struggled to make Emerald feel as though she belonged after her mother packed up her younger sister and fled. Jade Stone was worthless, and from what he'd heard, Ema's younger sister, Garnett, was going to give her mother a run for her money. Both women believed the world owed them simply because they were attractive. He'd often wondered why they thought that was enough. The irony was, neither of them held a candle to Ema.

"Do you think it's possible you've always known you belonged here as well? Maybe your soul recognizes Crystal as your home, but your head keeps getting in the way?" He could think of a hundred different ways to help her get out of her own head. Unfortunately, ninety-nine of those required a level of trust he had yet to earn. One aspect of dominance and submission he found the most rewarding was helping women let go, and knowing he'd given his partner that level of freedom was humbling.

Yeah… trust is important… and nudity… naked is critical.

"I suppose that's possible. I have been known to overthink things into oblivion. Sometimes, I wish I could let things go and just live in the moment, setting aside all the expectations other people seem so anxious to impose."

Josh might have misgivings about the mystical aspects of Emerald's life, but he damned well recognized a sliver of divine intervention when it was handed to him.

"Tell me what you know about dominance and submission, Ema." He deliberately hit on the topic without forewarning. One thing he appreciated about Emerald Stone was how easy she was to read. Pretense had never been a part of her personality. With Ema, what you saw was exactly who she was to her core. Her eyes widened, her pupils dilating until only a thin ring of green remained, and the sweetest cotton candy pink flush he'd ever seen stained her cheeks.

"I've read a few books, but I don't have any… well, I haven't…"

He wanted to push her boundaries, but it wouldn't benefit either of them if she wasn't comfortable enough to speak openly.

"Ema, I will never judge you. Nothing you can say will shock me. It's important you feel secure enough to speak your mind. There are a lot of perks to the D/s lifestyle, but I think you'll find open communication is one of the most valuable." Stepping forward, Josh held out his hand, waiting for her to place her small one atop his. Wrapping his fingers around hers, he helped her step away from the hot tub. He deliberately left her shoes behind, hoping she would start feeling more comfortable in his home.

Stepping into the most intimate of several seating groups surrounding the pool, Josh settled Ema in the chair his youngest sister swore hugged her every time she sat in it. Seeing Ema wiggle into the thick cushions of the chair made him smile. Josh sat on the edge of the coffee table, making sure their knees were touching. Leaning forward, he focused on her, ensuring she felt the full force of his attention.

"Everyone needs someone in their life who has their back without hesitation or judgment. We all need to know we can count on that one individual who expects nothing more than our honesty." As much as Josh knew Opal loved Ema, the older woman probably put as much pressure on her granddaughter as anyone. Hell, Opal and her sister had let their business fall into such a state of disrepair, Josh wondered if magic wasn't the damned store's only chance of survival.

From what he'd observed over the past few days, Ema was working hard to bring things in the metaphysical shop up to date. Josh found it amusing Ema was sending the two elderly women on errands, obviously meant to keep them out of her hair. He'd been in the local hardware store yesterday when they'd asked the owner for a left-handed monkey wrench. It had taken every ounce of self-control he could muster to keep from laughing out loud—Ema must be running out of legitimate requests.

"Let's start again." He held her hands between his own and fought a smile when she relaxed. If she thought he would back away from the conversation, she was in for a surprise. As a SEAL, he'd never backed away from a challenge. As the sheriff, it was rarely in anyone's best interest to step back, and as a Dom, it was unthinkable. He intended to get the information, but he wasn't opposed to changing his tactic.

"How many sexual partners have you had, Ema?" If he hadn't been completely focused on her, he might have missed the flash of something too close to embarrassment in her eyes before it was quickly masked. She tried to pull her hands out of his in a futile effort to put distance between them, but it was a move he anticipated and easily prevented. "I will always be honest with you, sweetness, and I expect the same courtesy. Answer the question, Ema."

"One." She spoke so softly he might have missed her startling response if he hadn't seen her lips move.

He worked hard to keep his expression from betraying how shocked he was by her revelation. *What the hell is wrong with the men in Boston? Are they all blind?* Josh realized how she had misinterpreted his silence when he saw a sheen of tears in her beautiful green eyes.

"I didn't date much, and the only boyfriend I had was more interested in watching television than going out. Hex me, most of the time, it felt more as if he was my babysitter rather than my date."

"I'm interested in hearing why you think so, and we'll definitely come back to it, but right now, it's important for you to know how honored I am to have been your only partner." He paused, giving her a few seconds to process his words. If their interlude at the lake was her only sexual experience, he looked forward to showing her what he learned since he claimed her innocence that night under the stars.

"Men don't seem to view me as a potential sex partner. My friends told me I give off a girl-next-door vibe that reminds them of their sisters." *Say what?* Before he could express his disagreement, she shrugged, "I understand if you want to call it a night."

"No, as a matter of fact, I don't think you understand at all. I'm not sure who fed you that line, but I want to assure you it's total bullshit. You certainly don't remind me of my sisters." The girl-next-door vibe might be true, but for him, that was a benefit. Tears breached her lower eyelids, rolling slowly down her cheeks. The look of relief in her eyes assured him they weren't tears of sadness.

"Asking about your sexual past wasn't meant to embarrass you, Ema. I want to make certain everything is perfect this time. Making sure you are properly prepared for my cock is not only my responsibility, Ema, it's also my privilege." He gave her a lecherous grin. "As I recall, I didn't do a good job of preparing you last time. Youth and inexperience are my only excuses." Shaking his head at his own naivety, he sent up a silent prayer he'd do better this time around. As anxious as he was to get her beneath him, it would be a miracle if he could hold off long enough to ensure her pleasure—damn, he wanted her.

"You said you have read about D/s, but it's important you understand every relationship is different." Taking a deep breath, he pushed ahead, not giving her an opportunity to back out. "Everything is open to negotiation except your safety. I'm not a 24/7 Dom, but there are elements of the lifestyle I find rewarding. Making certain your needs are met will always be my primary objective." Her cheeks blushed as a ghost smile teased the corners of her lips, and Josh knew what she'd found amusing. He'd been told by fellow veterans it took years for them to stop lapsing into what his mom called *soldier-speak*.

"I appreciate your concern for my safety, but I've been taking care of myself for a long time." He could tell she was mildly miffed. In the future, her snark would give him plenty of ammunition.

"Let me give you an example—your car." He wanted to laugh when her spine went ramrod straight. She'd inquired about the antique yacht on wheels yesterday, and he distracted her, asking if she'd spoken with Kit recently. He'd seen the two of them chatting on the front steps of the library, so he'd known it was a valid question. Josh smiled as he remembered how grateful he was to see the two women laughing together. It was a relief to know Ema had made a friend. The more ties she had to the community, the more likely she would be to stay.

Refocusing his attention on the example he planned to use, he fought a smile when he saw her wide-eyed look. How a woman who was brilliant in so many ways managed to be oblivious to the obvious dangers of the car she'd driven cross-country was inexplicable.

"Your car is a hazard, Emerald. The odometer reads almost two hundred thousand miles, and it only works part of the time. The tires are so smooth, it's tantamount to ice skating. The brakes are shot, and the muffler fell off when Buck put it on the lift."

"Lift? Why would he want to lift my car? I don't think she'd like that. It would feel as if someone was looking up her skirt."

Josh was used to hearing people personalize their cars and trucks, but Ema's observation was particularly interesting. The damned beast randomly changed color and had personality in spades.

"I have to admit she has some interesting personality characteristics. Her weight alone is probably her biggest safety advantage." Ema wasn't wrong about the car's heft. The guys at the garage swore their lift groaned when they hoisted the car into the air. "Did you know the car's body is Buick, but the motor and transmission are Cadillac? It's the damnedest thing anyone has ever seen."

"I'm not sure why that's important or why anyone cares." Shit, this time, she was genuinely insulted. Damn, this wasn't the direction he wanted the conversation to go.

"The car is remarkable in many ways, but in its current condition, it isn't safe. It needs new tires, and the motor should be replaced. You need a new exhaust system, and the transmission is making a sound no one can even identify." He watched as indecision moved over her expression, and she pulled her lower lip between her teeth.

"That sounds expensive. I'm burning through my savings faster than I ever dreamed possible, just trying to get the store restocked. Drat on a dead rat, everything seems to be piling up... and I don't want to use magic for anything that doesn't help others." Her last words were little more than a whisper, but he didn't miss them. She was getting sidetracked. Ema's focus had moved to the cost of fixing her car rather than his concern about her safety.

"You've missed the point, Ema. I was simply pointing out there are areas of your life where you need someone looking out for your wellbeing. I'll have high expectations when it comes to your safety—the only area I won't be willing to negotiate." Wrapping her hands in his, Josh smoothed the pads of his thumbs over the tender skin on the inside of her wrists.

"Let's focus on how the lifestyle will look for us rather than you cartwheeling into worry about your car. While I would prefer to get you something with a better safety rating, I'm not sure Buck and his crew would let me. They swear your car has a personality all its own." There was a damned understatement if he'd ever spoken one.

"Do you think they will let me make payments on the repairs?"

Since it was obvious she wasn't going to let this go, Josh decided to finish the discussion hoping it would help her focus. It seemed they would need to work on staying on topic as well.

"Ema, I'll cover the cost of the repairs. It's part of what I've been trying to explain."

"I'll pay you back as soon as I can. You're right, Berta is a character. When I test drove her in Boston, I walked down the street to a coffee shop to think over the decision. She followed me. The salesman told me he'd never seen anything like it."

Josh couldn't hold back his laughter, imagining the man watching in horror as the monstrosity drove itself down the street.

"Make sure you tell Buck's crew that story. They'll love it, and they have a story of their own. It seems Berta wanted a bath when she got inside their shop. Hoses kept moving, faucets turned on for no apparent reason, and their high-pressure washer repeatedly moved to her side, despite being locked in two different backrooms."

"No surprise there. She is a diva. Several times, she refused to move when I'd skipped her weekly trip to the car wash. She also loves changing colors inside and out. One day, she had rhinestone trim. Honestly, how pretentious."

Raising his hands in the universal sign of surrender, Josh could only shake his head at Ema's frustration.

Before he'd left home to join the military, he'd sworn magic was all illusion and no substance. Sure, there had been a lot of unexplained phenomena in Crystal, but he'd been young and arrogant, believing there was always a logical explanation. His time in the Navy taught him was to keep an open mind because sometimes, the most *reasonable explanation* is there is no reasonable explanation.

"A diva car with a color-changing fetish deserves new shoes, a motor, and a proper exhaust system. Her transmission will be a bigger challenge because finding parts has proven to be more difficult than anyone imagined. Until then, you can continue riding into town with me, or we'll find something in the garage out back."

His parents kept several extra cars and pickups in the mechanic's garage at the back of the property. Anything he lent her would seem boring by comparison, but at least she wouldn't be tied to his schedule. Every car and truck in the ranch's fleet of spares was in great mechanical shape, but they would definitely lack Berta's colorful personality.

The coming tourist season meant Josh would work longer hours. Since he didn't want her to look for an apartment in town, it was important to make things as convenient for her as possible. Josh could read body language and knew Ema was as interested in moving this conversation in a different direction as he was. There would be plenty of time later to discuss the lifestyle. Tonight, he simply wanted to make love to the only woman he'd never been able to forget.

"Now, let's get back to our previous discussion." Ema's pupils dilated, and her pulse pounded at the base of her neck. *Perfect.*

CHAPTER TEN

"STOP FUSSING AT me, Ruby. I'm doing my best, but damnation, this door gets heavier every time I try to open the blasted thing." Opal wasn't interested in listening to her sister whine. She needed help to open the damned door to the crystal room.

"If you made me walk down all those damned stairs only to traipse back up again, I'm going to be mad as an old wet hen." Ruby's glare might have affected a lesser witch, but Opal had been dealing with her sister's threatening expressions her entire life and knew there was no bite behind the bark. "What's so damned important you couldn't use magic to retrieve it? You've been acting weird. Well, I suppose that's a subjective assessment, considering you peg out most people's weird-o-meter without breaking a sweat."

"Are you trying to insult me? If so, you're wasting your time. I've never had a desire to fit into someone else's mold. Good Goddess, why would I want to do such a boring thing?" Opal shuddered at the horrifying thought. She'd never been afraid of the inherent dangers Aradia's descendants faced, but thinking about being dull was downright terrifying.

"Tell me why we are here, Opal?" Any hint of teasing

was gone from Ruby's voice. She was done playing. Ruby Stone was a brilliant alchemist who'd spent years working as a chemist for a large pharmaceutical company. Years she claimed tested her resolve to never harm a fellow human. When the company Ruby worked for started dabbling in genetic modification, she'd walked away without looking back.

"I need to find a truth screening crystal. Nigel is going to try something slick with Emerald, and I don't want her to be hoodwinked."

"Hoodwinked? Holy hex, you're slipping. There for a hot minute, you *almost* sounded your age." Ruby looked her sister up and down, taking several seconds to scan her aura before continuing. "You don't think it's possible Nigel has feelings for her? He's been her overseer for a long time, Opal. He's had a lot of time to develop a deep attachment. We both know she is incredibly easy to love."

Opal decided it was best to ignore Ruby's crack about her age, even if it chapped her ass. Damn, she loved that phrase. In her opinion, the world would be a lot more fun if young people were in charge.

"The crystal will help her see a person's true heart. I'd never take away her free will, but she holds the future of our coven in her hands, so it's important she make the best decision possible."

"Let me guess, you believe Joshua Bennett is her soul match."

"Of course, he is. I don't know how I missed it all these years. It's a small wonder Aradia hasn't erased my name from the family tree. Can you imagine how frustrated she had to be when I kept trying to find a wife for Josh? Holy hexes and horny-toads, I'm lucky she didn't send one of the knights to skewer me."

"Don't you think you are being just a tad over-dramatic? Aradia is probably lounging on a warm beach, grateful to be free from drafty castles. I'll bet she's basking in the sunshine, listening to the waves lap at the shore. Those fruity cocktails with little umbrellas go a long way to smooth a path to forgiveness. As Queen of the Witches and the guardian of their magical future, she is too busy to worry about your misguided matchmaking." Ruby continued babbling, but Opal tuned her out when the heavy door they'd been struggling to open finally groaned in surrender. Stepping through, Opal waved her hand, setting flame to the torches on the walls.

"Move your hands slowly over the smaller stones. It has to be small enough to put in a piece of jewelry." Opal was already moving her hands along the long tables set against the crystal walls. The mine beneath the store had been producing crystals for more than a hundred years. Some of the most powerful stones used by magicals around the world had come from the Stone Coven's mine.

"There are several over here that have potential, Opal. Their vibrations are high, but I don't believe they are high enough." Ruby was a gifted magical, but she'd never been as powerful as her older sisters. "Our coven member did a good job of sorting them, though I'm not sure why anyone bothered." Ruby had overseen the process as coven members spent more time working outside their homes, meaning they had fewer free hours to devote to magical activities. Not only did it make it easier for fewer people to handle sales, knowing the stones' vibration levels was a great way for the younger witches to enhance their magic.

"Sorting them was helpful when coven members first started working outside their homes. I miss the days of Ozzie and Harriet."

"Those boys sure could sing—they were lookers, too."

Opal laughed, leave it to her younger sister to think about the Nelson brothers. Ruby had never remarried after being widowed at such a young age. Opal's husband had been killed not long after they'd become parents. Their three-year marriage was the happiest she'd ever been, and it had taken years for her to feel as if she had her feet under her again. If it hadn't been for Ruby and Ola, Opal wasn't sure how she'd have managed the store, her duties as the head of their coven, and raised a child.

Skimming her hands over the section of stones Ruby identified, it didn't take long to find the perfect gem. "Thanks for your help. This one is perfect. I'll make a pretty piece, then hope, like Helen of Troy, it works. That blasted Nigel is a pain in my ass."

"Do you really think he plans to make Ema his? He's never kept a woman longer than a few months. He's a scoundrel, that one."

Ruby always gave Nigel too much credit if you asked Opal. The man's brain was controlled by his dick and his never-ending quest for power. On a level-playing field, anyone with an IQ over room temperature could see his bullshit coming a mile away. Opal planned to make certain Nigel couldn't mask his intentions from Ema.

"I think he wants to be aligned with her because he and every other opportunist wizard knows she is not only the firstborn in a seventh generation, but the power is magnified because this is the seventh cycle."

"Which amplifies everything. We've always known this day would come. The moment Ema pledges her heart to her soul's match, everything will change." Ruby was right, but Opal doubted anyone understood the future of witchcraft was hanging in the precarious balance.

The seventh cycle of seven was Aradia's answer to the dark side's pressure to take over the world of magic. The need for a system of checks and balances kept her from simply wiping those whose magic was self-serving from the face of the earth.

"Aradia tied the seventh-generation power to love for a reason. Without love, magic is too easily corrupted. Love makes people care about the future, but even love needs a little help now and then. Nigel cares for Ema, but he cares about himself more. He'd never be able to resist the lure of power, and Ema is too sweet to see his real motives if he tries to mask them."

"I agree he can be a charmer. Just look at the way he worked the room during our meet and greet." Ruby's comment went straight to the heart of what Opal had been worrying about.

The man was a master of illusion when it came to his heart's true intention. The Magic Council might not see Nigel for what he was, but Opal knew a chameleon when she saw one.

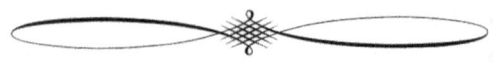

RUBY STONE LOOKED on in silence as her sister fought an internal battle. She'd never envied Opal's position as head of their coven. Guarding a huge crystal reserve, running a business, and years spent protecting a young woman who held the future of an entire generation of witches in her hand was more than any woman should be expected to take on alone. A lot had fallen on Opal's narrow shoulders.

Her older sister spent years trying to steer Emerald in the right direction, trying to train her when anyone could see the girl wasn't interested. Opal didn't think those around her understood Emerald's importance, but she'd always underestimated people's curiosity. Ruby, on the other hand, understood how snoopy people could be when they smelled a story.

The harder Opal tried to impress upon Ema how special she was, the more distant she became until the young witch put as much distance as she could between herself and her grandmother. Ruby remembered the day Opal told her Ema had become friends with two of the Adler sisters and had heard the relief in Opal's voice. The young shifters were also gifted magicals and had the best chance of changing Ema's view of magic.

"Are we staying down here or going back upstairs? I'm tired, and there are too many damned stairs for my old knees. I need a new potion. I'm thinking about trying to whip up something with weed." Ruby had been looking for an excuse to use marijuana, and this was the perfect excuse.

"That's so damned lame. If you want to relive your youth, go for it, but blaming your knees is really pathetic." Opal pulled her wand from her back pocket and whispered a short incantation. Ruby understood the Latin words Opal intoned, but the spell wasn't something she used since teleporting wasn't one of her gifts. Dropping into a chair as soon as they were in back in the kitchen, Ruby shook her head.

"Hex me, it's a tough call deciding what's the most challenging—huffing and puffing my way back up the stairs or getting all mucked up teleporting. Tomorrow, I'm going to one of those dispensaries. I already have a list of things I want to try." Looking across the table at Opal, Rudy slapped her hand atop the table. "Hey, are you listening to me? I'm talking to you, and you're staring at that damned rock."

"Can't you feel it? The crystal's power became magnified when we brought it up from the cavern."

"The whole cave felt supercharged, but I don't know why. We were just down there a few days before Ema came home, and it felt... well, dull is the word that comes to mind. Today, the hair on my arms stood on end." Holding out her hand, she added, "Let me see that for a minute." When Opal set the crystal in her palm, Ruby felt the energy course through her. Rubbing the unpolished stone over her knees, she could feel the warmth of healing loosening the stiffness of the joints.

"Great Goddess, my knees haven't felt this good since I sailed past the century mark. I'm still going to the dispensary, but I think my list needs to be tweaked." The irony in her words was wasted on her older sister. Hopefully, she could find some wacky weed that would send Nigel Lancaster back into his bat cave, so her sister would stop obsessing about the damned man.

A flash of light was the only warning they had before

Nigel appeared in a cloud of smoke. Theatrics—she shouldn't have expected anything less. It was as if they'd wished him into existence. Damn. Note to self, do not think or talk about the devil, or he appears.

"A hundred? Tell me, Ruby, how long ago did you pass that milestone? You don't look a day over a hundred fifty, so I can't imagine how your knees could suffer from any age-related affliction."

Ruby wanted to roll her eyes at the man's blatant attempt to flirt with her when they both knew he was wasting his time. She'd become a widow at a young age, and even though she'd had her share of male companions over the years, she found the whole concept of dating more trouble than it was worth. At this point in her life, Ruby had enough on her plate without adding any unnecessary complications, and men were a complication in anyone's view.

"Can it, Nigel. If that's your best pick-up line, it's easy to see why you are still single." Opal knew the man wasn't romantically interested in Ruby... or anyone else, for that matter. Nigel was a player and had been for as long as she'd known him. Unfortunately, that was far longer than either of them wanted to admit. He'd been acting the part of a cad for so long, it was second nature. "It's going to take all night to make the necklace for Ema if I have to do it alone." Glaring at her sister, Opal grumbled, "If you could focus on the task at hand, I'll bet we could wrap this up and still have time for cocktails."

"Do you have a drawing of what you want the piece to look like? You know Emerald's taste better than I do. If we're going to combine our magic, it's best if we work toward the same goal." Opal pulled the sketch from her pocket, spreading it flat on the table.

Nigel shook his head. "The latch will not work. She'll know something is up if it appears unusual. Emerald is much brighter than anyone gives her credit."

"Good thinking. We'll have to make it look like a regular latch but put a spell on it only one of us can remove."

"Don't you think the design is a bit pretentious for her? I've never seen her wear anything to draw attention to herself." Opal and Ruby had already put together their cover story. Anyone asking would hear how the piece was a welcome home gift. They planned to spell the stone with a charm to enhance the wisdom of the owner. It was close enough to the truth, and Nigel wouldn't have any reason to be suspicious if his intentions were in Ema's best interest.

"Hex, you might be right."

"For Goddess' sake. Why don't you simply ask Ema to carry the crystal with her? If she wants to make it into a piece of jewelry, she is more than capable." Nigel and Opal both glared at her, but Ruby pushed ahead. "You are treating her like a child. It won't work for you in the long run. She's too smart and independent to stay here if she has to surrender her free will." Narrowing her focus to Opal, Ruby continued.

"You think just because I didn't have children, I don't understand. I understand all too well what it's like to have decisions taken away by family." She'd always been overshadowed by her twin sisters. When she'd finally had enough, she moved across the country to get her doctorate in chemistry before working to improve the way the medical community used medications to heal patients. In the end, her decision to quit and move home had come down to ethics. Watching pharmaceutical companies focus on making money rather than health and healing was more than her conscience could take.

"You might be right. She definitely has a mind of her own. As much as I appreciate her intelligence, but I have to admit, it's damned inconvenient when it interferes with my plans for her. But it doesn't seem right to give her a plain rock for a gift." Once Opal started grumbling about how lackluster the gift would seem, Ruby knew she'd only won a small part of the argument. If they ever hoped to retire, Ema needed to be settled and focused on protecting the crystals beneath the store. Sighing, Ruby conceded a plain stone would be underwhelming.

Personally, Ruby believed Josh Bennett was their secret weapon. When she said so earlier, Nigel's aura changed colors for several seconds. The fleeting shift piqued her curiosity, making her wonder if there was a connection between the two men she hadn't heard about. How could he have developed such a strong opinion? She knew it wouldn't do any good to ask Nigel. The man seemed to equate secretive with sexy, obviously missing the memo this was a new millennium.

"I will talk to her after we get back from Denver. In the meantime, I'd like for her to enjoy a small token of our appreciation." Ruby wanted to gag—Opal was pouring it on pretty damned thick. Even Mr. The-World-Revolves-Around-Me raised a brow in question.

Opal was obviously planning to put off the conversation as long as possible. The shopping list Ema had given them was going to take them all over the city. They would be lucky if they didn't end up spending the night since Ruby adamantly refused to teleport between cities. *Why should I set myself up to feel as though I've been run over by a damned truck if I can avoid it?*

WALKING BACK THROUGH the kitchen, Josh grinned when he felt Ema's hand tremble in his. Pulling her around, so they stood face to face, he pushed a stray lock of her hair behind her ear. Studying her for several long seconds, the sizzle of sexual awareness and attraction built between them.

"Tell me what you want out of this, Ema." He didn't explain further—he didn't need to.

"I want you to make love to me, Josh. I want to feel the warmth of your bare skin against mine again... to know if your touch is as magical as I remember. You have a lot to live up to... my memory has set a high standard."

Josh grinned down at her, realizing she knew him too well.

"Challenge accepted." His hands around her small waist, Josh lifted her onto the kitchen counter. They weren't eye to eye, but they were close. He wanted to make certain she understood they would be on equal footing everywhere but the bedroom.

"That night at the lake, I asked you to trust me. Do you remember?" When she nodded, he added, "First lesson...

words, Ema. I need the words."

"I remember. It was easy to trust you." Her response could not have been any more perfect.

"There is nothing I value more than your trust. It's important you know how grateful I am for such a precious gift and how much I will always treasure it." Pausing for a few beats to make certain she understood how sincere his words were, Josh kept his hands at her waist before sliding them up until his thumbs were nestled beneath her breasts. The warmth of her body fused with his own, the sensation bringing a deep sense of calm, accompanied by the knowledge he was exactly where he needed to be.

"You trusted me with your innocence that night under the stars. I'm asking for that same level of trust again. What I have planned will be different this time. I hope like hell you'll find my skill level has improved." Grinning at her, he watched a pale blush paint her cheeks. Josh was suddenly battling the urge to bare her breasts and see if her nipples were the same cotton candy color he dreamed about. The moonlight at the lake was romantic, but his imagination had been forced to fill in some of the visual details over the years.

"There won't be a lot of rules tonight, but I have a few. First, rest assured you will be as safe with me tonight as you were all those years ago. I'd never hurt you, Ema." He could have sworn he saw a fleeting look of disappointment in her green eyes, but it was gone so quickly, he wondered if it had been his imagination. Hell, it was probably simply wishful thinking. "Second, if anything makes you uncomfortable, I want you to tell me immediately."

"Are you talking about safe words?" He was surprised

by her question but shouldn't have been. From what he'd heard, the erotic fiction genre had exploded over the past decade. She'd already admitted to reading about BDSM. Knowing Ema, she'd probably read more than a few hot romances and backed those up with research.

"I trust you, Josh, but... well, I heard..."

Josh wanted to push, to ask her what she'd heard despite having a damned good idea. He hadn't been as discrete as he should have been before he'd left Crystal. After the fiasco with Meghan, he'd adopted an almost religious devotion to condoms and a rock-solid aversion to any kind of commitment. His reputation spiraled out of control when he'd asked a woman if she enjoyed being tied up during sex.

Watching in silence as Ema fought an internal battle was painstaking, but the longer he watched, the more convinced he became that her hesitance was interest rather than concern. She shocked him when she finally asked, "Do you have silk rope in your bedroom?" For several seconds he could only stare at her in disbelief. His cock was much quicker to respond, going from semi-interested in the conversation to so hard, it felt like it would burst before he found his words.

"Talk to me, Emerald. Ask the questions I can see dancing in your intelligent eyes. No question is too personal, and no topic is taboo. I asked you to trust me, and that means I'm an open book." The statement sounded broader than he intended, but there was no use correcting it.

"I thought you were into kink. If you aren't, that's okay. I mean, it's not like I really have any experience either way, but it sounds... interesting. Reading about it is probably not the same as experiencing it, right? Hex, now I'm rambling. I hate it when I do that... although you'd think I'd be immune to the embarrassment by now. I just thought maybe you could help me find out what all the fuss is about... you know, with bondage and... well, other stuff. But I've probably screwed that up by showing you I'm skating on the outer rim of the sanity bell. Not hard to figure out why my social life has been a bust, is it? Oh, for spell's sake, my mouth and brain have suddenly stopped working together, and my mouth is running the show."

Josh almost laughed out loud at how much she'd inadvertently revealed. Knowing she'd hoped he'd be willing to introduce her to the lifestyle was a dream come true. If it had been any other woman, Josh would have questioned her motives and worried he was being set up. Emerald Stone was the least manipulative woman he'd ever met, which was damned amazing, considering her mother could write a book on the subject. Now that he thought about it, all the women in her family seemed to have a talent for getting others to do their bidding.

"Do their bidding? Wow. Are you a closet historical romance reader? Not that you should have to keep it a secret if you want to read erotica. I just figured your buddies would probably heckle you. Frickity frack, I'm sorry. I didn't mean to listen in on your thinking, but I can't really control it. Sometimes it just happens..."

Josh did the only thing he could—he kissed her. Sealing his lips to hers was the only way he knew to silence her rambling. Hearing her soft sigh and feeling the firm mounds of her breasts pressed against him was damned satisfying.

Ema's kiss was still as unpracticed as it had been years earlier, but there was something different—a soul-deep connection he'd never experienced with any other women. Josh wasn't sure how to describe the feeling, but on some level, his body responded to hers without his brain's help. Resisting the urge to shake his head to bring his focus back to the woman he felt spiraling toward release from nothing more than a kiss, Josh pulled back. He wanted to be able to see her reaction when he took control.

Moving her arms behind her back, he wrapped his large hand around her delicate wrists, shackling her easily. Josh smiled to himself when her eyes widened, and her respiration hitched. Her pulse pounded at the base of her throat, and he loved the way her pupils dilated. The flush of arousal spread slowly over the ivory skin exposed by her V-neck sweater, moving quickly up to her cheeks. The deep pink made him wonder what shade her ass cheeks would turn with the heated caress of his palm.

Josh was sexually dominant, but he didn't enjoy inflicting anything more than the edge of pain, enhancing a submissive's release. Bondage was his favorite form of play. A woman spread out like a feast, every inch bared to his touch, enhanced his own pleasure. He couldn't think of anything better than opening up a new world of pleasure for a woman who hadn't known how intense an orgasm could be.

"I love watching your reaction to this small introduction to bondage. It's the hottest thing I've ever seen. Your eyes dance with a need I know I can fulfill, and it's sending enough blood to my cock to make me light-headed."

When he set her on the counter, she'd been back far enough from the edge he didn't press against her when he pushed himself between her open knees. Using his free hand, Josh splayed his palm against the top of her ass cheeks and pulled her against the bulge in his jeans. If he didn't free himself from the confines soon, it would burst through the denim.

"Are we going to have sex in your kitchen?" Ema's eyes darted around the room, making him think she was worried someone would walk in on them. Under different circumstances, Josh might have taken offense that she didn't want anyone to see them in a compromising position, but Ema's lack of sexual experience made her vulnerable to concerns an experienced submissive would never consider.

"Part of trusting me is knowing I'd never put you in a position where I know you would be embarrassed."

"Me? Embarrassed? Oh, you misunderstood what I meant. I was worried about *your* reputation, Josh. You're a Bennett, for goodness sake."

Her comment blindsided him. Did she really believe he was subject to a perceived strict social structure in the small hamlet? Josh wouldn't deny the fact his family was wealthy, but they'd never used their money as a measure of their worth.

"I can tell by the look on your face what you're think-ing, and I'm doing a horrible job of explaining. Your family is admired for the wonderful things you contribute to the community, and I'd feel awful if I did anything to embar-rass them or damage your career. You're an elected official, Josh. Getting caught boinking me in the kitchen could hurt you in too many ways."

Boinking? Josh hadn't heard sex referred to as boinking since he was in high school.

"Sweetheart, I'm looking forward to making love to you, kissing every inch of your flawless, ivory skin, running my tongue through the wet folds of your sweet pussy, and fucking you until neither of us can remember our own name. But *boinking* is not on the agenda." He chuckled when she blushed such a deep shade of red, her face practically glowed. "We're the only people in the house, the doors are locked, and I set the alarm. Thank you for trying to protect my reputation, but I'm afraid that train left the station a long time ago."

"I've been gone long enough, I don't think I'm much of a liability... at least not yet, but I'm sure Granny Good Witch will pull me into one of her schemes soon enough. Someone shooting at me probably already cost me a chance to help with the Special Olympics, which sucks."

"We're getting too far off-topic... again. Just to clarify, the invitation still stands, and you'll be happy to know you have already passed your background check."

"What background check?"

"Sweetheart, you really need to read the documents you sign." He'd slid the authorization form in front of her one afternoon while she was on a call with a supplier. Ema scribbled her name where he'd pointed without so much as glancing at what she'd signed.

"Let's get back to your perfect reaction to having your hands restrained behind your back. That was hotter than hell, just so we're clear." Damn, that sweet blush was going to be the end of his sanity. "I'm looking forward to exploring every fantasy you've ever had but not tonight. Tonight is about reconnecting. I want to look into your eyes as you come and remember why I never forgot that night."

Pulling her into his arms, Josh tucked his hands beneath her ass, lifting her from the countertop, then turned and started down the hall. The heat of her sex pressed against his erection when she wrapped her legs around him. Setting her on her feet beside the bed, Josh reached for a small box of matches, intent on lighting the candles he'd placed around the room. He looked on in disbelief as Ema waved her hand, sending sparkles of light around the master suite, igniting the wick of every candle. Within seconds, the entire room was awash in pale-gold flickering light, and he was speechless.

"We're definitely having a conversation about *that* later."

Her hands moved to the buttons of his shirt, and the warmth of her fingers brushed against his bare chest as she opened the placket, sending another wave of blood rushing into his cock. There was so much blood pooled below his belt, it was a miracle he hadn't passed out. Tossing the shirt aside, Josh lifted her dress over her head and sucked in a breath.

"Fucking hell, Ema, you are gorgeous. I'm fighting like hell to keep from tearing off your sexy lingerie. I'm trying to remember to unwrap you like the gift you are, but I'm telling you now, it's killing me." Josh had a real weakness for sexy undergarments. He knew a lot of Doms didn't allow their subs to wear them, but he'd never understood why. Damn, he loved seeing a woman's body framed in silk and lace.

"Can we do slow and purposeful later? I haven't felt your hands on me for years, and I'm about to spontaneously combust."

Josh laughed softly as he shook his head. Damn, she never ceased to surprise him.

"I'd planned to savor you, but your plan sounds much better." Within seconds, he'd removed her pretty green undergarments and finished undressing. Pulling back the thick comforter, he smiled when her eyes brightened when he lowered her onto the emerald-green sheets. The bed was akin to sleeping on a cloud. The damned thing cost a fortune and was worth every penny.

"Your bed is amazing."

"One of the things I promised myself when I returned home was that I'd never again sleep on anything but the best bed I could buy. Every set of sheets I own is this color, Ema. The color of your eyes has always haunted me. I swear I dreamed in emerald-green for a damned year." Opening the condom he'd pulled from the nightstand, Josh rolled it over his length and held back his grin when her eyes widened.

"It's not going to fit."

"Sweetheart, it fit perfectly last time. Hell, it was beyond perfect. We'll go as slow as you need to." Moving over her, Josh decided it might be best to loosen her up with his fingers, but before he could shift positions, she grasped his shoulders and shook her head.

"This way, just like last time. Now. Please."

He didn't have a prayer resisting her heartfelt plea. Slipping his arms under her legs, Josh let her knees settle into the bend of his elbows. He moved his arms away from his body, opening her sex to his view, and was happy to see her pussy lips glistening with the evidence of her arousal. Positioning his tip at her entrance and pushing in, Josh groaned as her warmth surrounded him.

"Fuck me, you are so tight, sweetheart. Tight and hot. You are testing my self-control, Ema." When she started wiggling against him, Josh groaned. "We have to go slow, even though it may well kill me. I don't want to hurt you." His voice sounded rough and gravelly, but it was a small miracle he'd been able to speak at all.

Her vaginal walls were already rippling around his cock, and he wasn't even close to being fully seated. When he'd said she was tight, it has been a huge understatement. Reminding himself her body had taken him before wasn't helping deter the urge to plunge ahead.

Josh always regretted not taking better care of her the first time. He should have at the least asked if she'd had any sexual experience. Even as young as he'd been, Josh would have known to go slower. If Ema hadn't had sex since that night, he would not make the same mistake again. This time he'd make certain her body had plenty of time to adjust to his size.

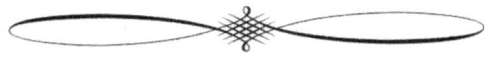

CHAPTER ELEVEN

W HY IS HE *torturing me? If he doesn't hurry up, I'm going to melt into a puddle.* Ema could feel the scorching heat building inside her. Need, unlike anything she'd ever experienced, started as a strange tingle of electricity racing up and down her spine. Ema heard the strangest sound echo through the room, but her body's urgent clamor for *more* stole her focus. The floor beneath the bed shook, making the bed tremble. For several seconds she was torn between trying to remember if Colorado had earthquakes and the relief Josh hadn't seemed to notice anything unusual.

"Let's see if your hot little pussy is ready for more, sweetheart." Josh's voice sounded strained, and a small part of her relished the realization he was as overwhelmed as she was. When she felt her muscles trying to pull his cock deeper, his hold on her tightened. "Let me set the pace, or I'll be forced to tie you to the damned bed." Her entire body reacted to his words, her vaginal muscles pulsing as she went liquid around him. "You're killing me, sweetheart. Your body is begging for something it isn't ready for, and it's getting harder and harder to hold off the need to sink balls deep into your heat."

Ema tried to slow her wildly beating heart, but her

body wasn't listening to common sense. She might not have had sex since their shared night of passion, but that didn't mean she hadn't found other ways to sate the intense need that had grown steadily since the first time they made love. During the past year, her barren sex life had cost her a small fortune in batteries for her favorite vibrator.

"We'll talk more about your battery consumption later, sweetheart." Emerald felt her cheeks heat to the point, she wondered if her face was going to burst into flames when she realized she'd spoken out loud. "Right now, I'm not about to question my good fortune." Ema almost cried with relief when he finally started moving.

Seriously? This is all I'm going to get? Shallow thrusts moving him deeper in excruciatingly small increments? Hex, it will take days for him to be balls deep.

Josh lifted her legs higher, the small shift in position was enough to make her body light up from the inside out. Feeling the hard outer ring of his cock head pressing against her G-spot sent a rush of cream to coat his length. If Ema hadn't been losing her mind as her body strained toward release, she might have been embarrassed by the wet sounds made by his cock shuttling in and out. Hearing his breathing change brought her back to the moment in time to feel his cock swell inside her. The large veins winding around his length, massaging her vaginal walls, the sensation was enough to send her hurtling over the edge.

Colors so brilliant they defied description flashed behind her eyelids, and she could have sworn she heard a woman somewhere in the distance scream Josh's name.

Every cell in her body felt as though it was shining in brilliant color as she hurtled through a clear tunnel. Nothing else existed at that moment. The change in her body's vibration caught her off guard. The shift in rhythm as she floated back down from the peak of her orgasm was oddly echoed by Josh's body. It only took her a few seconds to realize their hearts were beating in tandem.

Your hearts are joined, just as mine is with Conrad's. Two are stronger than one. Heed his counsel and seek shelter in his arms.

Who are you?

Aradia, Queen of the Witches.

"I'm not sure where you went, sweetheart, or who's voice was echoing through the room. When my brain comes back fully online, I'll be interested to hear your explanation. For now, I want to bask in the afterglow of the most intense sexual experience of my life." His body blanketed her, and despite the solid planes of rigid muscles pressing her into the mattress, the warmth surrounding her felt better than the comfy quilt Aunt Ruby made for her when she was a small child.

"I'll be happy to answer questions when my mind comes back online. You should probably know it may be a while. It's your own fault—you melted most of my brain cells." She felt the vibration of his chuckle a split second before he rolled.

Taking her with him, Josh pulled the comforter over them before her body had time to register the chill. She sighed softly, resting her cheek against his bare chest. Her brain was numbed by happy endorphins. Adding her brain's cocktail of contentment to the steady beat of his heart lulled her into a blissful slumber. The last thing she heard was Josh whisper a simple but powerful word as he kissed her sex-rumpled hair.

"Mine."

BOUNDING THROUGH THE front door of the store the next morning, Ema couldn't remember the last time she'd felt so invigorated. *Apparently, the rumor about great sex being the fountain of youth is true.* She came to a skidding stop when she noticed she wasn't alone. Ema panicked when she realized the man facing her had somehow gained entrance without unlocking the front door. When she took a step back, he shook his head as he held up his hands in the universal sign of surrender.

"I'm sorry I startled you, Emerald. Your grandmother and aunt let me in before they left. It seems you've sent them for a rather interesting and lengthy list of supplies."

"Who are you, and why are you here?" There was something oddly familiar about the man standing in front of her, but Ema couldn't put her finger on why. He was dressed in faded blue jeans and a polo shirt that stretched tight over a well-muscled chest, making him look younger than she suspected he actually was. Looking into his eyes, Ema saw an old soul—a stark contrast to his outward appearance. The man's attempt to appear younger was all the reason she needed to proceed with an abundance of caution.

Ema felt her eyes widen when an ornate wood and marble table materialized out of thin air between them. She wasn't an expert in antiques, but it was easy to see the piece was valuable. Running her fingers over the marble inlay, Ema smiled when she realized the surface was warm.

"It's beautiful. The marble is warm, and I assume that's a consequence of being transported from the third star east of Never-Never Land."

"As much as I appreciate the Peter Pan reference—and yes, I caught the connection to your concern about my age."

Damn, she was out of practice dealing with magicals. She should have known he'd listen in on her thoughts. Having grown up in a household where magic was the norm, Ema had perfected her shields to the point they'd been second nature. After living in Boston for a few years, she'd let down her guard.

"I'll save you the trouble of erecting the shields you believe so effective. They'll be useless against me, though they'll probably be fairly effective against most of the other witches and wizards you'll encounter." Nigel raised a brow as if he expected her to argue before giving her a slight nod of approval. Leveling a considering look at her, he slid a map she hadn't noticed across the table to her.

"For the record, my name is Nigel Lancaster. Now, let's get down to business, shall we? If you look at a map, you'll note the crystal mines around the globe are delineated by gold dots. The marks are in odd non-linear formations because there are vast and immensely powerful veins of crystal running beneath the earth's surface. Most people take little notice when they cross one of the energy-charged lines the magical world refers to as the power grid. The hair on their arms might stand on end or a shiver race up their spine, but for those who are affected by changes in the earth's vibration, the impact can be significant."

Ema studied the map for several minutes before looking up. "Why isn't there a dot for Crystal?" Studying the map while she waited for him to respond, Ema ran her finger along the line of dots between Boston and Crystal. It seemed odd the marks were all remarkably close to Interstate 70. There wasn't much distance between the dots until you reached western Kansas. After that, there were larger spaces between them. The presence of powerful crystals was probably the reason she'd been able to drive for so many hours without resting.

"The crystal cavern beneath this store belongs to the coven and has never been actively mined for anything other than their personal use. The coven was granted permission to sell stones mined without mechanical help, so their efforts would never be large scale. The Council of Magic agreed the significance of the crystals beneath your quaint little town should be kept secret, although their reasons differed from coven members. The enormity of the mine's power has never even been shared with the magical community… until recently."

"If it was kept secret for so long, why reveal it now?"

"A member of the Stone Coven left after a heated argument with your grandmother. It seems the young woman didn't understand why the coven was struggling financially when they were sitting on a virtual mint."

Ema learned early in her marketing career, there was a lot of power in silence. If you waited long enough, people would become uncomfortable and keep talking, even when they knew it wasn't in their best interest. The man sighed and shook his head, chuckling.

"Your power may be more diverse than the Magic Council knows, Emerald. You are right about the power of the line helping you make the long trip, but your assumption I wouldn't have continued without you manipulating the silence is off the mark. Those tricks work with nonmagicals or those with limited power—they're useless against any of the witches and wizards you'll be facing."

"Facing? Are you talking about customers at the store? I hope you're a fortune-teller because we're going to need a powerful customer base if we're going to save Spellbound." It was a wonder the wide plank floor didn't burst into flames beneath her feet for making such an outrageous understatement. If they didn't get the store up and running within the next couple of weeks, they didn't have a prayer of saving it. She'd been trying to avoid using magic for anything other than cleaning, but it was getting more difficult, and the pressure to get the store up and running continued to build.

"You will get all the help you need to make certain the store is up and running by the end of the week." Ema stared at him in disbelief. The news sounded too good to be true, and, in her experience, gifts usually had strings attached—particularly gifts of this magnitude. "I know you have no reason to believe me, but I promise you won't be disappointed." He paused for several seconds, and she wondered if he was going to tell her the help would require her sacrificing her firstborn child or something equally outrageous. "Good heavens, requiring children as payment went out of vogue centuries ago. I swear young people read fables and retain the most useless pieces of information rather than the moral lesson."

"There is something oddly familiar about you and this conversation. I don't know why, but I'm getting goosebumps trying to place you."

"We've met before, but you were young, so I doubt you remember."

"Wait, if we've met when I was a child, how old are you?" Magicals were good at concealing their age, and knowing his actual age would go a long way to explain who he was. One of her issues with the world of magic was the duplicity you faced at every turn. Things were rarely as they seemed, and most of the time, it too much trouble to sort through the nonsense to find the truth.

Before she left Boston, Ema suspected her grandmother was exaggerating her illness to lure her home but hadn't been willing to take the chance. Now that she thought about it, the nonmagical world wasn't any better—that's why it had been so easy to walk away. Her employer appeared upfront in the beginning, but the longer she'd worked there, the more deception she'd seen. Nigel Lancaster's smooth as butter voice brought her back to the moment.

"Age is just a number, Emerald. You should never let the number of times you've circled the sun define you." He hadn't answered the question, but his response was so typical for those in the magical community, she knew it would be useless to argue the point.

"So, another coven wants to mine the crystals and cash in. The Magic Council is opposed because they... what?

Want it for themselves? The Council doesn't want me to trust the other coven, but I'm supposed to blindly trust you? Help me out here. I'm trying to unravel this mystery, but nobody is leveling with me. My granny and aunt are always talking in freaking circles, some woman who claims to be the Queen of Witches talks in my head, and I'm standing over a crystal mine everybody is fighting over, but no one will tell me why. It's beyond frustrating to be the only one who is frick-fracking clueless. How about someone gives me a copy of the damned script?" Slapping her palm down on the map in frustration, she looked up to discover Nigel had vanished into thin air.

What the hell?

"What's going on, sweetheart? I don't know who you were talking to, but you sounded damned put out. I could help you work that stress right out of your system. I have several excellent ideas." Josh's arm encircled her torso, tightening just below her breasts as he pulled her back flush against his chest.

"I have no idea where he went." She looked left and right in disbelief. Why had he magically disappeared just as Josh arrived?

"Who?"

"Nigel Lancaster, or at least that's what he said his name was. He was talking... well, he was supposed to be talking to me about the crystal cavern beneath the store, but he was talking in circles. From what little I've been able to gather, the cavern's value has been a well-kept secret until recently. Beyond that, I can't get a straight answer from anyone." Josh turned her in his arms until they were facing one another. Ema felt an unfamiliar pull at her heart when their eyes met and wondered if he felt the same shift in the energy pulsing around them.

"Was he the target of your anger? The entire room was practically vibrating with your frustration."

"Yes. I felt like he was dancing around whatever he wanted to tell me. My grandmother and aunt have been doing the same thing. Don't even get me started on my granny's phony illness. The woman is positively shameless."

"Is it possible she was desperate?" Josh's question rang truer than she wanted to admit.

"Desperate for what?" Ema had considered the possibility but didn't know what possible explanation her granny had for straight-up lying.

"Could be one of several things, but I have a hunch it's a combination of things." When she didn't respond, Josh lifted her onto the table. The few inches she gained in height weren't as important as the heated desire she saw smoldering in his blue eyes when he pushed her knees apart to step between them. "I've asked around, and it seems Spellbound has been hovering on the brink of bankruptcy for several months. Has she told you how precarious their financial situation is?"

Ema wasn't surprised to learn her grandmother hadn't shared the details but felt her heart seize, anyway. Had her granny thought Ema would avoid moving home if she'd known the store was failing? It was humbling to think her grandmother might consider her was as shallow as her mother and sister. If someone was standing in front of the store, handing out five-hundred-dollar bills, Jade and Garnett Stone might consider returning to their small hometown—hell, even then, it was questionable.

"I would have come sooner if I had known how bad it was. No, she hasn't told me, but I'd have to be dumber than a box of rocks to not see things are teetering on the cusp of disaster. Why didn't she just tell me the truth?"

"Pride." Josh's answer was simple, and Ema understood the truth in his response. "Opal has spent her entire life trying to make up for her daughter's selfish behavior. No one ever believed she was responsible for Jade's egocentric actions, but your granny seems determined to bear the burden." Pushing a lock of her hair behind her ear, Josh chuckled. "Opal once told me you are destined to save the coven."

Ema was shocked to hear her grandmother had shared anything magical with Josh since she knew how skeptical he was about things he couldn't see or touch.

"My grandmother has told me tales about my heritage my entire life, but she's never given me enough information to make any of it seem real. The man who was here earlier was spinning a yarn about the crystal mine, but he vanished just before you came in, which makes me wonder why he would want to avoid you."

"It isn't uncommon for people to go out of their way to avoid law enforcement officers, but I have to admit I'm baffled about this one."

"There was something familiar about him, but I don't know why. I'm typically good with names and faces, but there are spells to erase the memory of encounters."

"Why would he want to do that?"

"I don't know, but I have an idea how I can find out." Ema hoped her Book of Shadows would reveal the truth.

When she returned to the guest house after work, she'd ask the book to show her why Nigel Lancaster made her feel as if they had met before. It wouldn't matter how powerful his magic was, he wouldn't be able to cast a spell over her book. It was the only thing no one could take from her. "My book will tell me." She could see the questions in his eyes and was grateful he kept them to himself.

"I have a few things to wrap up before I can leave. Since you don't know who the man was or what he wanted, I'd rather you waited for me." It hadn't surprised him when Ema borrowed the oldest car in the mechanic's garage. It was in great condition, but it didn't have four-wheel drive, and Josh considered it too light for mountain driving unless the weather was perfect—which was damned rare. "There is a weather front moving in. The fog is already causing problems, and I don't want you driving on mountain roads under those conditions. I'll have the guys at the garage lock up the car you drove and take you home."

"If we keep this up, they'll need to add on to the garage. I'm turning the place into a parking lot."

Josh chuckled and shook his head.

"They'll consider it a small price to pay for the privilege of keeping Berta a while longer. I suspect they have your car in tip-top shape but aren't looking forward to parting with her. It seems they are winning a lot of money, laying bets on what color the car will be the next time they check. I should probably bust their asses for gambling without a license, but they're having so much fun, I hate to spoil it."

Ema snickered and wondered how the garage's crew endeared themselves to her temperamental automobile.

Berta didn't usually like strangers, so hearing she was helping the men win money spoke volumes.

"Do I want to know what she's doing?" Holding up her hand, Ema shook her head. "No. Don't tell me. I'm simply happy she's playing nice." The car was enchanted, and her disposition wasn't always as cooperative as it should be, so Ema wasn't joking when she said she was pleased Berta was behaving.

"Do you smell smoke?" Josh blinked in surprise, glancing at Ema as they drove through the security gate leading to his home. The alarm he saw in her expression was all the explanation he needed. Stomping on the accelerator, he heard her gasp as the truck lurched forward.

Tossing his phone to her, he instructed Ema to call 911. It would take emergency services ten minutes to reach the ranch under ideal circumstances, and tonight was anything but ideal. He listened as Ema relayed the information, cringing when he realized the orange glow was coming from the guest house. When his truck came to a rocking stop, he turned to tell Ema to stay in the truck, but she was already halfway out the door.

Emerald Stone was damned fast when she wanted to be. Josh was shocked at how quickly she'd sprinted across the yard. When he caught up with her, he was shocked to find Ema standing halfway between the main house and the small guest quarters where everything she owned was engulfed in a fire so hot, there wasn't a chance in hell there'd be anything left.

Arms extended, palms up, Ema chanted so softly, Josh couldn't make out the words. He stared in utter amazement as the front door of the small bungalow opened. The large book she'd called her Book of Shadows hovered in the air just outside the door's smoldering frames. If he hadn't known better, he'd have sworn it was assessing the surroundings before it bounced side to side as if relieved to be outside. Floating on an invisible cushion of air, the thick book slowly made its way closer, finally settling in her open arms.

"I'd have never believed it if I hadn't seen it myself. Fucking hell, that was one of the most remarkable things I've ever seen."

Ema's small hands shook as they skimmed lovingly over the surface of the embossed leather cover. Josh could only shake his head in wonder. From what he could see, the damned thing wasn't so much as singed. The distant wail of sirens heralded the incoming emergency responders, but he knew everything else she owned was going to be lost by the time the fire trucks arrived.

"Sweetheart, I'm so sorry. I don't know why the fire suppression system didn't activate. I promise to replace everything you've lost." She waved her hand as if dismissing his concern. When she finally tore her gaze from the brilliant blaze, her eyes glassy with tears, Josh felt his chest constrict at her pained expression.

"I'm sorry, Josh. I know this is my fault. I'm not sure why someone is so determined to see me leave Crystal, but it's unfair of them to put you and your home at risk."

Holy hell. Was she fucking serious? She was worried about him while every piece of clothing and memento she owned was going up in fucking flames?

Josh was as baffled as she was about a motive. He didn't know who was responsible, but he damned well planned to find out. Wrapping his arm around her shoulders, Josh led Ema under the covered patio. The sheltered area was closer to the backdoor of his home and would offer her more privacy when the firefighters arrived.

Taking the heavy book from her arms, he set it on the corner of the long metal and glass outdoor table, then did a double-take when the table vibrated. He was anxious to hear more about the book Ema referred to as her most valued possession, but that discussion needed to wait. Turning her so they were facing one another, Josh focused all his attention on Ema, trying to ignore the crackling of the nearby flames.

"This is not your fault, Emerald. I don't know who is responsible or what their motive is, but I promise to do everything in my power to find out." When she started to speak, he shook his head. "Don't argue with the local sheriff, sweetheart." He was relieved when her shoulders relaxed beneath his touch. "I have to say, you've certainly livened things up since you arrived." He wouldn't have been surprised to see her grandmother on someone's radar, but knowing Ema was the target was baffling.

"You're right about my granny. She has made a few enemies over the years." Josh shook his head in amusement and wondered if he would ever get used to her responding to observations he hadn't made out loud. "I'm tired of being left in the damned dark by a couple of nursing home rejects."

Josh couldn't hold back his bark of laughter and could only imagine how many calls he'd get if either of the Stone sisters became a resident of the local retirement home. *Heaven forbid.*

CHAPTER TWELVE

O PAL STONE STOMPED into the small kitchenette, giving the antique oven a swift kick. She might be old, but she could still kick hard enough to make the metal clang and set off the mini-light show of her tennis shoes.

"Well, I guess if you are going to dress like a toddler, everyone should expect you to act like one." Ruby's disapproving tone did nothing to improve Opal's foul mood.

"Be grateful these shoes make me smile. Otherwise, I might go completely postal. What the hell is happening? Ema is going to take off like a damned streak if this shit doesn't stop."

"Well, Nigel is responsible for the window fiasco, and Ema might have figured that detail out on her own if you hadn't cleaned up all the glass and masked his magic so quickly. Josh was unhappy with you, too."

Ruby was really getting on her nerves—nothing like an annoying younger sibling who always seemed to be right to put the icing on a craptastic day.

"Did you call Ola? She needs to get her happy ass up here and help. I'm tired of trying to pull this mess together. That damned Ives Coven is a menace. I thought Lizzy had more sense than to fall for Danny Ives. He isn't smart enough to manage the mine, even if we handed it over. You can bet your ass he's behind the efforts to scare Ema away." They'd both known trouble would follow when one of their former members moved in with the ambitious leader of a rival coven.

"Burning down the Bennett ranch guest house was careless and stupid. The Council needs to do something with him before this thing escalates." Opal was fed up with Danny's continued attempts to take over the Stone Coven.

"The Council is aware of the problem, Opal." Audric Stafford's voice came from the bottom of the stairs, and Opal wanted to toss a chair down the dark entrance to their embarrassingly small apartment. Maybe it would bounce off his head and knock some sense into her long-time friend. "Give it up and come down here. I'm not getting any younger, and I want to talk to you before I head home. I swear I'm getting too old for this shit."

With a quick flick of her wrist, Opal was standing alongside a man she'd known since they were kids. Their friendship stood the test of time because they genuinely liked and, more importantly, respected one another. Opal glared at Audric before calming herself enough to speak.

"Danny Ives magical signature was all over that damned fire. I took a few of Ema's mementos out the back and let her summon her Book of Shadows." Audric's soft chuckle annoyed her because she wasn't sure what the damned man found so amusing.

"You didn't save any of her clothes?" Audric's amused question was teasing rather than a sincere inquiry.

"Good Goddess, no. She's always dressed like a near-sighted, color-blind librarian with a glass eye. If I didn't love her to distraction, it would be embarrassing." This time, Audric laughed out loud as he shrugged.

"She's lovely, and now that she is bound to Joshua Bennett, I hope his sense of style influences hers." Ruby coughed in what Opal was convinced rated as the lamest coverup of ill-timed laughter in history.

"The guest house is a loss, but there is a bright side— Ema will move into the main house sooner rather than later. I'll be speaking with her tomorrow morning. Don't forget we've had various spirit protectors watching over her since she was born. They've already started revealing themselves to her, but the results have been mixed. She seems delightfully oblivious at times but accepted Red Cloud's protection without question."

"I wish she remembered Nigel." Opal didn't make any effort to keep the disdain from her voice. "He wants her as a partner, but it won't be anything other than a working relationship with occasional benefits. The revealing crystal she is wearing should help."

Audric raised a brow in question. Leaning against the door, his tailored suit made him look like he'd just stepped off the pages of GQ. Damn, the man was still one of the most handsome men Opal had ever met. Audric Stafford hadn't aged a day in the last hundred years—it was damned annoying now that she thought about it.

"Nigel is an asshat. I doubt he has any idea how to love anyone other than the jerk he sees in the mirror every morning. We're hopeful the necklace Ema is wearing will help her see through his smoke and mirrors routine." Ruby's assessment was as accurate as any. Opal grinned when her younger sister crossed her arms, the simple shift pushing her breasts far enough north they returned to the zip code they'd occupied decades earlier.

"I agree, Nigel is... well, shall we say self-serving?"

Opal rolled her eyes at the head wizard's understatement.

"Any woman who assumes Nigel will consider *love* a part of their partnership will be in for a boatload of heartache. The man is a cad. If you Google the term, you get his picture. Did you hear him tell me he'd return after his pedicure? For heaven's sake, it's not like his neatly trimmed toenails are going to save our coven." Opal shuddered as Audric and Ruby laughed.

"Dad, next time you ask me to stop by, I'm going to ask more questions. First and foremost, I want to make certain we aren't discussing toenails and how they might save a coven. Call me prudish, but some topics should always be considered off-limits."

Opal rushed forward to wrap Gigi Stafford in a hug. When she finally released the younger woman, Ruby stepped forward.

"It's great to see you again, Brigitte." Rudy's sincere words made the young witch smile.

"Ruby, you look wonderful." Taking in her surroundings, Gigi waved her hand in a circle, sending glittering lights from her fingertips. When the sparkles cleared, a lovely seating arrangement, complete with a small table of snacks and wine, was front and center. "Let's sit down, and you can fill me in. It's been a long day, and since we're discussing the Stone Coven, it's sure to be a lengthy, interesting story."

Opal nodded as she settled into one of the comfortable

chairs.

"I'm going to hurt anyone who tries to take this chair out of here." When Gigi laughed, Opal leaned her head back and sighed. "It's been so long since we had comfortable furniture, I'd nearly forgotten what it feels like. I tried to spell a chair like this but couldn't seem to get it right. Damn, I want to retire and sit on a beach someplace, sipping drinks served by a clothing-challenged cabana boy with a hot bod."

"Don't be ridiculous. You'll never retire. You're too much of a busy body." Ruby's words weren't spoken with any real heat, and there was probably more truth to them than Opal wanted to think about.

"That's just rude... even taking into account your usual low standards in this regard, that comment was rude." Opal had never understood why both her sisters considered her fair game for their snark. Ola and Ruby both had college educations they believed made them smarter than the sister who'd been determined to continue Aradia's legacy. Damn it, how did they expect a seventh generation to be born without her having a family?

"You each had a role to play, Opal. Having a family was yours, and even though your daughter wasn't all you'd hoped, she made at least one perfect choice—she left Emerald with you." Audric's observation soothed her in a way nothing else could.

Opal knew she'd done her best with Jade. Unfortunately, nothing had ever been good enough for her only child. Jade was the only thing that mattered to Jade—she was the center of her own universe. Garnett was proof positive the old saying about the fruit not falling far from the tree was based on a universal truth. Fortunately, Emerald was a spectacular exception.

"Let's get to the nitty-gritty... I'm tired and looking forward to sleeping in my own bed before next week."

Opal smiled at Brigitte. The gifted young magical had already agreed to mentor Emerald, and Opal couldn't imagine anyone better. Gigi had always been a powerful magical, and her commonsense approach and never-say-die attitude made her a formidable ally and a terrifying enemy.

"Several of our members have joined the neighboring coven." Before Opal could continue, Gigi snorted and shook her head, the younger woman's expression reflecting the same disgust Opal and Ruby felt for the group whose numbers were growing too rapidly for it to be occurring naturally.

"Danny Ives is a butt plug. He wouldn't know integrity if it walked up and slapped him on both flabby cheeks... and I'm not talking about the ones on his porthole face. If they ever hold an election for the man least likely to get it up, no one else will stand a chance."

Opal looked at Audric, noting his obvious surprise.

"I'm interested to know what sort of run-in you've had with Mr. Ives, Brigitte." Audric's tone was level, but Opal could feel anger vibrating around him. Evidently, the head of the Magic Council had also met the asshat who wanted to assume control of the crystal mine.

"He hits on anyone he believes might further his agenda... and I mean anyone. Ives isn't particular about gender, appearance, or moral compass. Danny Ives only cares about taking what he feels is owed to him and making his dick happy. He's a toad, and I'm not talking about his weight. He must be using some kind of spell on the younger members of his coven—there is no other explanation for his popularity or their loyalty."

DANNY IVES WATCHED the video monitor he'd set up across the street from Spellbound and cursed. It was always easier to spy on nonmagicals. Hell, even lower-level witches were a cakewalk compared to the Stafford's. He'd been able to see the four individuals sitting inside the vacant store until they started talking, then the damned camera went completely dark. Using the joystick in front of him, Danny panned left and right, growling when the picture cleared as soon as Spellbound was no longer in the frame.

He needed to get this project wrapped up. Setting fire to the Bennett's guest house was supposed to have provided enough distraction, he could get into the store and cast a spell clearing his path, but Opal Stone was proving to be a bigger pain in his ass than he'd expected—and that was saying a lot. He'd known the old hag would put up as many roadblocks as possible, but the whole thing was spiraling out of control. How the hell did one small woman, whose fashion inspiration obviously came from a color-blind clown school reject, manage to play her cards so close to her chest? And to add gas to the fire, Audric Stafford's wildcard daughter was now involved—just fucking dandy.

One of the few mistakes he'd made since joining forces

with the dark magicians was not recognizing Brigitte Stafford at a party. He'd been enjoying himself with a number of different partners from various covens when he'd spotted a woman watching him with what he'd mistaken for sexual interest.

It wasn't until after she'd threatened to relieve him of his testicles, he realized who he was dealing with. She'd not only rejected his offer, the fucking lunatic woman snarled the threat while dangling him upside down several feet above the bar. Trying to mask his identity several months later when their paths crossed again hadn't ended any better. Even though she'd spared him the public humiliation of their previous encounter, he'd been forced to find his way home from deep in the Amazon rainforest. Since teleportation wasn't his strongest magical skill, he'd ended up in too many shitholes to count before finally landing in Crystal. If he never saw another snake or insect in his entire life, it would suit him fine.

Setting the guest house behind the Bennett ranch house on fire had been easy. His mistake had been doing the deed in person. Getting in and out of the property had proven a bigger challenge than he'd expected. Danny was surprised at the sophistication of Joshua Bennett's security system. Evidently, former Special Forces operatives were paranoid bastards. Sending a low voltage magnetic pulse to the system took it down long enough for him to get in, but backup generators rebooted the electronics within seconds. Once reset, the system entered a damned twilight fucking-zone of enhanced security, meaning he'd essentially been trapped inside the perimeter.

The fire was blazing out of control as he'd stumbled

through the woods at the back of the estate. He'd planned to be back in town before the Stones reconvened at the store. He needed a few minutes to cast the spell, then mask the magic. The best part of the plan was ensuring Ema lost her Book of Shadows. The loss would diminish her power and influence for years, if not forever. Making Ema Stone vulnerable meant she'd be more likely to align the dwindling numbers of her family's coven with his. Merging the two groups would give him access to the valuable crystals protected by the Stone Coven.

Danny didn't have proof, but he suspected the extraordinary monetary potential of the mine wasn't the only reason it had always been kept a closely guarded secret. He'd recruited several of the Stone Coven's members to gather information, but the younger members he'd been able to pull away from Opal and Ruby Stone's sphere of influence weren't able to provide anything substantial, aside from the two witches' insistence Emerald's return would be their saving grace.

Danny wasn't sure how long he'd been staring at the blank monitor when movement on one of the other screens caught his eye. Josh Bennett's pickup was barreling into town, moving considerably faster than the local Sheriff ordinarily drove unless he was responding to an emergency call. The truck slid to a stop in front of the magical shop, and Emerald Stone bailed out of the passenger door before the vehicle stopped rocking. Sprinting to the door with Josh on her heels, Ema flicked her wrist toward the door, her magic opening the heavy wood and glass entrance without turning the knob.

Damn, he wanted to know what was happening inside

Spellbound. What the hell sent Opal's granddaughter into such a full-blown panic? Cursing the blackout Audric Stafford placed over the blasted store, Danny leaned back in the leather office chair, scanning the various monitors. Now it was a waiting game. Backing Ema Stone into a corner where her only option was to join forces with him would require time and finesse. Unfortunately, the dark magicians pulling his strings weren't known for their patience or tolerance for mistakes. Since he didn't want to become the target of their frustration, he needed to figure out what the hell was going on.

Scanning the monitors, Danny noticed a lone figure walking down the wooden sidewalk. The figure's height and the length of stride made Danny think it was a man, but the dark full-length trench coat with the hood pulled low over the stranger's face made it impossible to know for sure. Danny let his attention move from the screen for a fraction of a second, reaching for the joystick to zoom the camera in, hoping to get a better look.

Returning his attention to the monitor, Danny was surprised to see the man staring into the camera, his finger pointing directly at the lens. There was a blinding flash of light so intense, it took several seconds for the damned dots exploding in his vision to clear enough, Danny could see the lens had shattered. The tight spiderweb of cracks blurred the picture, and nothing was recognizable.

"Fucking hell, who was that?" A younger member of his coven rolled his chair closer and with a few keystrokes, rewound the security footage. Slowing the playback, the young man worked to enlarge and enhance the image captured the moment before the bright flash shattered the lens. Once he'd captured and enhanced the image, the other man shuddered. "It's as if he is looking right into my soul. That's creepy."

Danny agreed. He might not know the man's name, but that didn't keep him from feeling the magical power surrounding him. There was an air of challenge surrounding the man staring into the camera, and it was impossible to miss the anger in the bastard's expression.

"Whoever he is, that's a cool trick and impressive since our cameras were well concealed. I put that spell on myself, and this guy didn't hesitate to walk directly up to it. Damn, he didn't even look around to find the other units. Look... he took them all out with one shot." The young man looked at Danny, his eyes reflecting something between admiration and fear. "Anyone powerful enough to pull that off certainly would have left behind traces of his magic."

Danny was already on his feet and moving to the door. As the strongest magical in his coven, he had the best chance of identifying the magical signature. He'd need to proceed with caution and wondered if the man had taken time to clear the area of any traces of his presence.

One of the few advantages Danny saw in living in a small town was the fact he could drive downtown in five minutes. *Who am I kidding? You can drive anywhere in town in under five minutes unless people are standing in the middle of the street chatting. What's with that?* Sure, the streets were remarkably wide for a mountain town, but it seemed like it would make a lot more sense for people to carry on their gossip sessions in the safety of their front yards.

Walking down the wide wood-plank sidewalk, Danny

knew before he'd even gotten close to the ruined camera, the wizard had already erased every clue to his identity. He wasn't surprised—any magical capable of taking out a concealed security system with little more than a pointed finger would be too gifted to make the mistake of leaving his calling card. Pulling his phone from his pocket, Danny sent messages to several contacts for information about an outside magical in town. He suspected the man had entered Spellbound but had no way to know for sure.

Frustration steamrolled through him like a freight train. There was too much on the line, and now the damned situation had become exponentially more challenging. The worst part of tonight's nightmare was not being able to identify who'd thrown a curveball into his well-laid plan. He tried to focus on the progress he'd made. Taking out Emerald Stone's Book of Shadows was a huge step in the right direction. Before he could get back into his car, Danny heard a door slam. Even in the damned streetlights were working against him tonight. *I don't know who convinced the city council they should buy this many pole lanterns, but the blasted things look like runway lights. The halogen bulbs are probably visible from space.*

Watching the petite woman rumored to be genetically linked to some ancient super-magical move down the sidewalk, he wondered what had her feathers so ruffled. Danny had never been interested in history—what was in the past couldn't be changed, so he didn't see any reason to study it.

His mother spent years harping about how those who failed to learn about the ancients were doomed to repeat their mistakes. He'd always rolled his eyes when she wasn't looking, muttering 'whatever the hell that means,' under his breath. Now, watching Emerald's reflection in the glass of a nearby store as she stormed across the street. Right now, it would be helpful to have a better understanding of what he was facing.

Turning to face her, Danny was surprised to see the undisguised rage in her eyes. He'd met her once years ago but doubted she would remember. He'd been surprised by how unremarkable and plain she appeared. Maybe he'd expected too much. The rumors he'd heard about how gifted she was supposed to be were misleading. Instead of the stunning witch he'd assumed would accompany the reputation, he'd met a pale young woman with glasses two sizes larger than appropriate for her ordinary face, dressed in clothes she must have found on the bargain rack of a local farm supply store.

The woman shaking her finger in his direction was anything but plain. She wasn't dressed in a designer outfit, but what she wore made her look professional and well put together—even if she smelled faintly of smoke. What caught his attention was the energy swell he'd felt a few seconds before she closed the gap between them. He could practically feel the heat of fury rolling off her. Emerald Stone was literally vibrating with anger, her green eyes shining with pent-up frustration. The only thing he could think of was how beautiful she was. Gone was the mousy woman he'd made a point to introduce himself to several years earlier, and in her place was a woman who had come into her own whether or not she knew it.

"You. What were you doing in the woods behind the Bennett estate?"

Woah. He sure hadn't expected that—how had she known? He'd cloaked himself in invisibility. His magic wasn't strong enough to maintain the illusion for an extended period, but it had only taken him seconds to move beyond the security cameras that paranoid bastard, Josh Bennett, set up every few feet. "Stop trying to figure out how I knew you were there and answer the damned question."

He needed to head this train wreck off before she derailed all his well-laid plans. Damn it, she'd been fucking shit up since she arrived. Why the hell hadn't Frank Black kept her in Massachusetts? The incompetent nimrod had one damned job and hadn't been able to manage it. His position at the art brokerage firm required absolutely no skill whatsoever—and he'd still gone down in flames. His bosses had been forced to hire him, his damned wages paid for by the dark magicians hellbent on acquiring the crystal mine beneath Spellbound. All Black had to do was keep his girlfriend interested enough to ignore her damned grandmother until they'd overpowered her crazy ass, and he'd failed.

Danny understood the man's lack of sexual interest in Ema until he'd seen the passion in her eyes as she stormed across the street. She might be mad as hell at him, but he knew there was a fine line between love and hate—all he needed to do was push her from one side of the narrow boundary to the other.

"Good evening, Ms. Stone. You seem a bit... rattled. What's going on? I heard there was a fire at the Bennett estate this evening. Are you alright?"

CHAPTER THIRTEEN

"DON'T PLAY STUPID." Ema stared at the fool standing in front of her. She wouldn't be surprised if his nose started growing like fucking Pinocchio. She was disappointed when nothing about his ugly mug seemed to change other than his leering gaze skimming over her like an unwelcome caress. He looked her over as if she was a piece of meat before his beady little eyes moved slowly back to her face.

The man was everything she loathed—his penchant for playing fast and loose with magical ethics, his complete lack of respect for history, his ruthless pursuit of power within the magical community, and his mistaken impression he was some sort of sex god—and now he wanted to pretend like she was the village idiot?

"It's not an act." Her grandmother's voice came from across the street. Damn, the woman could still hear better than anyone Ema knew. Danny Ives had been causing trouble for the Stone coven for several years, so it was easy to understand her granny's disdain for the weasel standing in front of her.

"Opal, I can understand your animosity. You've lost a good number of coven members over the past couple of years, and you blame me for their lack of loyalty when it has always been their decision to move."

If he kept using that condescending tone with Granny Good Witch, there wouldn't be anything any of them could do to save his sorry ass.

"Danny, if Ema says you were behind the house, I don't doubt for a minute that's exactly where you were. What I want to know is why you were so close to my home at the same time someone set fire to the guest house where Ema had been staying." Josh sounded much calmer than Ema knew he was—his voice was tight, and his aura was blazing bright red, a sure sign he was a split second from throttling Ives.

"I was in my office and heard the call go out over the scanner. I had no idea the guest house burned. That's unfortunate. I hope you were able to save your personal belongings."

Ema went instantly still. Watching him carefully, she could feel his disdain for her grandmother and his shifting emotions about her. She knew the instant he realized Audric Stafford was standing nearby. Everything about Danny Ives's body language changed when he recognized the head of the Magic Council. Gone was the casual, almost flirtatious arrogance of a man who was convinced he'd destroyed everything she owned.

Focusing all of her energy on him, she let her awareness float into his mind, watching and listening as his mind replayed his evening. He hadn't cared about all the people he'd put at risk. All he'd wanted was to create a distraction and derail her by burning her Book of Shadows.

The asshat's plan was riddled with holes, but he'd been so focused on returning to Spellbound to cast a spell, giving him entrance into the cavern, he'd overlooked all the obvious obstacles. He considered destroying her Book of Shadows a bonus, knowing it would have crippled her as a magical and essentially eliminating her as a future complication. She was going to strangle his arrogant ass with her bare hands.

As soon as the thought moved through her mind, Audric stepped between them. Emerald knew he'd used magic to move so quickly, but the seamless shift in position was still damned impressive.

"You should have let her shred him. I haven't seen anyone drawn and quartered in a long time." Flicking a glance to where her Aunt Ruby stood with her arms crossed over her ample bosom, it was impossible to miss the mischief shining in her eyes.

"He's always spoiling people's fun. My sister and I have complained about it for years. Of course, she was busy raising the perfect child, leaving me to shoulder the heavy burden of testing our father's limits. You might have met my niece, Charlotte. She is married to Austin Adler. Their baby boy is the apple of my eye. He won't be an insecure twiddle-dick like Danny-boy. Did you know he was recently making inquiries in Mexico about having his dick enlarged? Word on the street is the doctors at several clinics told him they needed more to work with."

In Ema's view, Gigi Stafford had just been promoted to superhero status. If she lived to be five hundred years old, Ema was certain she would never experience another moment quite like this one. Danny Ives turned to the woman leaning against a streetlamp, fury radiating from his every pore. Until that moment, Ema had been convinced Gigi was making the story up, but his anger was as good as a confession.

"My cock is just fucking fine—not that you would know since I have more sense than to dip it in a hag." Ives's mocking tone belied his embarrassment.

It took every ounce of self-control Ema could muster to keep from laughing at how easily Gigi lured the dimwit into her trap. How the man managed to put together a growing coven was a mystery unless he was nothing more than a figurehead—which seemed more likely by the moment. Ema sensed his intention to strike a split second before he moved. Her magic was powerful, but she'd been beaten to the punch by Audric.

Ema quickly realized even though she'd heard people talk about how the world seems to slip into slow motion when the shit hits the fan, experiencing it firsthand is something else entirely. Before Danny could move, Audric froze him in place, magically locking the man into a state of suspended animation. Ives was not only precluded from moving, but he also wouldn't be able to use any of his senses if Audric sent him deep enough into the suspension. Glancing at Josh, Ema wasn't surprised to see him looking at Danny with something between horror, satisfaction, and curiosity.

"He isn't dead, is he? I'm not sure how I'd fill out the paperwork if he was." Ema understood Josh's position. It couldn't be easy for him to take everything in... particularly when he was already struggling to accept the existence of magic. He refocused his attention on Audric and chuckled. "Is this some kind of crash course in magic? I feel like you are tossing me into the deep end."

"Wow, I'm usually the one accused of the whole baptism by fire thing." Gigi sauntered closer to stop in front of Josh. "I admire your rope work. I saw a demo you did a couple of years ago at Club Isola." Ema watched the interaction closely, sensing there was more happening than was apparent.

"Good try, but I have never done a demo at Ian's club, despite him asking me several times. I know a test when I come up against one, Ms. Stafford. My memory isn't infallible, but I remember the first time I saw you. The Black Forest region of Germany, three years ago. I corrected one of your knots from the sideline, and you weren't pleased."

Ema smiled when she saw Brigitte's casual shrug.

"You're right on all points. It was a test, and the knot was lame. Your friendship with Emerald came to the attention of the Magic Council, and I was charged with making certain you were... well, let's just say, there are people in positions of power who were anxious to find out whether or not you were suitable." Unfortunately, Brigitte's answer was probably more honest than Josh knew.

"Glad to know I passed. If you decided I was suitable, it seems like you should have done a better job of covering my ass."

"Your exemplary record of successful missions is something of a legend among your SEAL colleagues, Joshua." Ema wasn't surprised to learn Audric Stafford had done his homework. Men didn't attain Audric's level of success without being prepared and well-informed.

"Teammates." Josh's one-word correction made Gigi

snicker, earning her a negligent shrug from her father.

"We helped you all we could. There are rather strict rules about interfering in the natural flow of fate." Shaking his head, Audric took a deep breath. "Before you ask, no, we weren't responsible for your last mission. There were magicals present, and many of them were ours. There were many more on the scene who had a vested interest in your failure."

"Why do I feel like he was targeted because of me?" Ema felt like the world was closing in around her. Josh moved behind her, using his strong arms to anchor her against his chest. She'd been in the midst of explaining to her grandmother, aunt, and the Staffords what she'd seen in her vision when she sensed Danny Ives outside. Ema had forgotten to grab her jacket when she'd seen the cocky bastard sauntering up the street.

"Don't worry about me, Ema. I'm perfectly capable of taking care of myself. Knowing who I'm up against gives me a heads up. Since we're having this conversation in the middle of the street after midnight, with one of the local losers standing like a damned statue a few feet away, I assume he is somehow involved in this fiasco."

"He tried to burn my Book of Shadows. He started the fire as a distraction, so he could get into the store, but he knew my book was in the guest house. The asshat wanted to cripple me as a magical."

"Please tell me you have proof."

"Of course, she does. Tell him, Ema. You heard the little twizzle dick bragging about it in his head, didn't you?" Ruby moved close enough to whisper close to Danny's ear. "You're going to make another trip to Mexico as soon as you can. If you get your penis extended, you'll be able to recruit more young witches. The hospitals in the center of Mexico are your best bet. Ask the local cartel members for recommendations."

Ema slapped her hand over her mouth to keep from bursting into the riotous laughter bubbling to the surface. Brigitte was doing the same while Audric merely smiled. Ema's grandmother shook her head, muttering under her breath, "And everyone thinks I'm the evil sister."

"Ladies, I believe the jury is still out on which Stone sister caused my hair to go prematurely gray." Audric's comment made Ema grin.

Ruby's subconscious suggestions to send Danny Ives into a pit of vipers was forgotten as they all turned to stare at the man who'd probably turned gray centuries earlier.

"Danny is dangerous because he's made promises to members of the contingent of dark magicals. Accepting a large down payment from them has put him in an untenable situation."

A flicker of light on either side of Audric was the only warning they were given before two enormous men suddenly flanked the Magic Council's esteemed chairman. Dressed in black fatigues, which made them look every inch the soldiers they were, Ema couldn't help but stare up at the two men. Her grandmother's voice brought her back to the moment, though it didn't take Ema long to reconsider.

"Holy shit, how tall are you guys? Damn, if I was only a few years younger, I'd give you a run for your money."

Ema watched in horror as her grandmother's clothes changed before her eyes. Gone was the ratty coat she'd grabbed as she'd stormed out of the store on Ema's heels, and in its place was a pair of neon green sweatpants hiked up so high, the elastic waistband must have been tucked under her boobs. The blinding jacket was equally obnoxious, the brilliant pink reflecting the light of the streetlamp, competing with her light-up tennis shoes.

"A few years? That's rich. And who the hell dressed you, a drunken Shriner with a sense of humor? I swear to the great Goddess, you give bag ladies everywhere a bad rap." Ema wasn't sure when Ola arrived, and from Josh's surprised expression, he was as stunned as she was. Ola turned her attention to Danny Ives and frowned. "He's such an asshole." Nodding to the two men standing on either side of Audric, Ola asked, "Are they my muscle for this transport? Please tell me, *yes*. I swear your new human resources director is my hero. Give the woman a raise."

"You're a shameless hussy, Ola."

"No news there." Ruby's shrug was in contrast to the mischief sparkling in her eyes.

Ema grinned. It felt good to be back on familiar ground. This banter had been a regular occurrence anytime the three sisters were together. She'd always envied their easy comradery, so different from her relationship with her own sister. Ema was convinced Garnett was born green with envy. In Emerald's opinion, her sister had wasted her entire life being pissed because she wasn't the firstborn.

It was baffling. Ema couldn't understand anyone wanting the responsibility she was coming to see as more of a curse than a blessing. Ema and Garnett had never been close, and Ema moving back to Crystal wouldn't help the situation. There wasn't anything she could do about the way her sister felt, so she made a conscious effort to push it from her mind.

Ema started to ask where they were taking Danny, but before she could get the words out, they were gone.

"I don't suppose you plan on bringing him back, so I can question him about the fire?" Josh was clearly frustrated they'd whisked away his only suspect in the fire behind his home.

"You wouldn't be able to prove he'd been there. Danny isn't as dim-witted as he first appears, and he's had some skilled help. He used magnetic magic to blank out your tapes."

"Magnetic magic?" Ema knew Josh's question was legitimate. She also knew he wasn't going to like the answer. Stepping out of his hold, she turned to watch his expression as Gigi explained—making a mental note to ask the other witch to back off a bit. At this rate, Brigitte would send Josh Bennett running as far away from Ema as he could manage in their small town.

"Essentially, it's a narrow beam of magnetic energy much like the magnetic pulses terrorists use to take out critical elements of their enemy's defense systems."

Josh stared at Brigitte as if she'd grown a second head before shaking his head in something that looked like a cross between defeat and frustration.

"I need a drink." Josh ran his hand through his hair, a sure sign he was struggling to assimilate everything he was hearing. "Hell, do I even want to know why the magic world is using such sophisticated weaponry?"

Audric chuckled under his breath, but Gigi, Opal, and Ruby laughed out loud.

"Josh, for such a looker, you sure can be dim. Who do you think introduced your research and development people to magnetic pulse weapons?" Shaking her head, Granny Good Witch added, "I swear nonmagicals always think they invented everything."

"Let's go back to the store. I'm hungry. I've whipped a little buffet. I bet there isn't an all-night eatery for miles." Gigi was right. By the time any of them drove to a larger town, the sun would be up. Walking into the store, Ema's stomach rumbled when the smell of her favorite breakfast foods surrounded her.

"This whole thing gets weirder by the minute, but I'm warming up to the perks." Josh looked from the buffet to Gigi. "The guys from the fire department will be rolling back in before long."

"Done. Now, let's eat."

Ema didn't doubt for a minute the local fire crew was going to be stunned when they returned to the station. Brigitte Stafford didn't appear to be the type of woman who did *mediocre*. Ema was certain anything the other woman put together would be over the top.

The small group spent the next hour eating and rehashing the evening's events. Audric explained the Magic Council's plans for Danny.

"We have been waiting for him to give us an excuse. We needed to see an overt act of aggression toward the Stone Coven before we could step in. Simply recruiting from your membership wasn't enough, even if we knew what he intended."

"Setting fire to the guest house was enough?" There was a ring of sarcasm in Josh's tone she was certain he'd made no attempt to disguise.

"No. His attempt to burn Emerald's Book of Shadows is considered a... what do you nonmagicals call the worst crimes? Damn... something about big letters. Why didn't the world stick with Latin? It never changes."

"A capital crime?" Josh grinned at the older man, clearly amused by his struggle with American legalese.

"Yes, that's it. Deliberately destroying a witch's most sacred possession is a high-level offense in the magic community."

"Yeah, and arson is a biggie. You know... it's the whole witches and fire thing." Gigi's off-the-cuff remark had Josh's jaw-dropping in disbelief, his incredulous look making Ema laugh out loud.

"I guess I can see why the fire thing is a sticking point. Damn, this whole fiasco is pinging my weirdo-meter into the stratosphere."

Ema felt the weight of the world settle on her narrow shoulders. Josh wouldn't be dealing with any of this if she hadn't moved back to Crystal.

"Look at her face. Duck me." Gigi shrugged and grinned when her father shook his head. "If it's good enough for autocorrect, it's good enough for me." Turning her attention to Ema, Gigi tapped her long, polished fingernail against the table. "Stop assuming none of this would have happened if you'd kept right on driving through Colorado. You have the added power of the crystals since you are here. Didn't you wonder why it was so easy for you to call your book out of a burning building? Those damned books are heavy. That was some hefty magic, girlfriend."

Ema was stunned when she stopped to think about the evening's events. Gigi was right about how easily she'd moved her book out of the burning building. She hadn't given it a second thought... she simply whispered the words and waited. It had been years since she'd actively practiced the craft, much less uttered an incantation strong enough to lift her Book of Shadows, yet she'd done so without a moment's hesitation.

"See that? The light of understanding is dawning in those pretty green eyes." Gigi lifted a glass of wine that magically appeared in her hand.

The mock toast had Josh shaking his head. Reaching for Ema's hand, he laced his fingers with hers.

"Let's head home. I want to stop by the firehouse and see if Ives was careless enough to leave me anything useful. Maybe I'll get lucky. It might be a small-town department, but there are a couple of damned fine investigators on the crew. If there was anything left behind, they would have spotted it. Hopefully, we'll have enough to prosecute him—assuming Mr. Stafford returns him in one piece."

Emerald had been away from the magical community for a while, but she knew Danny Ives wouldn't be returning to Crystal. It was unlikely he'd ever return to the United States. After being deprogrammed, he would be settled in a minor magical role, safely ensconced within the Council's headquarters. Hearing Josh refer to the Bennett mansion as her home set loose butterflies to flutter in her stomach. It would have seemed more intimate if Danny hadn't burned down the blasted guest house.

CHAPTER FOURTEEN

S TEPPING INTO THE shower, Ema let the hot water from the rainfall showerhead pour over her. She'd eaten two of the largest cinnamon rolls she'd ever seen before leaving Spellbound. Now she was teetering on the cusp of a sugar crash of epic proportions. If she didn't get herself in gear quickly, Josh would find her standing in this same spot tomorrow morning. His offer to shower in one of the guest suites had been generous but disappointing.

"Stop whining. He gave up his own amazing shower so you could enjoy it. Josh is graciously sharing his beautiful home with you, even when you've proven you are a trouble magnet of the first order. A little gratitude would go a long way, Ema."

"Do you always talk to yourself in the shower, sweetheart? Is this a regular occurrence... a small quirk I should be aware of?" Ema's shriek of surprise reverberated off the marble walls, and she slipped in her effort to move quickly. Josh didn't miss a beat, wrapping his arm around her upper torso before she dropped to the floor. "Easy, baby. Let's not make a run to the emergency room tonight."

"Holy Hannah, I'm sorry I screamed. I was giving myself a pep talk and not paying attention." There were times when she felt like two different people. One looked and spoke like the professional woman she'd been for the past several years. The next moment, she was steamrolled by the insecure young girl who tried in vain to make her mother love her. Hades, maybe her personality was splitting. The way things were going, she would probably end up with a dozen women living inside her head. They made a movie about someone named Sybil who flipped a script all the time, right?

"Were you really disappointed I offered to use the other shower, sweetness?" He leaned down, speaking the words close, letting the warmth of his breath caress the sensitive, damp skin behind her ear. The simple move made her knees weak and stole her ability to form more than a one-word response.

"Yes." The answer was easy, even if it might be more difficult to explain all the reasons. She watched as he reached around her, letting the automatic dispenser drop shampoo into his palm. What had seemed like an outrageous extravagance when she'd first seen it made perfect sense now. He hadn't needed to release her to dispense the sage and sandalwood scented product. Despite her best efforts, Ema felt her heart sink as she wondered how many women he'd showered with in the past.

"What was that thought?" When she didn't immediately respond, he turned her so quickly, her head swam. "I'm not kidding Ema, tell me what just went through your mind. Your entire body went rigid before sagging. I felt your sadness wash over me, and I want to know what the hell brought it on." She hated admitting her insecurity but knew Josh wasn't the type of man to let something go once he'd keyed into it.

"I wondered how many other women have stood in this spot... how many you must have showered with to know how convenient automatic dispensers would be. I know I don't have any right to ask, and maybe if I wasn't so damned tired, it wouldn't matter. When I push myself past reasonable limits, weird stuff becomes magnified and strange things happen. And I'm worried about the warrior in the guest house. A fire wouldn't harm a spirit, right? If he's survived all these years, surely a small inferno wouldn't be too much for him to handle."

"We're going to address every point while I wash your hair, but let's start at the end. What warrior?" Ema appreciated Josh's matter-of-fact approach. He hadn't acted as if she'd lost her mind, he simply asked her for information.

"I noticed him the first night I was here. He was standing silently in the corner of the bedroom. I felt safe with him watching over me as I slept. I know it probably sounds strange, but I knew he wouldn't hurt me. I woke up earlier than usual this morning, and there was a knight in his place. I suppose it makes sense they would work in shifts. Anyone assigning guardians to watch over me would obviously know about my penchant for being clueless and walking headlong into a shitstorm."

"You never cease to surprise, sweetheart. Someday soon, I want to introduce you to Daniel Lamont, who will want to hear your story. He was born and bred in these mountains and knows more about the Native American history, folklore, and culture of the groups who lived nearby than anyone I know. It will be interesting to hear if he has any insight into who the warrior might be. If I was taking bets, I'd put my money on Audric Stafford for help to identify the knight."

Josh's strong fingers massaged her scalp and finger-combed the lather through the long strands of her hair as he spoke. His gentle care made her eyes burn with unshed tears.

"As for your concerns about the automatic dispensers... training and combat injuries taught me the value of the small devices that allowed me to maintain some degree of independence during recovery. After the first time I had to ask for help to take a shower, I started making notes. By the time I retired, I had a whole list of special modifications I wanted to be certain were made during the remodel I was planning. You'll notice those small enhancements now and then." The low timbre of his voice and quiet chuckle were more comforting than she wanted to admit.

"As for my previous sexual experience, I won't lie if you ask, but I'd prefer it wasn't something we discussed right now... or ever. No man with any integrity wants to discuss his past exploits with the woman he wants to make his own. I've never brought another woman here, not since the house became mine."

Ema let out the breath she hadn't realized she was holding and leaned against his muscular chest. She hated the way her old insecurities surfaced at the most inopportune times.

Wait! What? Did he just say he wants to make me his?

This time, there wasn't anything subtle about his laughter.

"Come on, let's get you dried off and into bed. I can only imagine how tired you must be to have let that tidbit slip by. We'll dry your hair a bit before I braid it for you. A loose braid will work perfectly for what I have planned."

Ema's body went from teetering on the verge of collapse to supercharged sexual awareness between one breath and the next. She wanted to ask what he had in mind, but everything she'd read about dominance and submission emphasized it was the Dominant's option to share information. Mulling everything over in her mind to the point of emotional overload, Ema was surprised to find herself standing at the edge of the bed.

"I have no idea where you go during those little mental road trips, and it terrifying to think about how easily you could be led off the edge of a cliff."

I'm not usually such a flipping space cadet, but it's so easy to just let everything go when I'm with you. Ema felt the energy in the room shift and tried to take an instinctive step back but found herself pressed against a solid wall of heated, bare skin before her feet could move. She barely registered he was moving before she was flat on her back, staring into Josh's sky-blue eyes, his face mere inches from hers.

"I've told you before, but I'm happy to repeat it. Your trust is my most treasured possession. Hearing you say you feel safe in my care is the highest compliment you could ever pay me. There will be times when I want you to stay in the moment, but I'll do a better job of letting you know when your focus is important. As we learn more about each other—all those little pieces of information people gain when they live together will make it much easier for me to avoid any trigger points—even those you might not know about."

The longer he talked, the further Ema felt herself drifting from the conversation.

Who knew Crystal's most eligible bachelor would be so chatty? Good grief, can we dive into the deep end of the psycho-babble pool later? If you'll just make me come and let me take a nap, I promise to examine every nuance of trigger points. Geez Louise. Get on with the fuckery.

Josh moved lightning fast, flipping her onto her stomach and wrapping a slender strand of nylon rope around her wrists, securing them together above her head before tethering them through a notch she hadn't noticed in the headboard. She instinctively tested the binding with several quick tugs, making Josh chuckle.

"Some bindings will tighten if you resist, but we haven't reached that level of trust yet, so feel free to pull to your heart's content." Josh's voice had taken on an edge she hadn't heard before, and she hadn't missed the sudden uptick in the energy around him. "What we have reached is a point where your unspoken insolence has surpassed what I'm capable of ignoring."

Damn it to demented dust bunnies, she really needed to remember to shield her rambling thoughts. The books she'd read hadn't mentioned how quickly a Dom could shift directions. *Note to Ema: Keep demanding snark to self.*

Emerald's entire body felt like it was heating from the inside out, and her face was flushed a brilliant shade of red when she realized how wet her pussy had become. It would be mortifying if he noticed the cream she could feel coating the outer lips of her sex.

"Is it too late to apologize?" A heated caress laid on the fleshy part of her ass was as clear as any answer could be. The slap hadn't hurt, but the sound of his palm colliding with the flesh of her ass startled her as the smack echoed around the room.

"I'd tell you to stop talking, but if I leave you to it, I'll know where your head is. Hearing you demand a release gives me a lot of ammunition, sweetheart. Let's not start bartering orgasms for conversations."

What? Talk about taking a left turn at the third star and following it until morning. How had he come to such an absurd conclusion? Using a trick she'd learned when dealing with clients, Ema took three steadying breaths while making a concerted effort to block her thoughts. The last thing she needed was to tip him off about how self-conscious she was about her reaction to the swat he'd given her.

"I already know how much you enjoyed the swat, sweetheart. Your body gave you away before your brilliant mind had time to catch up. Every inch of your flawless skin is flushed, your breath hitched before you moaned ever so sweetly, and the earthy scent of your arousal wrapped around me, sending my control hurtling toward the edge. I'm not sure why I can hear you, but I have to say, it's damned helpful." His soft laughter made her relax as he tucked two pillows under her lower abdomen before securing each ankle to a bedpost. Anticipating another swat or caress, Ema squirmed when several seconds passed without him touching her.

"Stay still. I want to admire you. I've waited years for this moment—years spent wondering what color my handprint would be on your pearlescent skin. I can't tell you how often I wondered what shade of pink your pussy lips were when you're aroused. One of my favorite fantasies was imagining how your pussy lips would look with dewy beads of your cream highlighting the sensitive flesh. I've always believed the ancients had it right when they described a woman's sex as a rose. Yours is a perfect deep red."

Ema felt a warm rush of air waft over the bare flesh of her exposed pussy, the sound of his sigh adding to the eroticism surrounding them. She buried her face in the soft cotton sheet, hoping to hide the blush heating her face. *I wonder if my ass cheeks would blush if he hadn't already warmed them?*

"I'm not sure I'm comfortable having my bare butt poking up in the air. Maybe, if it wasn't so—" She stopped abruptly when his hand came down in another quick swat. He hadn't hurt her, but there was definitely enough heat in the slap to get her attention.

"Be very careful, Ema. I'm damned protective of what I consider mine, and I won't take kindly to hearing you speak disparagingly about yourself." Ema didn't respond— the truth was, she couldn't speak around the lump in her throat. "Now that we've established a couple of boundaries, I want to explore what your body enjoys.

"Don't be surprised when your sex responds to things your head isn't ready to admit turn you on. Don't let what you think you should find pleasurable override what sets your body on fire. Don't fear what looks like something a bad girl would brag about in the locker room. Put yourself out there and try every single thing that appeals to you." Ema was pleased when Josh finally surrendered himself to telepathic communication. In her view, it was a huge step forward as he began to embrace things he couldn't see or explain.

Oh, goodie. I've been promoted to Guinea pig. Cringing when she heard the snark in her unspoken response, relief flooded her when Josh merely laughed.

"Let's see how long you're capable of those clever quips, shall we?" The snick of something that sounded like a bottle opening stilled any reply she might have uttered. When she felt something slick slide between the cheeks of her ass, Ema froze.

"Stay still and stop worrying. We're playing, remember? Close your eyes and let your body speak for you."

Ema didn't hesitate to follow Josh's command, closing her eyes quickly. Much to her surprise, instead of giving her a chance to hide from his knowing gaze, losing her sight opened her other senses. The smallest brush of air gliding over her bare skin alerted her Josh was moving. A nearly silent rustle of fabric indicated he'd dropped the towel wrapped around his waist. Gasping when his fingers slipped between the cheeks of her ass, it took Ema several seconds to recognize the cool sensation she thought was lube was becoming warmer by the second.

"Have you ever experimented with anal stimulation, sweetheart?" Holy hexes, nothing like pole vaulting right up to the tough questions.

"No, but I've read there are supposed to be a lot of memories buried within the sensitive tissues." She remembered rereading that section of the book several times, unsure how to process the information. It didn't make any sense to her. Why would that area of the body be a storehouse for emotions?

"You're doing great. Relax. It isn't your job to analyze everything into oblivion, Ema. You don't have to understand why something feels good to enjoy it."

Those simple words were an eye-opening moment for her. Ema had always been driven by an insatiable need to learn. She suspected it was a consequence of trying to be perfect. Her inner child still clung to the misguided belief, if she was *better*, it would make her mom love her.

LISTENING TO EMA'S rambling thoughts was both a blessing and an exercise in frustration. The insight was priceless, the level of intimacy quickly forming a connection deeper than any Josh had ever imagined possible. The consequence was how difficult it was for him to keep his growing disdain for Ema's mother and sister to himself. Understanding the true depth of the emotional toll their behavior continued to take on Emerald made him furious.

"Emotion manifests itself in a lot of different ways, sweetheart. The lesson I want you to learn is it doesn't matter why something feels good or gives you the edge of pain that enhances pleasure. What matters is enjoying the moment. Don't be stalled by analysis paralysis. It's my job to think through the scene. Your part is to accept the pleasure I give you and let me know immediately if you feel overwhelmed, either physically or emotionally. If you say wait, I'll pause so you can ask questions or catch your breath. If you say stop, I will."

Josh didn't want to rely on safe words until he was convinced Ema wouldn't let her deep-seated desire to please override her personal level of emotional and physical comfort. The line between overthinking what he said and becoming overwhelmed by the dance of destruction his fingers were doing around the sensitive rim of her rear rosette was razor-thin. Josh knew he was riding the line perfectly when Ema lifted her pretty ass, trying to press closer to his touch.

Substituting warming oil for lube meant Ema's body would register the sensations as sensual rather than intrusive. He'd learned during visits to kink clubs around the world there were exceptions to every rule. Most Doms adhered so closely to the *begin as you intend to go* rule, they overlooked opportunities to layer pleasurable memories, so those were what a submissive remembered when they ventured deeper into scenes. Josh looked forward to their first trip to a club. It would give him a chance to find out what turned her on and offer Ema a glimpse at a side of herself he doubted she knew existed—but that would not happen until he was convinced she was no longer a target.

Fantasizing about their first kink club visit was a great distraction from the intense throbbing in his testicles. The brief delay had given him a chance to rein in his out-of-control desire, but now it was time to give Ema the release her body was clamoring for. Grabbing a wet wipe, Josh cleaned the warming gel from his fingers. He didn't want to inadvertently expose her pearly clit to that level of stimulation just yet.

"Please. I need you to touch me. My head is spinning, and the noise from all your thinking is distracting when all I want is to feel your cock shuttling in and out of my pussy. Face it, your cock is huge. It's never going to fit in my ass without magic."

"It will fit. The magic required won't be what you're thinking. Proper preparation is the key, but that's a discussion for another day." Leaning over, so his chest pressed against her back, Josh whispered against the sensitive shell of her ear, "I'm clean, Ema." She'd already told him she was protected, and suddenly, all Josh could think about was how much he wanted to sink balls deep with nothing between them. The head of his cock was poised at her entrance, but since he hadn't donned a condom, he waited for her response.

If he hadn't been completely attuned to every nuance of Ema's body, he might have missed the slight flexing of the muscles of her forearm a split second before her fingers twitched. Before he had time to ask what was happening, he watched what looked like a cross between glitter and fairy lights explode around them as his body thrust forward. Before he could pull in a breath, Josh's mind went numb. Ema's vaginal walls flexed, massaging his length with so much rippling strength, his mind went blank for several seconds. He'd never had unprotected sex, despite his gold-digging high school girlfriend's claims otherwise.

The feeling was intense on multiple levels. For the first time, Josh was forced to fully acknowledge the power of magic—or he would if he ever regained the ability to speak.

CHAPTER FIFTEEN

"I SWEAR, YOUR driving gets worse by the minute." Opal's snarky tone didn't faze Ruby. She'd been dealing with her bossy older sisters her entire life. She was equally immune to Opal's glare.

"Says the woman who hasn't had a license since Herbert Hoover was President."

"A driver's license is silly. I didn't forget how to drive just because that little card expired. It's another tax, I tell you. Face it, driving a car is like riding a bike—once you master the skill, it's something you never forget how to do. Blasted bells, you don't forget a skill simply because the government decided your permission to perform it has expired."

"That may be true, but it's still the law. If Josh ever checks, he's going to pull the keys on your scooter."

"Stop nagging and drive. I swear you are worse than Ola. Rules, rules, rules. You're preaching to the woman who has spent her entire life living Aradia's Rule of Seven… I should be allowed a bit of leeway on something as trivial as a driver's license. I swear people would be so much happier if they were easier to get along with… like me."

The car swerved violently to the right when she fell

into a coughing fit. By the time Ruby finally brought the car to a stop at the edge of the road, she was thumping her forehead against the steering wheel.

Ruby looked up just as the entire car began spinning slowly away from beneath them... or were she and Opal levitating? A split second before she heard the telltale whoosh of teleportation, Ruby had the sinking sensation of impending bad news. She wasn't typically a gifted clairvoyant, but the sensation of gloom and fear crashed over her like a tsunami. Ruby might not know where they were going, but whoever summoned them was powerful. Pulling two gifted magicals into a transport if they were unprepared or resistant required significant magical strength.

"Sorry about that, Ruby. I know how much you hate teleporting, but it was the easiest way to get everyone together quickly." Ruby recognized Ola's voice before the smoke cleared around her. Muttering under her breath, she mentally reviewed the news feed article she'd read recently about untraceable poisons. When her head stopped spinning, she'd start on her damned shopping list.

"What the ever-loving hell? Don't you have to have a person's consent to drop them into a damned tube and shoot them..." Josh paused, reaching for Emerald when she swayed as the smoke surrounding her cleared. "Careful, sweetheart. I don't know about you, but that was a first. I was getting ready to throw steaks on the grill when the floor fell out from under my feet, and I landed in what looks like a subterranean conference room." Taking in the amused expressions of the men and women standing nearby, he shook his head. "Ema, we're going to have a long chat about transportation protocol."

"That'll be a monumental waste of time." Ruby didn't care how snarky her comment sounded. She was annoyed at the abrupt nature of their summons to the hidden Magic Council headquarters and even more frustrated knowing the only way home was another teleportation. "The entire lot of them are going to nod and swear it won't happen again, then do as they damned well please the next time they want you front and center."

"Stop whining. I swear to all things mystical, every other magical on the planet sees the value of hopping from point A to point B without the nightmare of airport security and being trapped in a metal tube with a hundred other people." Any remorse Ola had felt had clearly evaporated.

"Jesus, Joseph, and Mary, this day just vaulted to the top of my *you will not believe this shit* list."

"I'm so sorry, Josh. I don't know why Aunt Ola brought us here, but it must be very important... at least it had better be."

Ruby sighed when she saw the unshed tears in her niece's eyes. Damn, damn, double-damn. She should have kept her mouth shut. No doubt her grumbling added fuel to Josh's frustration. Ema deserved Ruby's support, and now she felt like a first-class heel.

Ema glanced at Josh before dropping her gaze to the floor. "I swear my life was almost normal when I was in Boston."

Josh pulled Ema around so they were face to face before tipping her chin up, forcing her to meet his gaze. It seemed like she was spending a lot of time being spun around so Josh could remind her none of this was her fault.

"Ema, the timing of this experience might not have been perfect, but I can't deny it's been damned interesting." Unconcerned about their audience, Josh pulled Ema close, pressing what started as a chaste kiss against her lips. The temperature in the room went up several degrees as Josh deepened this kiss to the point, Ema's swayed in his embrace.

"Damn, I haven't seen anything that hot for so long, I'd almost forgotten how much fun it is to watch." Ema felt her face flush with the heat of embarrassment. Brigitte Stafford's words yanked her back to the moment. Ruby could understand Ema's untenable position and felt a pang of sympathy when her great-niece looked as though the other woman had doused her with ice water. Gigi gave a disinterested shrug before adding, "Don't mind me. I'm not judging... simply envious." Blowing out her breath, Ema straightened her spine, and Ruby smiled as the young witch seemed to pull strength from thin air.

Emerald has no idea how powerful she is... or how influential she will be. I relish the opportunity to watch her fulfill the prophecy and grateful beyond measure the legacy didn't fall to Jade. It's humbling to admit, but my niece is damned hard to love.

EMA'S HEAD WAS starting to pound—the sheer volume of all the telepathic communication inundating her was staggering. Grateful Josh's hands were still wrapped solidly around her upper arms, Ema took several steadying breaths, letting his strength restore her own.

"Can you block out the noise?" His quiet question surprised her.

Over the past few days, she'd thumbed through her Book of Shadows, seeking guidance, and had been shocked to discover many of the previously blank pages filled with detailed descriptions of the various ways mirrored souls could recognize one another. She'd inaccurately assumed the growing bond was being solidified by their passionate love life and was surprised to learn the answer was more cerebral.

Intimacy was the key—the emotional connection they'd both felt before they'd made love the first time was why she and Josh felt a pull they didn't understand. Every encounter they had since bound their hearts closer together. At first, seeing the intimate details of their physical relationship mentioned in her book was oddly intrusive, but reading about their emotional connection had been even more unnerving. It hadn't taken Ema long to understand why the spell Aradia cast upon her descendants inspired so much jealousy. When memories from last night's mind-blowing sex in the hot tub floated through her mind, she felt Josh's grip on her upper arms tighten possessively.

"You need to rein it in, sweetheart. My control isn't an inexhaustible resource, and even though I'd enjoy doing a rope demo with you, this isn't my audience of choice." Josh's teasing tone was enough to bring her back to the moment and send a rush of heated desire to her sex.

Turning her attention to the people taking their seats around the large conference table, Ema felt an odd sense of dread. She might not have paid attention during her grandmother's lessons, but common sense was all Ema needed to know they hadn't been teleported to the council's underground lair to receive good news.

"You're right, Ema, this is an emergency. Unfortunate and unprecedented. We've never had anyone escape before."

"Escape? You whisked away my prime suspect before I could even question him, then lost him?" Ema felt Josh's frustration as it pounded through the room like a bass drum. On the outside, the only visible change was the slight narrowing of his eyes. If he'd been in a room filled with nonmagicals, no one would have known how close he was to losing his temper. Several seconds of silence followed before Josh sighed and shook his head.

"Let me guess, it's a long story, but the bottom line is, the son of a bitch had inside help, this is unprecedented, and no one has any idea how a traitor slipped through your impeccable security screening." Ema heard a ripple of snickers and knew Josh nailed it.

"Well, dad, I hate to say I told you so, but I'm not above it. We all knew he'd see through any bullshit story your people tried to sell him. Although I have to admit, I expected you'd at least get a chance to make a sales pitch."

Gigi's sarcasm wasn't lost on anyone, but Ema appreciated the other woman's ability to defuse Josh's mounting anger. Audric leaned back in his luxurious leather chair, elbows propped on the chair's thickly padded arms, his fingers steepled beneath his chin. The lines of wisdom bracketing bright eyes, usually dancing with amusement, looked wearier than she'd seen in the past.

Ema was surprised when the crystal in the necklace her grandmother and Aunt Ruby made for her heated against her skin. With clarity she'd never experienced before, Ema knew instinctively what she needed to do. Leaning forward, she held out her hand to the elderly wizard and was relieved when he only hesitated a second before placing his slender fingers in hers. The crash of fatigue hit with such force it made her wonder how he was still functioning. Exhaustion, worry, guilt, embarrassment— every emotion rolled over her with equal force. Whispering a healing spell, Ema tightened her hold on Audric's hand when he tried to pull back.

Ema hadn't thought about one-on-one healing in so long, she'd forgotten it was one of her magical gifts. Even now, it hadn't been a conscious decision. She'd merely wanted to comfort a man she'd grown fond of when it was easy to see how distressed he was. By the time she released her hold on his cold fingers, the digits were warm, and his face had more color than it had a few minutes earlier.

"You do Aradia proud, Emerald. I'm looking forward to seeing your skills develop. You will surpass all of our expectations. The sky is the absolute limit for you, dear." Audric's voice seemed to gain strength as he spoke, his eyes widening as if his own voice surprised him.

The crystal around her neck was still warm, and she had the oddest sensation it was allowing her to see the man behind the title, getting a glimpse of the powerful wizard most people weren't privy to. Straightening in his chair, Audric looked as though he was gathering the last remnants of his composure before continuing. The transformation was mesmerizing.

"We brought you here because we thought you deserved to hear about Ives's escape in a face-to-face meeting. I'm grateful for your healing touch and thrilled my old age has finally been put to good use. Being the catalyst to remind you of this special gift was an honor, my dear. My daughter is a healer. Unfortunately, Charlotte is forced to take on the illness or injury, then heal herself."

"It may not sound like a huge difference, but it is. You pushed your healing energy into Dad without absorbing any of his utter exhaustion, and you did it without breaking a sweat. Training you will be the easiest task the council has ever given me." Audric's words had warmed her heart, but Gigi's were a huge boost to her self-confidence. Ema had the impression Brigitte Stafford was difficult to impress, and knowing she'd earned even a small bit of her respect was damned humbling.

"Ema has always underestimated her skill. I also believe many of us have failed to give Opal the credit she deserves. It seems Ema learned much more than any of us realized." Ema gave her Great-Aunt Ola a huge smile, appreciating her kind words for her twin sister as much as the back-handed compliment she'd given her.

"As much as I appreciate everyone complimenting Ema, can we get back to our problem? I'm certain you consider Danny Ives a threat to Emerald, or we wouldn't be here. If you summoned all of us here, you've left Spellbound unprotected. I don't want all of Ema's hard work ruined by a man hellbent on kissing the ass of some... what did you call them the other day?" Josh's attention was shifted to Gigi. He'd obviously spoken privately with her about Danny Ives, and Ema was anxious to hear about their interaction.

"Ives is being driven by dark forces, but the important thing to remember is a soul can't be *led astray* as so many people seem to believe. A person's soul has to be willing—coercion will never prevail if the soul is pure."

"That isn't to say most people don't have a price—because they do." Audric's added bit of wisdom felt like the missing piece of the puzzle. In Ema's opinion, Danny's price had been the promise of power and adoring women, the two things he could never attain on his own. "Mr. Ives is going to find life much more difficult now. We've frozen all of his assets, including accounts he probably thinks are untouchable." For the first time, Josh's smile looked relaxed as his blue eyes danced with obvious amusement.

"I've known Danny his entire life. He has always been a pain in the ass, but it's only been in the last few years he came to the attention of authorities. No one has figured out where his money is coming from. He's built up a small community, and most of the locals have expressed their concerns the cult of crazies would eventually turn violent."

"It was a legitimate concern. Danny amassed a substantial fortune and has been surprisingly smart concealing it in off-shore accounts," Ola added. Ema knew her aunt was considered an expert in finance and investments, but she'd never heard her talk about anything remotely professional.

Ema glanced around the room, noting the number of people present seemed to remain the same, but the faces changed. The shifting of participants was bordering on weird when she finally noticed a familiar face. Nigel

Lancaster kept popping up at the oddest times, and she couldn't shake the feeling there was so much more to the man than she'd been told. The crystal around her neck began heating against her bare skin, and Ema focused on Lancaster, wondering why everything about the man seemed shrouded in secrecy.

CHAPTER SIXTEEN

J OSH FOLLOWED EMA'S gaze, shocked to see his old friend standing nearby. What the hell was Mikel Snowden doing here? Pushing to his feet, Josh ignored the curious looks from the others in the room as he closed the distance between them with a few long strides. Extending his hand and giving the other man a broad smile, Josh greeted his friend.

"Mikel, I don't have any idea why you're here, but it's good to see you. Damn, it's been a long time, man." Before his friend and former neighbor could respond, Ema spoke from behind him.

"Wait? What? Why did you call him Mikel, and why do you know a wizard?"

"Wizard? He was my neighbor when I lived on Catalina Island. He told me he was traveling for work, which was why he wasn't around that often...."

"I'll just bet he did." Ruby's interruption was all it took for things to start making sense to Josh.

"You were spying on me, weren't you? Checking to make certain I was suitable for... that's what all the questions were about. Jesus, Joseph, and Mary, I thought you were hinting at a poly-marriage like the Lamonts or Wests. Hell, I felt bad for not letting you know I was moving. I even suffered a brief pang of guilt when I got a chance to connect with Ema, knowing I could never share her with you or anyone else." Priding himself on his ability to remain calm and collected in any situation, Josh cringed when he realized how much he'd inadvertently revealed to a room filled with people—some he barely knew.

"Well, well, this just gets better and better. So far, we've learned Danny Ives outwitted some of our best escorts—and I'm not talking about the kind wearing fishnets and G-strings. We've witnessed Emerald's ability to heal with little more than a touch, and now we've discovered Ema's overseer has an alter ego. What else have you been up to, *Mikel?*" Brigitte Stafford's voice dripped with sarcasm Josh suspected was supposed to camouflage her disdain for the man he knew as Mikel Snowden, but it wasn't working.

"All technically true, though taken slightly out of context." The other man pushed away from the wall he'd been leaning against and stepped out of the shadows. He moved with the same cat-like grace Josh admired when they'd been friends several years earlier. There'd been times Mikel's steps were so soundless, Josh wondered if the man's feet were touching the ground. "A downside of being tasked with overseeing Emerald's magical training and safety was the need to be clandestine." Turning his attention to Josh, he quirked a brow.

"Would you have shared the details of your desire for Emerald if you had known I was her overseer?" Turning his attention to Ema, Mikel—no, Josh needed to start thinking of him as Nigel Lancaster—the man's expression softened. *As soon as I get back to my office, I'm going to find out everything I can about the bastard.* "The reason you felt an odd sense of familiarity when we *met* recently is easily explained. We've met many times over the years, but I erased those meetings from your mind, leaving little more than the lingering sense of comfort you'd feel the next time I visited."

"So... something creepy between *Fifty First Dates* and the little flashy light things from *Men in Black*. Dandy. My life turns out to be a cross between a sappy rom-com and an old sci-fi flick. This is just pathetic. Everybody thinks being a witch is cool... after all, you get to move shit around without touching it, mix exotic ingredients into great potions that occasionally blow up." Josh wanted to laugh out loud at Ema's list of perks. He appreciated her sense of humor under what were less than ideal circumstances.

"What most nonmagicals don't see is an organization run by people who are hundreds of years old. Magicals don't think a thing about having their noses so far up in your business, when you fart, their ears wiggle."

Josh finally lost the battle to keep from laughing out loud. Leaning his head back, he let the stress of their current situation drain away. Ema wrinkled her nose in disgust aimed at the situation, making her look like a disgruntled teenager. Damn, she was cute.

"Well, there's a mental picture I could have done without. Honestly, Emerald, some things are best left unsaid." Opal rolled her eyes at her twin's condescending rebuke.

"Don't listen to her, Ema. Ola has always been old. Even when we were kids, she was old."

"It's the matronly clothes she wears." Ruby's eyes glittered with amusement, the youngest sister clearly enjoying the opportunity to annoy her sister.

"Could be those orthopedic shoes. Damn, those are ugly. She'd probably be a lot nicer if she had a pair of sequin high-tops." Until now, Josh had held out hope the Stone women harbored a thread of sanity buried somewhere deep inside, but it seemed little more than a foolish pipe dream.

Shifting his attention to Ema, Josh noted the way her head was tipped slightly to the side, a move he knew meant she was listening to someone's thoughts or a woman's voice she claimed often guided her when she was struggling to sort out something particularly troubling.

She was wearing the crystal necklace she hadn't taken off since receiving it recently. When he'd asked about it, she'd shrugged and grinned, then explained her granny and great-aunt swore it would help her see the truth. Josh was quickly learning those claiming to be magicals often spoke in more abstract terms, so he wasn't sure if Ema meant the literal truth or the truth of someone's heart. Either way, he'd been unconcerned because his heart and words were aligned with the woman he wanted to spend the rest of his life with.

The thought no sooner moved through his mind than Ema turned her gaze on him, surprise and happiness visible in her expression. Good heavens, hadn't she been listening to him?

Of course, I've been listening, but a girl never tires of hearing a lover's vow of devotion. Being loved is the highest honor, and I'm grateful beyond measure for yours. Be assured, I'll always magnify your love and send it back to you tenfold. Of all the Universe's gifts, the ability to love is the greatest.

If he wasn't convinced his mom would never forgive him, Josh would have grabbed Emerald's hand and sprinted to the nearest justice of the peace. He'd told his parents and sisters Ema was back in his life, and they were thrilled and already pushing for an invitation to dinner. His family all knew and liked Ema. He would face a lot of pressure to make things *official,* and cheating them out of the chance to help plan a wedding wasn't a risk he was willing to take. He was looking forward to watching the women in his family try to finesse Emerald into shortening whatever timeline she set. Shaking his head, Josh almost laughed at his presumption she'd even consider marrying him.

"I appreciate you updating us on the escape. What are you doing to bring him back in?" Josh wasn't trying to be rude, but nothing about this summons made sense. Audric Stafford tipped his head as he seemed to be listening to a voice no one else could hear. The elderly wizard was as spooky as he was amusing. Someday, Josh hoped the two of them could sit down and have a long conversation about history.

"We're using every tool available to locate Danny. He is indeed a threat to the Stones, but he is also in danger. Dealing with dark magicians is a double-edged sword. The rewards can be enormous, but the expectations are ever-increasing. Those funding the Ives coven won't hesitate to make an example of him. We're talking about people with unlimited resources and no moral compass. They are ruthless, and until now, they've erased the memory of anyone we brought in."

"Seems to be a *thing* in magic circles, doesn't it?" To his credit, Lancaster had the good grace to duck his head in response to Ema's unrestrained sarcasm.

"As hard as it is to imagine, Emerald, I believe Nigel had your best interests at heart. You haven't been particularly interested in magic until now, so any oversight from our community would be seen as interference." Ema stiffened beside him, but Josh knew Audric was right. "As for you, Josh, Nigel's assignment was clearly outlined when it was given. Your magical gifts are untapped, which means you were essentially an unknown."

"Your interlude at the lake put you dead center on the Council's radar. There are metaphysical explanations related to Ema's status, but in this case, the simple explanation is so much more fun." Gigi's grin didn't bode well. Josh might not know the woman well, but he didn't need to in order to see how much she was enjoying his unease. With a wave of her hand, Brigitte laughed. "Don't worry, no one is going to discuss the particulars, but suffice to say, your fates were sealed that night. Personally, I would guess Aradia was involved long before that point, but I'm equally sure she'll only reveal it to the two of you."

The whole situation was racking up *weird shit* points at an alarming rate. He'd heard them mention Aradia more than once, so he'd researched the name online. The Queen of the Witches was known for her bravery and brilliance in battle. There was a lot of disagreement about when and where she'd lived, but most sources agreed she was still a powerful force in the magical world. He only found one reference to the seventh-generation gifted magical and a quick calculation—assuming women were in their twenties when they had their first child—which put Aradia's age somewhere in the neighborhood of twelve hundred thirty. At that point, Josh had shaken his head and stopped reading. He had to give the Stones credit. They obviously came from hardy stock.

"Your car is parked in your garage, Opal. You can move back into your family home, your renters have suddenly decided to move on, and you'll find your financial situation is greatly improved as well." Before Opal or Ruby could comment, they vanished into thin air. Josh shook his head, wondering if he would ever be completely comfortable with the smoke and mirrors theatrics.

"Theatrics? I'll have you know we're well-respected in magical circles. Smoke and mirrors, indeed." He'd have worried Ola Stone was indeed offended if he hadn't seen her wink at Ema.

"We're sending the two of you back to the Bennett Ranch." Audric directed his next comments to Josh. "We've enhanced your security. Remember, Aradia's Knights may not look exactly the way you'd expect them to." Josh opened his mouth to ask what Stafford meant, but the words were lost in the whooshing sound of air rushing around him as he found himself hurtled through the same brilliantly colored tube he'd arrived in. It was probably too much to ask they'd use a blasted elevator like normal people.

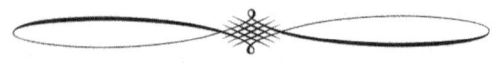

EMA WATCHED AS Josh disappeared and wondered how quickly she was going to find herself living above the store. Listening as his mind raced during this ridiculous meeting, she'd wondered how long it would take him to tire of the chaos that was a growing presence in her life.

"Stop worrying, Emerald. Josh is smitten with you and has been since your first night together." Ema smiled at Gigi, grateful for her reassuring words.

"Josh overestimates his ability to prevail in this situation. Like everyone, he has hidden magical skill, but he'll call it intuition. Your instinct will be to protect him at all costs, Ema." She detected a note of sadness in Nigel's voice and wondered why. "For what it's worth, it was never my intention to hurt you—quite the opposite, in fact. One day soon, we'll sit down and have a long conversation. I hope we can find meaningful ways to work together as partners. I believe you'll find me a useful resource."

Ema wasn't entirely sure what he meant but wasn't going to take time to ask. Knowing Josh was already in his home was unsettling. Was he okay? Had he weathered the trip home and his first teleportation?

"I'm willing to give you a second chance because I know you and Josh were friends once." *As strange as it sounds, that means more than my discomfort about have my memory erased by whatever hocus pocus you used.* For the first time, she watched a genuine smile spread over his handsome face. His eyes darkened, and she knew he'd been listening. *Damn, I'm out of practice blocking. I really need to step it up.* Amusement flashed in his eyes a second before the floor felt as though it disappeared from under her feet. Sliding through the brightly lit tube she knew would take her to the Bennett Ranch, Ema heard Nigel's soft laughter.

"It won't work, sweet girl, but you are welcome to try."

DANNY IVES STOOD in a thick section of trees outside the Bennett Ranch's secured perimeter. Using the small but powerful binoculars he'd conjured minutes earlier, Danny watched for any sign of Josh or Emerald. He hadn't seen anyone, so at least one thing had gone right. Whoever enhanced the ranch's security hadn't been fooling around. Fuck, his fingers were going to be blistered from when he'd touched a small section of fence. Cursing his stupidity, he secretly wished he hadn't slipped away from the two idiots Audric Stafford assigned to escort him to his magical lair.

It wasn't fair to blame the guards. They'd been over-whelmed by the dark magicians who'd shown up to explain in great detail what would happen to his family and friends if he didn't finish the job he'd been paid for. Danny didn't have any close family—certainly not any he cared enough about to protect—but over the years, he'd made friends who stuck by him and didn't deserve to suffer for his mistakes. He wasn't known for having a conscience, so he'd leveraged his reputation to buy time.

In his infinite arrogance, Danny painted himself into a corner so tight, he was only left with two options. He could try to contact Audric Stafford and surrender, or he could complete the mission and become even more indebted to the group of dark magicals intent on destroying anything or anyone standing between them and the crystal cavern beneath Spellbound.

Seeing the telltale flash of light he knew signaled teleportation, Danny didn't have to wait long to find out who'd arrived. Joshua Bennett blinked several times before scanning his surroundings and shaking his head to get his bearings. Danny had never been fond of Josh, but he had to admire the way he weathered being magically rocketed from one place to another.

Without missing a beat, Bennett tossed steaks on the grill before stepping back through the open patio doors. A second flash of light led Danny to believe Ema had arrived despite the car she'd been driving sitting in front of the store.

Yesterday he'd been across the street when Opal and Ruby left through the front door, so he'd gotten a quick glimpse of the unfinished space. Today he'd stopped by on his way to the ranch and been shocked to see the windows uncovered.

The outside of the building was in pristine condition, repainted and repaired, making it look historic but well-kept. The shelves were stocked, and even from the sidewalk, it had been easy to pick up the pulsing energy of residual magic. There were too many magical signatures to sort one from another, but it was apparent Stafford had sent a full crew to finish up what Emerald had been trying to do, using as little magic as possible. From what he'd heard, she'd tried to live as a nonmagical in Boston, though for the life of him, Danny couldn't figure out why.

Of course, you don't understand. Independence and autonomy are lessons the soul learns when it wants to advance. The unfamiliar woman's voice moved through his mind, the undisguised sarcasm dripping from each word. *My voice is unfamiliar because I rarely trouble myself educating those who see no value in history or those who inaccurately believe they control their own destiny when they are so obviously incapable.*

To refocus on the couple he could see setting the table through the open doors, Danny shook his head, hoping to push the woman's voice from his head. He might not know who she was, but it took a strong magical to project into the mind of another magical—particularly one who wasn't open to the communication.

Watching Josh and Ema, he almost envied how easily they worked together. The two of them seemed to be oddly in sync, as though their moves were choreographed. He'd rarely seen a couple so at ease with one another. Danny had met many couples who had been married for decades, but he never saw any of them exhibit the same fluid movements. Not only was he curious about their odd familiarity, he was also baffled why it seemed to matter. What would it be like to have a woman in his life who looked at him the way Ema looked at Josh? And why the hell did he care?

Danny had never given a rat's ass about finding a woman of his own, preferring to keep his encounters purely sexual with no regard for what tomorrow might bring. Determined to get his mind back to the task at hand, Danny inched his way forward. Whispering a spell, he felt the cloak of anonymity fall over him and knew his outward appearance bore no resemblance to his real self. Getting close without being recognized was critical if he had any hope of scaring Ema into leaving Crystal.

CHAPTER SEVENTEEN

Ema was relieved when she arrived at the Bennett Ranch, and Josh didn't treat her any differently. She'd been worried everything would change, and he would decide she was more trouble than she was worth. When Ema mentioned she had, once again, left a vehicle in town, Josh chuckled and assured her it was already taken care of.

"If I knew how to cook, I'd bake something for the guys at the garage. I feel bad for abusing their generosity."

"You want to make them happy? Leave your crazy color-changing car with them for a few more days. I swear I haven't seen them this excited about a car in... well, forever. They are determined to figure out how she was able to open locked doors. They don't seem too interested in solving the mystery of her changing colors since it's making them a mint."

Their easy conversation had been one of the things that initially attracted her to Josh, and Ema was grateful that hadn't changed over the years. Pushing her plate away, she leaned back in her chair and sighed. "I'm going to have to spend the rest of the evening in your gym working off all those delicious calories."

"I can think of a lot more pleasurable ways to burn them off, sweetheart." Ema felt her face heat and couldn't hold back her giggle when Josh waggled his eyebrows. "We'll worry about our naked workout later." Nodding to their empty wine glasses, he took their plates to the sink, then grabbed the wine bottle and a small covered plate she hadn't noticed earlier.

"Grab the glasses, and let's go outside. There isn't a cloud in the sky, and I want to look at the stars while we talk." Draining the first glass of wine Josh poured for her, Ema shrugged when he raised a brow in question. "No reason to be nervous, Ema. I just need some answers if I'm going to process what happened today." He refilled her glass and gave her a look she didn't have any trouble interpreting. Ema didn't move to pick up the glass despite the temptation to numb her nerves.

"You look like you're ready to bolt, baby. Come here." Without waiting for her to move, Josh scooped her up and set her on his lap. Wrapping his arm around her waist, he handed her the glass of wine she hadn't yet touched and grinned. "It's not the most expensive wine in the cellar, but it didn't come out of a cardboard box. Try to savor it."

"Sorry, I was nervous. I know how you feel about magic, and I've been dreading this conversation."

"Stop. I know where you're headed with this... I don't know how I know, but I do, and you're wrong. I may have never fully believed magic was possible, but hell, at this point, it's impossible to deny." Ema relaxed for the first time since she'd realized they were standing side by side in a conference room she'd known immediately was buried deep in the bedrock of the Magic Council's headquarters. "Tell me about Aradia." Before she could respond, the crystal around her neck started to vibrate and heat to the point she pulled it away from her skin to keep it from burning the sensitive skin at the base of her throat.

"What the fuck? What is she doing here, and how the hell did she slip past my security?" Ema turned to look at the man walking in their direction, stiffening when she recognized Danny Ives. Wait, did Josh say she? Why on earth hadn't he recognized Danny?

"Stop right there. Don't you dare come any closer." Ema's shouted warning fell on deaf ears. Ives continues stalking toward them as Josh got to his feet and tried to shield her from view.

"Why are you here, Meghan, and how the hell did you get past my security?" Josh's voice boomed around them, his anger almost palatable. Ema's mind was scrambling to make sense of the scene playing out in front of her and to keep the crystal pendant hanging around her neck from scorching her.

Grabbing a cloth napkin from the table, Ema wrapped it around the hot stone and stared in astonishment as Danny morph into Josh's former flame, Meghan Morris. Letting the stone fall from the thick cotton, Danny was once again clearly visible. She didn't have time to appreciate the spell her grandmother and aunt had cast on the beautiful necklace, but she was grateful for their foresight. Her granny might be a wildcard, but she had an uncanny ability to know what people needed long before the situation arose.

Freezing Josh with magic was too risky for more reasons than Ema had time to consider. The conversation they needed to have would take much longer than the few seconds they had before Ives was within range to wreak the havoc she could hear rattling around inside his head. Desperate to ensure he understood what they were facing, Ema pulled Josh's hand until she could wrap his long fingers around her crystal pendant. Josh's eyes widened in surprise, and Ema wasn't surprised to hear his muttered curses.

"What the fuck? Ives? How?"

"Magic." She'd explain more in a few minutes, but first, she needed to take care of a little business. Taking a page from Josh's playbook, Ema uttered a few words, then watched as Ives was bound in silk rope. A ball gag like the one described in her erotic romance novels kept Danny from speaking any of the spells she'd heard rolling around in his pea-sized brain. His snarl let her know she'd broadcast her assessment farther than she'd planned. Josh looked at her with amused pride reflecting in his eyes.

No gags for you, sweetheart. I don't like them. Even if I did, I wouldn't give up listening to the soft moans and gasps of pleasure you make when I'm buried balls deep in your heat or teasing your lovely clit out from under its hood.

Josh's thoughts raced through her mind in a fraction of a second, leaving a blast of heat in their wake. Ema appreciated how their connection seemed to grow stronger every day, the growing link empowering her and magnifying her magic. Resting her hand on Josh's forearm, Ema sent up a silent prayer to the Universe for him to remain calm. She didn't have time to explain or wait for the help she'd summoned to arrive.

Shifting her focus from Josh to Danny, she was surprised by the mixed emotions she felt swirling around him. Anger was predominant, but it wasn't all directed at others.

His anger was so pervasive, she doubted he had any idea how to diffuse it. Trying to sort through the barrage of angry telepathic energy flowing in all directions was an exercise in frustration. Dropping the gag at his feet, Danny surprised her with a warning rather than a threat.

"They're coming. I'm not alone. Your power will be wasted in a dying coven. We're offering you a chance to have your name etched in gold in every history book from this moment forward. You will be rich beyond your wildest imagination, and your descendants will never want for anything." The more she heard, the heavier Ema's heart felt.

A dark mist appeared behind Danny, floating silently toward where the three of them stood. Josh's snarl of frustration beside her pulled her attention to where he stood.

"Promise me you won't do anything rash. If I have to choose between protecting myself or keeping you safe, I'll move heaven and earth to shield you." She saw his eyes widen in surprise a heartbeat before softening.

"We're going to have a long chat about roles and boundaries." *Preferably with you tied to my bed and sated to the point, you'll agree to anything I say.* She appreciated his mischievous grin. The look reassured her he wasn't angry she was going to take the lead. As the mist started taking shape, Ema groaned. As if dealing with Dastardly Danny wasn't enough of a pain in the ass, the last person she wanted to add to the toxic mix surrounding them was Mr. Zero Personality, Frank Black.

"What? No warm greeting for an old flame?" Frank's mocking voice reminded her how much she appreciated

Josh's sincerity.

"I'm surprised to learn you are a magical, Frank. To be honest, I didn't think you had enough personality." She'd been a doormat during their entire relationship but had promised herself she would never back into the same pattern. After spending the past few days with Josh, Emerald was already aware of how much had been missing from her life. Frank had never listened to her the way Josh did.

"Your disdain is noted, Ema. It's unimportant, but noted." His sarcasm had the opposite effect he'd been hoping for. Ema could sense Josh's anger and was grateful when she felt him move closer to her. Standing to her side but a half step behind, his body language sent a clear message to the two men in front of them.

A vague memory of one of her grandmother's lessons teased the fringes of Ema's mind. Her granny had been trying to explain the sizzle of electricity she would feel before all hell broke loose, but it hadn't meant anything to her at the time. She damned well understood it now. The crackle of power was so strong, the hair on her arms stood on end. Time seemed slow as people materialized out of thin air. The number of men and women in long, flowing black cloaks was more than a little intimidating.

Perfect. You are a magnet for magical power. My legacy burns brightly in your soul. My name is Aradia... my knights and I stand with you.

Between one breath and the next, Emerald's entire world shifted on its axis. Lightning struck the ground to her left, the clap of thunder making Ema scream in surprise. As the smoke cleared, Emerald was shocked to find a woman standing so close, their shoulders were nearly touching. The first thing Ema noticed was the woman's clothing, then brilliant green eyes, eerily similar to the ones Ema saw each time she looked in a mirror, met her gaze.

"Proper introductions will have to wait until after we clear the evil from this sacred ground." Before Ema could ask how she thought the two of them could defeat the dozen or more men and women flanking Danny, a line of light extended to their right and another to their left in a flash so brilliant, spots danced in Ema's vision for several seconds.

"Fucking hell. Somebody want to catch me up? Who are all these people?" Josh wrapped a protective arm around her shoulders, his words laced with confusion and concern. Ema understood his uncertainty. Hell, she was having trouble wrapping her head around what she saw, and having grown up with Opal Stone, she'd seen impressive displays of magical power more often than she cared to admit.

The first person revealed as the smoke cleared was the Native American warrior she'd seen in her room that first night in the guest house. She'd only seen him a few times since, but Ema knew he was the same man. Other warriors stood shoulder to shoulder with Knights, Samurai, Ninjas, Persian Immortals, and Navy SEALs.

"Jesus Christ, my whole fucking team is here. How is that possible? Even magic can't bring back the dead." Ema understood the bewilderment in Josh's voice. It had to be difficult for nonmagicals to understand how thin the veil is between this world and the next.

"Joshua, please forgive me." Aradia's quiet apology

barely registered before Josh was gone. *On damn, he isn't going to be a happy camper when he makes his way back to the ranch.* Aradia grinned at Ema, the lighter expression making her look as though she was glowing from the inside out. "Don't worry. He can see what's happening, but you won't be distracted by his questions or your need to protect him."

Turning back to the witches and wizards facing them, the woman swirled her fingers in the air, colorful sparkles of light flying from her fingertips. Ema's eyes widened in surprise as a wand matching the one Aradia held formed in her own hand. There was something elegant about the way Aradia moved, a fluidity much like what she'd observed with Josh. The other woman gave her a warm smile so much like the Emerald's own, it was startling.

"Years of training. Warriors are the same, no matter their time or place in history. You have much to learn, but your keen observation skills will make the process much easier. Let's cleanse this area before Audric arrives."

Ema barely had time to blink before Aradia leveled her wand at the dark magicians who'd been held off by the warriors flanking them. Emerald had been so focused on her conversation with Aradia, she hadn't paid attention to the surging tide of power surrounding them.

What do you want me to do?

Let the power of light move through you. You will magnify the magic if you allow it to flow freely through you. Aradia's words were empowering, even if they were a bit too vague for Ema's comfort.

I'm all for on-the-job training… but damn!

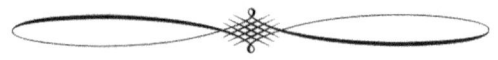

GIGI GRINNED AS she listened to the thoughts racing through Ema's mind. Aradia had asked them to stand down unless things deteriorated. It hadn't surprised her when the Queen of Witches sent Josh to wait with them. What had surprised her was how intense his focus was on the scene unfolding in front of them.

"I feel like I'm being torn in two. Seeing my unit was a kick in the gut, but knowing they are protecting the woman I want to spend the rest of my life with is more than I could have ever asked for."

"And the flip side?" Gigi wasn't naïve enough to miss the hesitance in his voice.

"Knowing she *needs to be protected* and the humbling realization I'm not able to help is sobering and damned frustrating."

Gigi damned well wouldn't insult Josh's intelligence with empty reassurances. It was a simple fact the man was a warrior to the depths of his soul, but until he discovered his own magic, he would need to let the spirit warriors protect Emerald.

When her dad turned his attention to her, Gigi noted a sparkle in his eyes she hadn't seen in a long time.

"It fills my soul with hope to see these warriors lined up to fight evil. The dark side has been slowly gaining ground for two centuries. It's high time our side brings more balance in the world." With a quick glance toward

Josh, Audric shrugged. "Waiting for Emerald wasn't easy. Giving her time to come home was excruciating, especially since we knew Frank Black was working both sides."

"Ema knew there was something wrong with her boyfriend but mistakingly thought his lack of interest in some way was her fault. I don't understand why any man wants to make a woman feel unworthy? You don't want her? Fine. Move along. Don't lay your pain at the feet of someone who bears no responsibility for your plight." Gigi wasn't sure how much Josh knew about how poorly Frank Black had treated Ema, but judging by his body language, he knew enough to make anger pulse around him like a bass drum.

"Agreed, but remember, every experience molds us in some way. Fire tempers steel, Brigitte." Gigi wanted to roll her eyes at the phrase her father used so often, she and Charlotte swore they were going to have it engraved on his headstone someday. "Pay attention and learn, daughter. This battle will be over so quickly, you'll miss it if you blink. Aradia doesn't suffer fools. The two standing front and center are about to learn a valuable lesson."

"They are stooges. Moe seems to be missing, but Curly and Larry are on full display. Aradia is going to incinerate them. It'll be fun to watch but certainly won't be an all-day event." For the first time since Aradia sent Josh to wait on the sidelines, Gigi saw a ghost of a smile in his expression.

CHAPTER EIGHTEEN

E MA TRIED TO tune in to what Danny was whispering to Frank, but there was so much negative energy swirling around her, it was impossible. She'd panicked when she realized she was the center of a dark energy storm. Looking at Aradia helped calm Ema's nerves—the other woman didn't look the least bit concerned.

"Who leads this contingent?" Aradia's voice filled the large yard, booming over the roaring of swirling wind. A cloaked figure moved to the front, but his hood made it impossible to make out his face.

One of the first things you need to learn is how to identify witches and wizards by their magical signature. The man standing in front of us is Herschel Franklin. He is a distant relative of Benjamin's, but you would never know it. Herschel has no integrity, and he couldn't pour rain out of his boot if there was a diagram on the heel.

Ema bit the inside of her cheeks to keep from laughing at Aradia's observation. Somehow, the joke made her seem more approachable. Over the past couple of days, Ema had asked her grandmother and aunt to clarify a few points about the legacy they'd spoken of so often. Everything they'd told Ema about Aradia made her seem so regal and brave, a warrior who famously led an army of knights to victory despite being in labor.

"Aradia, I'm surprised to see you taking such a keen interest in an untrained magical whose personality pales in comparison to her insane grandmother." Emerald heard a snarl she would have sworn came from a feral animal if she hadn't known the unladylike sound came from her. Before she could lunge at the man, Aradia laid her hand on Ema's arm. That simple touch was all it took to calm the raging storm of Ema's anger.

"Herschel, I'm disappointed… but not surprised. You really should do your homework." Aradia's voice was calm. Her lack of concern calmed Ema as much as it seemed to enrage the man she was talking to. "Emerald's power is an untapped well deeper than any of you can imagine. I know my warning falls on deaf ears, but heed it, nonetheless. Until she is ready, we'll stand shoulder to shoulder. We'll protect our brothers and sisters when they are downtrodden. We'll teach each other and share the journey with anyone who wants to see the world shine in the light of universal good. And we'll stand against those who oppress others—whether it's for personal satisfaction or financial gain."

"If you are explaining these basic principles to him, he is a disgrace to his family name and magicals everywhere." Emerald didn't make any effort to whisper. She wasn't sure what prompted her to take a swipe at the leader of the dark forces, but the words slipped out as if they'd moved through her rather than been planned. Ema was beginning to understand what it felt like to let magic flow freely through her.

Think of yourself as a conduit or channel. The magic is in you. Training will teach you ways to tap the energy and direct it more efficiently. Aradia's voice moved through Emerald's mind, comforting and encouraging her. Ema couldn't help but wonder how different her life would have been if she had a mother who'd loved her unconditionally? A mother who'd help guide her magical growth with her wisdom and experience.

The truth hit her full force—she had. Her grandmother had stepped up when her own mother had failed. Love and gratitude warmed her heart despite the energy surrounding her, which swelled to the point her focus seemed to be razor-sharp.

Ema felt the wizard's intent to strike a fraction of a second after Aradia. There was obviously a lot to be said for experience. That microsecond delay in her reaction would have meant the difference between life and death, but Aradia's hand was already in motion when Ema felt Franklin's intent. Before she could react, the man disintegrated in front of her.

The line of warriors flanking them moved so quickly, Ema could only stare in wonder. The dark wizards tried to fight Aradia's knights but were subdued quickly, the battle was history within seconds. Injured magicals were quickly whisked away so quickly, Ema had trouble keeping track. When a tall man dressed in full knight regalia moved to Aradia's side, Ema saw the woman's body language soften.

"Conrad, my love, I'd like for you to meet Emerald Stone." Ema extended her hand to shake his, but Conrad went to one knee, kissing the back of her hand. It took her several seconds to realize why she immediately felt at ease in his presence when his size alone should have been intimidating. Conrad reminded her of Josh, his chivalry and warrior spirit reflected in the warm glow of his aura.

"It's a pleasure to meet you, Miss." It had been a long time since anyone called her Miss, and Ema found herself amused rather than annoyed by the term she knew he'd meant to be respectful. "I've heard so much about you, I feel as though I know you already." It was a nice sentiment, but she was at a distinct disadvantage. Damn her rebellious nature for not taking any interest in her granny's lessons. He leaned close and whispered, "None of us listen when we are young. Being foolish is one of the many privileges of youth." Ema grinned and let out the breath she hadn't realized she was holding. She appreciated Conrad tactfully erasing some of the guilt she felt.

Looking to her right, Ema was surprised to see Josh standing among his former SEAL team. Their conversation appeared to be animated, but Ema noticed there wasn't any of the usual backslapping and handshaking she knew usually took place with soldiers and wondered why. When she realized she'd spoken the observation aloud, Ema blushed.

"It's a perfectly reasonable question, Emerald. I'm happy to answer any and all questions—it's the only way you can learn." Spinning around, Ema found Gigi standing right behind her. "The higher evolved a magical is, the easier it is for them to maintain a physical presence. Without a substantial physical presence, they can't touch someone on this side of the veil. We surrounded Josh with some of our finest warrior knights on this side of the veil. Even though he considers the mission a dismal failure, the Council sees it differently. Those warriors were charged with saving Josh… for you."

Ema's head was spinning as she tried to make sense of the barrage of information. Knowing Josh lost his entire team was heartbreaking. Hearing the brave men lost their lives to protect the one man the Universe selected for her stole her breath. Seeing what she suspected was only a small part of Aradia's army made her wonder how much of her future was already mapped out. *I feel like an actor in a play where everyone else has the script, and I'm left to wing it.*

"It's more like you are a pawn on a chessboard." Ema snickered at Gigi's subtle reminder she needed to work on shielding her thoughts. "The bad news? You aren't one of the planners… yet. The good news? You aren't responsible for all the details… yet." Gigi cackled at her own joke, making her look so much younger and more approachable than she'd appeared when they first met.

"I get that a lot, you know. People don't see me as approachable… strange, but true. I'm actually a lot of fun; just ask my latest submissive. I'm sure he'd be happy to tell you… if I let him." Gigi flashed a bright smile before brilliant colored smoke began swirling around her. "Places to go, people to annoy." The woman's voice echoed in the distance as she slowly disappeared from sight.

Shaking her head, Ema turned back to where Aradia and Conrad stood, talking quietly. "How long will it take me to get used to people popping in and out to tinker in my business?"

"If you're lucky, you'll never become blasé about the wonders of magic. After all these years, I still find myself struck dumb by the mystical mysteries of my lovely partner." Ema noted Conrad hadn't referred to Aradia as his wife and wondered if unions in the magical world were different somehow.

"You have so many wonderful things to learn, Emerald. Enjoy the journey. We've cleared the road of the first obstacles, but there are many more to come. We'll be back when you need us. Until then, spend time among the crystals. Use them appropriately. Draw strength from their energy. Let love light your path... listen to your heart, but take your mind with you. If you allow the two to work in tandem, they'll never steer you wrong."

"It's been two days, and I'm still trying to wrap my head around getting to talk to my team again." Josh leaned back in the lounger, staring at the inky night sky. It reminded Ema of the night at the lake. They'd talked for hours before their mutual attraction morphed into a sexual experience that changed both of their lives in more ways than they could have ever imagined. "I know I haven't been very supportive when it comes to magic—it's never been easy for me to believe in anything I couldn't see."

Ema had never taken Josh's skepticism personally. This was something he needed to work through himself. Talking seemed to help him process everything, so she kept her thoughts to herself. "Seeing my team, hearing their story... it was one of the most humbling experiences of my life. The only part of that entire night I didn't have trouble believing was their declaration we were destined to be together. My team's sacrifice is almost too much to take in, and knowing they are still watching my back... and yours... damn, it's so much more than I could have asked for."

"I've learned so much about Aradia's Knights over the past two days. Their warriors on both sides of the veil are a unified force for good. The dark side of magic has run rampant for over a generation. It's scary what happens when the people who can make a difference sit back and let things happen because it's not politically correct to speak up. I've learned part of the Stone legacy is to stir the pot, so to speak." She was still embarrassed to admit how much she could have learned from her granny if she'd been paying attention.

"So, basically, you're supposed to finish what Opal started?" Josh's question made Ema laugh. It was no wonder the Universe thought he was perfect for her. His ability to see the big picture and cut to the chase was refreshing. Without waiting for her to answer, he asked, "Are you ready for the grand opening? I have to hand it to you, the store looks amazing, and your website is kickass."

Ema felt her cheeks heat, blushing at the praise. She'd worked hard to plan everything. Hex, she'd filled several Big Chief tablets with outlines. Everyone made fun of her for using the old elementary school staple, but she didn't care. The wide lines and long paper worked perfectly for her. The magicals the Council sent to help appreciated her notes, and the small team was able to pull everything together in record time.

Ema wasn't sure how long she'd been lost in thought. Thinking about ways to ensure the store's success was a black hole, and she'd fall into all the ways she could improve. One thought led to the next, and before she knew it, an hour had passed, and she was still sitting in the same spot. Josh's amused voice brought her back to the moment.

"Since you're so good at planning, I have another project for you to consider."

Turning when she heard the rustle of clothing, Ema gasped when she saw Josh kneeling on one knee, a small, black velvet box resting on his outstretched palm. Opening the small box, Josh smiled when her eyes widened in surprise. The diamond ring sparkled under the stars, catching the soft light of the full moon.

"Will you marry me, Emerald Stone? I know we are already considered life partners in the magical community, but for my benefit, let's make it legal as well. I can't imagine my life without you in it." A tear rolled down her cheek as she let her emotions reflect the enormity of the moment. "You can plan whatever kind of wedding you want. Large. Small. Simple. Elaborate. My mom and sisters will be thrilled to help." She could hear the uncertainty in his voice when he continued, "Damn, Ema, say something."

"Yes."

The End

Books by Avery Gale

Spellbound
Spellbound – The Knights of Aradia

The Adlers
Brooklyn
London
Austin
Paris
Cleveland
Asia
Kensington
Israel
Bronx
Catalina

The ShadowDance Club
Katarina's Return – Book One
Jenna's Submission – Book Two
Rissa's Recovery – Book Three
Trace & Tori – Book Four
Reborn as Bree – Book Five
Red Clouds Dancing – Book Six
Perfect Picture – Book Seven

Game On – Book Four
Well Bred – Book Five

Mountain Mastery
Well Written
Savannah's Sentinel
Sheltering Reagan

The Christmas Painting
Taking Out the Mother of the Bride

I would love to hear from you!

Email:
avery.gale@ymail.com

Website:
www.averygale.com

Facebook:
facebook.com/avery.gale.3

Twitter:
@avery_gale